Hi Susa
Schio,
Start the Book wondering
a valley or lake!
Have a great spring

Incarnation

SARAH GERDES

ISBN: 1-7329503-0-X
ISBN-13: 978-1-7329503-0-6

Printed in the United States of America
First American Print Edition 2018
Cover design by Lyuben Valevski
http://lv-designs.eu

DEDICATION

This book is for the people of Ouray, Colorado. The locations, mine, restaurants and hot springs are real and wonderful. A good many characters are loosely based on people who still live in town, including the high school basketball coach who married us on the top of an Ouray mountain. May it always stay remote enough to keep the rest of the world from vacationing…at least at the same time.

ACKNOWLEDGMENTS

A big thank you to Dr. Eric Wallace and his acclaimed (and multi-patent-holding) research scientist wife Shay. Both were instrumental in helping clarify and refine the details of DNA mutations to ensure believability while maintaining the fictional aspects of this book. I am so grateful for their insight and guidance.

Incarnation

PREFACE

Wind whipped up the jagged mountain edge, gusting over the granite, tipping the man-size tires of the thirty-ton loader inches off the ground. The massive vehicle bounced up then down, dropping with a thud of finality, jarring driver and passenger.

Kyle's teethe clenched tighter than he thought possible. The trip had to be made.

"You sure this is the place?" Joe asked in a low, constricted voice, his fingers gripping the wheel as he stared out into the dark night. The frantic sound of the wipers had little effect on quarter-sized snowflakes assaulting the windshield.

Kyle stared out into the darkness. *The truth is here. I can feel it.* The old miner who confessed his secret had been one inch from the bottom of finishing off the fifth of vodka when he slurred out the words that led Kyle to make this trip. The man had nothing left to lose by telling Kyle. The yellow in the old timer's eyes meant he was dying anyway.

"It's here," Kyle told Joe, his voice flat, eyes narrow. *It would be me who lost everything*, thought Kyle, *or gained it all back*.

He caught the sideways flash of a glance from the driver and knew what it meant. It was the same look he'd gotten since he was young; the look that said he spoke more forcefully than he should, that he knew more than he'd been taught in school and somehow, neither were acceptable. Yet it was the same indecipherable quality that made adults listen and take him seriously.

Kyle ran his thumb along his jawline. He was seventeen, old enough to drive but too young to vote, an angry fate that had robbed him of the chance to have a say in the leadership of the country by a month. Now he'd have to wait nearly four more years to make a difference in a new government. One that would give back his face.

His face. The one that was stolen and replaced with a government-issued, handsome but completely non-descript mask. One without defining characteristics, but a perfect combination of his parents.

But it wasn't just him. The government had taken the face of everyone else in the country, replaced with homogenous incarnations they could control and manage, a way of erasing personal identities with the ease of swiping a credit card.

Kyle pushed his fingers out straight and strong, resisting the urge to clench up as the loader made its way around a narrow corner. He felt the slide as a wheel slipped then caught.

"Off the edge there," Joe said. Kyle visualized the cliff, a sheer, sheet of rock, two-thousand feet down. If the dying miner had told Kyle the truth about the information stored in the abandoned shaft, it would be worth it. The man would be a legend and Kyle a hero.

Back and forth the truck went, making its climb up a road belonging to a defunct gold mining operation. In the sixties and seventies, the mine had been one of the top-producing sources of precious metals in the United States. Long before the last global war broke out and the country faced anarchy, the mine had been purged of its precious trove, leaving miles of empty tunnels and a small town with fewer than five hundred people. During the winter, it was barely a pit-stop on an infrequently traveled highway, boasting two bars, a gas station and grocery store, all mainly used by tourists who paused for a soak in the natural hot springs. It wasn't until the annual ice climbing event in February that the town came alive. The summers were always busy, when visitors from all over the world came to test their off-road four-wheeling skills on the extreme mountainous terrain. They mingled with the monied set from Telluride, not far over the hill from where he was now. Kyle was one of the few natives of Ouray, born and raised by his hippie mom who gave up on society in her twenties to live the 'free life' in the small mountain town. Ouray sat on Colorado's edge, near where the corners of four states meet, a bragging point of local tourist officials. Who would have thought this mine shaft in his town would be the hiding place for the government's most dangerous secret?

"We're here."

The truck jerked to a stop, as though it had hit a rock larger than itself. Joe reached above his head, flicking a switch. A beam of light blasted the side of the mountain and Kyle felt Joe's eyes on him. The man had been driving the massive orange vehicles up and down the mountain pass road his whole life. Now he made do as a handyman, but it was hard scraping out a living in the small town, so he bartered for services, and this was Joe's return payment for Kyle fixing his transmission last week.

"You do this, you're going to be on the run the rest of your life."

Kyle stared at the boarded up mine shaft. His heart pounded so loud in his ears he barely heard the man's comment.

"Only if they find out it was me," he responded, his voice flat, and hard. *And then they have to catch me.*

CHAPTER 01

"I'm waiting ten minutes," said Joe. "You're either back or you're finding a different way down. They might already know we're here." Kyle nodded, pulling his hoody over his head, his surgical gloves as tight as a second skin. He yanked the drawstring around his neck and bolted out, gripping the ice-cold metal.

He went around the back of the vehicle, keeping close. The drop-off was inches away in one direction, the vertical wall of the nine-thousand-foot mountains on the other. He visualized the tops of the peaks, each crest and dip. He knew them as well as he knew the scars and indents on the back of his hands. As a child, he'd spent many nights here, gazing up at the snow-covered tips, wondering if they touched the sky. The thought had taken away his fear, giving him peace when he'd had none.

In the time since, he'd hiked the hills, usually off the trails, going where he wanted. Government patrols had originally dotted the landscape but had gotten lax over the years, content in the knowledge that the free-spirits in the remote part of the state were more interested in creating stained glass than exploring underground tunnels. Kyle figured he knew the mountain paths better than the park rangers and would have hiked up himself had it not been winter and the driver owed him a favor.

"Look for the old mine shaft door, but ignore it," the miner had told him in his liquored-up state. "The entrance is through the old security building, through a door by the electrical panel." Kyle had been by it dozens of times, usually squatting against the metal to catch a break against the beating sun in the summers. The closest trail was no more than a car-length from the south edge of the building. Now Kyle winced against the pelting snow, shining the light in to the darkness until it glanced off metal. The drunken man had given Kyle a code; the one that he said would never be changed; couldn't be changed. He'd pled with Kyle to commit it to memory, and Kyle had.

Kyle found the square metal panel on the side of the building, feeling for the number pad. It was alphanumeric, and the miner ended his confession with a warning.

"You put in the wrong code twice and the alarm goes off. Silent. Underground. The helicopters will hunt you down in minutes." Kyle's heart pounded in his chest, and for a split second, he tried to tell himself that the old man's ramblings could be wrong, but that didn't hold. The building was here, so was the pad. The alarm was likely real. So was the danger.

Kyle took a breath and pressed the keypad with the sequence he'd memorized. Nothing. He waited, his breath stopped, wondering what to do. Try again? Had he gotten the code wrong? He waited, the blustering wind a giant hand pressing him into the door. He placed his fingers on the keypad and was about to push the numbers a second time when he heard a whoosh. He jerked his hand away, pointing the light to his right. The rippled, metal wall retracted, a dim, greenish glow from within turning the snow into a hail of gumdrops wanting to take shelter from the elements.

"It will not shut," the miner had told him. "You must manually close the door from within." But where? The miner hadn't told him that part. Kyle's heart was beating at a pace now matching the seconds on the clock. He'd burned several minutes: he didn't have many until his ride left without him.

He flashed the light up and down both sides of the wall, relieved when a two-by-two size box caught his eye. It had a single, black button, void of a lock or turnkey. He pressed it, ready to bolt if it was a panic button. The door silently slid shut at the same time he heard *Foom-foom-foom*, a sound like spits from a gun equipped with a silencer. Lights lit up a tunnel the height of a truck and just as wide.

This was it. He was going to make a run for it or he was going to leave now. He glanced at his watch. Six minutes left. Before he knew he'd made up his mind, his legs took off.

His rubber-soled boots gripped the turf-like floor covering, making a scratching sound. The walls and ceilings were covered top to bottom with metal, making him feel like he was a rat stuck inside the intestines of a much larger carnivore. He continued to build up speed when the air temperature changed and he skidded to a halt.

"Holy…" he breathed, unable to finish. The room was exactly what the old miner had described; a gymnasium-sized room lined with metal cabinets, each one waist high, three drawers deep. He stepped towards the closest one, reaching out his hand, ridiculously afraid the grey yellow might shock him.

Alabama. Alaska. Arizona…

A bead of sweat trickled down his forehead, making its way between his eyebrows and to his nose.

He gripped the handle, glancing around the emptiness, fighting the irrational fear someone was lurking in the dark, ready to shoot him for what he was about to do.

Breaking the law? Check. Federal crime? Check. Death penalty or life spent in a dungeon without seeing the light of day? Check.

It doesn't matter. I have to know.

He found Colorado and opened the drawer. His chest barely moved and the sweat felt frozen. The clear, plastic sheets were organized by year, starting thirty-seven years before. Time enough for his parents to lose their identities, more than sufficient to soften memories of their individuality. And him and his generation? *We never had a chance.*

He pulled out one clear slip cover. Within each square slot was a silver block, the size and shape of the sugar cubes used at restaurants. He removed it, turning it over. The surfaces were hard and smooth. He pressed. Fire proof. Water proof. Perhaps it was titanium, damage proof. In other words, indestructible.

The miner had been telling the truth. Instinct told Kyle he had only a precious few minutes left. He found the year he wanted, lifted the cover and removed the blocks and slammed the drawer shut, making sure it closed completely. He was about run when he stopped. On instinct rather than thought, he opened the drawer back up and pulled out a cover from California, slammed it shut then jogged down the aisle, intent on finding New York.

Main…Masters.

Masters? It couldn't be. Adrenaline shook his fingers as he slid open the metal drawer. Six cubes. One or all? With a swipe they were gone. To make his theft look legit, he went to New York and picked a cube at random.

He was already running as he slid the blocks inside an inner pocket, awkwardly zipping it closed. He hit the top of tunnel at full-speed, skidding against the metal as he slammed his palm down on the bank of lights with one hand and hit the black button to open the sliding metal door with the other. It whooshed open, the wind and snow attacking his face, knocking him back. He steadied himself against the wall, pushing into the wind that threatened to hurl him over the edge.

*Ten…twenty…*Kyle counted, moving to the spot where the truck should be. *Thirty…*he stopped cold. The truck wasn't here but the edge was. He frantically shown the light around the entire area, the beam doing a poor job of cutting through a shield of snow that had become a blizzard.

Whoop..whoop..whoop. The muffled sound coming up the valley gave him the split second he needed to flip around, diving back towards the south side of the shed. *Military chopper.* The whooping sound was getting louder, the resonance deeper.

Had the old miner wanted Kyle to get caught? No, the man had wanted him to succeed. He had been drunk and desperate. He'd either forgotten or hadn't known about another internal trigger.

Kyle scrambled on his belly, his arms extending out like a crab, moving at a diagonal to the side of the drop off, searching desperately for the trailhead, worried for Joe. The tire tracks would be covered from the snow; no trace there. It was a short, two minute drive down, with several tunnels. If fate were on Joe's side, and the universe really was endowed with an all-powerful being who wanted to exact justice, the escaping truck would be blessed with an invisible cloak of rock when the chopper flew overhead. If it didn't, and Joe was caught, Kyle's identity would be extracted through needle.

Kyle didn't dwell on the possibility. The road wasn't an option; he'd take the faster, more dangerous route down the mountain hillside.

He shimmied to the edge, sure he'd found the path.

The whooping was coming around the mountain, and Kyle clenched his lips, put his arms out over his head, palms touching, and dove.

His chest took the brunt of the hit, his elbows next and then his palms, cutting a line down the center of the snow-covered path. It had been a lighter than normal snowfall, the powder thick enough to take away the worst of the sting but not so deep that it slowed him down.

The path itself was safe enough; no drop offs or ledges that didn't already have safety poles. He used his hands as deflectors against the smaller boulders like a bobsled going around corners. He banked to his left and hit a barrier, instantly pivoting to the other side. When he'd started exploring the area, his mom had told him hikers had put up the rudimentary poles and nets to save themselves the hassle of falling off after they'd smoked their pot. He cursed as his right hand smashed into a metal post, anger and gratitude mixed as he thought of the hikers who had just saved his life.

As he slid, he wondered if the men in the chopper had gotten out or even landed.

No way. No room. The wind and the snow were too fierce. They'd get stuck, he thought, hoping he was right.

His inattention was ill-timed. His chin cracked against the stone edge and another hit went to his chest. He rolled to the right, protecting his precious cargo. Bad move. A rock connected with the back of his skull. He turned, spread his legs, and with the other hand, tried grasping for a branch or tree, anything to stop his momentum. He caught a branch and felt the pull of his forearm. It was enough. Curling his legs in, the snow bunched under and around his knees, creating a mound in front of him.

He spit snow and blood from his mouth, feeling the back of his head. It was wet, the moisture between his thumb and forefinger black. Small cut, nothing major. He crouched, absorbing his surroundings. The lights from the Bailey house, closest to the base of the mountain, were a few hundred yards away. No dog. No noise.

Kyle felt the objects in his jacket. D had been right so far; that meant these cubes stored data, more than any house-sized memory bank could hold. But how to get it off? He thought of the person who would know. He had to get back to town before the curfew hit. Local law enforcement was much more relaxed in the mountain towns than in the cities, but the residents knew better than to flaunt the privilege.

Once he reached the end of the trail, he looked either way for signs of movement, took a deep breath and bolted.

CHAPTER 02

Kyle sprinted down the Bailey's gravel driveway, cutting across the main road. The bright red, green, and blue Christmas lights strung along the gutters of the home lit the otherwise dark street, showing the ground was barely covered with snow. The storm was just now descending from the top of the mountains, gaining intensity as the temperature dropped.

He pushed up the sleeve on his jacket. 9:05 p.m. He slid his hand under his hood, touching his head again. He reached down and wiped the blood on the ground, making a black smudge. He couldn't remove the gloves yet, he still needed them.

Keeping to the west side of the road and under the trees, he ran south until he reached the large maple tree that stood on the corner of the baseball-field sized lot to the south of the hot springs. The pool shut an hour ago and it was Matt's night to close. He'd be long gone.

Sprinting towards the back door, he'd never been so thankful for the job he'd had since he was old enough to pass the life-guard test. It had helped him afford the sports-related fees when his parents' job hadn't, and put a few extra bucks in his wallet throughout the year. It was going to help him now.

Two feet away from the south entrance, he took out the key he always kept with him.

"Thank you for not listening to me," Kyle whispered out loud to Barrett, the owner who was nowhere to be found. Kyle, who had been after him to get rid of the archaic key system in favor of an electronic card, exhaled with relief. Electronic meant tracking in and out. A key meant no one would ever know he'd come or gone.

He washed his hands twice, then tore off the gloves, darting to the laundry room where the cleaning crew kept their supplies. He lifted the lid of the trash can where used gloves were placed. Everyone who worked at the springs took turns cleaning. This was one more pair with his DNA, just like all the others he'd thrown away for the last six years. Trash day was Monday, another bit of luck. If the gloves left residue on the button he'd pressed or cabinets, they'd soon be gone.

He went to his locker, changed into his workout gear then put his head under the sink, carefully rinsing the blood from his hair and neck. Washing the basin clean, he put his head below the automatic hand dryer and two minutes later, retrieved the cubes.

Where to put them? He'd be a fool to keep them on him.

The fish pond. He found two plastic Ziploc bags, inserted the cubes into one, closed it, then inserted it into the other. Shutting off the light, he walked out of the main office area, alongside the rectangular pool area to the fish pond. The original owner had been a lover of tropical fish and had isolated part of the springs, converting it into a warm-water refuge for imported turtles and koi. The entire place smelled slightly of sulfur, but neither tourists nor turtles minded.

Dropping at the edge, he tilted one of the big, slime-covered rocks and slid the cubes underneath. A fish brushed the back of his hand, right where it had knocked the pole.

"That hurt," he muttered.

"Kyle, that you?" Kyle's heart pushed into his throat until he recognized the voice. It was his boss, Barrett Maloney.

"Hey, boss," Kyle answered casually, his voice at odds with his heart rate. "Just checking on Fred here," he said, stroking a nearby turtle.

"Didn't Matt close tonight?" Kyle stood.

"That's why I'm here. Wanted to make sure he got it all right. We learned what a new guy means to the turtle population." His boss grunted and walked to the edge of the fence. His eye was on the water more than Kyle, muttering about the legalities of acquiring new turtles with the government restrictions.

"Thought you'd already be with Ashley," said Barrett, giving Kyle a knowing smile. The darkness didn't hide the slightly leering look in the older man's eyes, nor did it disguise the envy that seemed to ooze along with the comment. Ashley was the prettiest thing in the town of 500, and everyone knew it, including Ashley.

"You know better than that," Kyle answered dourly.

"What? She saving puppies from the frozen lake tonight?" They both laughed. It wasn't enough to be tall, rail thin and live in the largest private residence in town. She was constantly bringing home any stray she found.

"Friday is formal family dinner, actually. I'll take a pass on that one."

Barrett gestured to the exit and they both began walking towards it.

"You're one lucky hombre, my friend. I'd endure a dinner with her family if I were you, assuming it was going to get me where I wanted to be." Kyle went along with the man's laughter, slightly grossed out at the idea of the older, pot-bellied man with his girlfriend.

Kyle opened the lock with his master key and joined Barrett on the other side, locking it behind him. "Right. And you'd find yourself on the end of a 12-gauge shotgun."

Barrett laughed dismissively. "I've heard about her father's collection but don't think he could hold it on his shoulder. Too girly, like his daughters."

"I treasure being male too much to take a chance. Besides, my dad warned me never to underestimate a father's protective instincts."

They walked past the swing set and slides, along the concrete path that framed the baseball field and paralleled main street.

"Wanna join me for a drink?" Barrett asked. "I mean, not a real drink. You don't do that, I know. But just hitting Ty's. We got time."

"Sure," Kyle said, blowing the snow away from his mouth. He guessed the chopper was still up in the mountain and the searchers were going through everything. Did they have fingerprint equipment? Unlikely. They were probably armed and ready for a fight, not dealing with forensics.

He schooled himself from turning back to the pond. The most important thing he'd ever attained in his life was under the water, with Fred the turtle.

As they walked, lights shown from behind and Kyle heard the sound of an on-coming car. Thirty seconds later, it came abreast of them, the window rolled down and they slowed in time.

"Hey Sheriff," Barrett respectfully drawled. The Sheriff nodded, leaning across the seat.

"Kyle, that you?" Kyle leaned down and waved. *Breathe. Answer casually but be polite. Standard Kyle.*

"Slow night, Sheriff Dearden?" Kyle asked.

"So far," Dearden answered. "Heading to Ty's?"

"Where else?" Barrett replied. Not many of the teens hung out at Ty's and it was by choice. Other than the owner's kid Billy and Kyle, the town's teenagers favored the bowling alley at the edge of town or getting into trouble at home while their parents were out at the bars. But Kyle had another reason he wanted to be at Ty's tonight. He knew Billy would be there; the only person he could talk to about his…situation. It was also his alibi, assuming he ever needed one.

"Can't report what I don't see," Deardon replied with a wink barely visible under his dark, arched eyebrows, acknowledging Kyle's destination and his implicit approval. His thick cheek moved, showing a visible mass and Kyle suspected he had a plug of chew inside. "Kyle, your dad up at the Elks Lodge?"

"Is it cold outside?" Kyle asked in return.

"Good enough," Sheriff Deardon said, rolling up his window. A crackling of static and tense orders came from within the vehicle as the window was near the top. Kyle saw the Sheriff's hand practically rip his shoulder mic and curse loud enough for him to hear. The tires spun and the car fishtailed as he turned in the middle of the road, heading back the way he came, the only way to access the mountain road to the mine.

"Looks like no drinks for him," Barrett muttered without sympathy.

They crossed the street to the east side of the road, toward a modest, one-story egg-shell blue home with a thin line of blue lights at the top. It was the length of a trailer and about as wide, and it marked the beginning of Main Street. The sign outside read "Windows to the World Stained Glass," and a thin woman with shoulder length blond hair was bent over a table in front of the rectangular window. She appeared to be inserting pieces of glass in a lead frame, and as they watched, a bone-like hand lifted and adjusted the light down, closer to her project. She then took a drink from a mug and continued her task; neither her eyes or head moved.

"Your mom ever stop working?" Barrett asked, as if he didn't know her work habits as well as the rest of the town.

"She's got a project on deadline." He told Barrett about the new window commissioned by a church in Oregon. It was comprised of more than a thousand tiny pieces, all hand cut and soldered. "Too bad they aren't going to pay her what it's worth." She never did charge enough, and it infuriated Kyle. She created Tiffany lamp replicas so good no one but the experts could tell they weren't the real thing, but she refused to charge more than the cheap versions at the local store. *She worked so hard.*

"Hey, Mom!" Kyle yelled. She looked up, smiled and waved. He pointed up the street and she nodded, the next instant her head was down. She had a different schedule than Dad. He liked to get up at the crack of dawn, walk five miles through the trails, drink a half pot of coffee and work on his intricate wood floors until seven at night. Then it was quitting time. Mom, on the other hand, liked to get up late, work late and shut down right about the time the sun came up. The balance meant that Kyle always had a parent around and available, as quirky as they both were.

Kyle glanced across the street at the austere grey Victorian. The house didn't fit in, the authentic versions built by the original homesteaders. This was too modern, like the architect read the book but put a New York gloss on it. Kyle saw the man of the house, Stuart Fine, stand and raise a toast.

Kyle walked faster, which set Barrett laughing.

"Hey, slow down. Your girlfriend's not going to be sitting at the window, watching you hit the bar."

"No, but her dad might be." When the Fine family moved into town, Ashley's dad had tried to buy his parent's home, wanting it for the large backyard that butted directly against the base of the mountain. Nothing but rocks, goats, bears, and the best view in town. When his parents didn't budge, Stu purchased the lot across the street and erected the Victorian.

The uncharitable men in town muttered it was a monument to his own ego, with plenty of rooms that no one entered with dirty shoes. But size didn't seem to be the real issue. It was more like it didn't fit in, just like Stu. From the raucous fights Kyle heard in the summers when the windows were open, the missus wasn't real happy about leaving her California country club and social life.

Still, Stu wasn't a complete jerk. In fact, both he and his wife did all they could to assimilate. They walked to town and bought local, mostly for staples like milk. It wasn't until Kyle got inside their home that he saw they lived a very different existence than the rest of the town folk. At least they don't rub it in people's faces.

Except for the few they invited over.

Kyle envisioned Ashley sitting at the table, her preferred spot to the left of her father, who always occupied the far end. From there he'd look at the other nine people, Ashley being the first and the last. Her long hair would have curls at the end and probably be pulled back from her face, the way her dad liked. The light off the three-foot-wide crystal chandelier would glance off her perfect face, and she'd be the hostess in training, taking her direction from her stern mother who insisted on linen napkins and silver in the formal dining room.

The only one missing was Ruth, the older sister who lived in Montrose, thirty minutes north.

Kyle wasn't opposed to formality for the appropriate occasion. When invited to Sunday dinner, he dressed as well as he could afford. He used good manners, but even sitting at that house was stress-inducing and uncomfortable, like he was a coarse pinecone tilted awkwardly on a silk couch.

"Maybe the dinner tonight and the strangers in that room have to do with the mine," Barrett hypothesized. "All those rumors about new activity flying around."

Kyle honestly didn't know. "That's why they are called rumors. Nothing's going on up at the mine or the whole town would know. They're probably just relatives."

"Yeah, and I gotta admit Stu's presence has served a purpose."

"So true."

Regardless of his personality quirks, Stu had done well for the town. After the mine ended operation, the government required Daimonte clean up the mess caused from decades of tailings left over from the drilling. It had nearly devasted the local water supplies, muddied the valleys and left dangerous gorges that skiers and snowmobilers had stumbled into and died. Stu was the executive Daimonte assigned to restore the area, thereby reclaiming the land, giving it back to nature. Stu had employed any able-bodied resident stupid enough to hook himself to a wire cable and straddle open shafts plummeting hundreds of feet into the ground.

Kyle was first in line. It paid a thousand a week and took balls of steel. The summer Kyle turned 15 and hit 5'10", he applied, seeing only the numbers on the other side of the ravine, not the death shoot below him. One year and four inches later, Kyle learned Ashley was interested in him, and before he so much as walked her home, he was smart enough to approach her dad. Stu had approved, but made it clear he expected more from Kyle than good grades and an athletic scholarship.

"I'm counting on you to use your judgment with my daughter," Stu had told him in his quiet, intense way that came with a thin-lipped delivery. Barrett might think Stu was incapable of holding a gun, but Kyle had every confidence the man had the connections to get a college application rejected or a basketball scholarship nixed. If that happened, Kyle had twelve thousand dollars in savings. Not enough for an Ivy League school, but he had the backup plan of an academic scholarship with a low-income grant; two benefits of being poor and smart.

Kyle blinked his eyes against the larger flakes.

Two homes past his own, they crossed a nearly-invisible concrete bridge covering a trench created for the massive water runoff in the spring. The elevated grade continued until it reached the center of town then leveled out. Across Main Street, old stables stood beside new art galleries, the influx of up and coming artists pushed out of Telluride setting up shop in a place where their Avant-guard talent and lower prices gave way to higher sales.

"Looks like the bar is hoppin," Barrett remarked as they neared. Of course it was. Nowhere else to go other than the Elks club, and that was usually filled with guys like his dad, who liked a beer with a pull-top can and preferred shuffle board to flat screens. Ty's joint catered to a younger crowd from out of town, who watched the fights on pay-per-view and spent four times what they needed to for a cold one.

Or to the locals who got a discount, and out-of-towners never knew.

Kyle shivered. As long as he sat in the front, behind the blacked out window and kept his head down, no one bothered him. The town protected its own, and Kyle wasn't an underachieving druggie, but an athletic standout who was determined to be the first in his family to go to college, and not let a misadventure with alcohol or unexpected pregnancy derail his goals. That gave him a pass, at least at the local bar.

Barrett held the door open and Kyle led the way, telling him he'd see him at the pool tomorrow before veering to the left.

CHAPTER 03

Kyle stopped short, seeing his usual spot taken by guys from over the hill in Telluride. You could always spot them. The jackets had names which to Kyle meant a car payment. No one around here would wear brands even if they could afford it.

Low key and cool. That's how we are. They could call us backwards and broke. *And for the most part, they would be right.*

He turned to the only other place he could safely sit knowing what he'd find before he saw it: Billy, sitting in the corner, hunched over a computer, pencil in hand, frantically writing something in a notebook on the table. Billy was the only person giving him a run for the valedictorian award, a rivalry that had started in the seventh grade.

"Hey," Kyle said, shaking the snow from his collar before he got to close. "Mind if I join you?" Billy pointed the tip of a pencil at the empty chair. Billy worked alone, usually on the weekends, and usually in the front of the bar. Better than being alone at home, Kyle guessed.

Kyle took in the patrons as nonchalantly as he knew how, giving the small room a passing glance, quick enough not to perturb anyone. Just because he was a known entity didn't mean all the older men wanted him to see their stupid antics or hear their off-color remarks about the local women.

He didn't see who he was looking for.

"Have you seen D?" he asked Billy.

"He's down at the retirement home," Billy answered without looking up. Kyle took off his jacket and he leaned back in his chair.

Kyle's stomach grumbled, and he wondered if he could keep anything down. He felt the tension building deep in his gut, like a volcano coming alive after a million years of dormancy.

Out of nowhere, Billy put the pencil down with force.

"Ok. You are giving off some seriously bad mojo and I gotta concentrate here."

"I need some food." *And some help*, Kyle thought, now debating if he wanted to risk getting Billy involved, but already knowing he had to. In fact, after listening to D's secret, his first thought had been that D was senile. His second thought had been of Billy.

Billy looked him up and down, a raking glance that took in far more than they should. "Then get some," Billy said, pencil motionless, waiting for Kyle to move. The distant wail of sirens stuck Kyle's butt to his seat, and out of the corner of his left eye, he saw red and blue lights flashing. His heart gave a pound so loud it rung in his ears. "Change your mind?" Billy asked, irritably.

"Don't know what I want, is all," he replied, pretending to look at the menu above the bar, attempting to squint down the blood that rushed to his head. *Concentrate on the letters, not on the siren.* There was no way they could track him in the snow, even if the helicopter had landed and assuming his footprints or body-slide down the trail could have been followed. Then to the waterpark? No way. It was right across from him anyway. He would have seen the lights. No, they weren't after him. Not yet.

"You get in a fight with whatser-name?" Billy asked, at the same time examining Kyle's face as if it might have visible claw marks.

"She's at dinner with her family," he responded automatically.

"My bad," Billy said without a bit of remorse. "You don't care enough about her to fight, at least not that I can see."

"Excuse me?" Billy's head was already down again and Kyle let it pass. He needed some answers. With a full stomach, he'd get the fortitude to talk to Billy about what was really on his mind.

"I'm going for the potato skins. Want some?" Billy declined, and Kyle felt for his wallet. It...*oh, no.* It had been in his back pocket when he went up the mountain. Had it fallen out on his slippery slide down the hill? During the jog to the springs or was it at the springs itself?

Calm down. Lost wallets happened all the time and his contained little besides identification. One credit card with a five hundred dollar limit he used only for emergencies and twenty bucks, his student body card and driver's license. Still, all it took was one person to find it and they'd be after him. Kyle tried to take the optimistic outlook. It might be buried in the deep snow until next spring. In the meantime, he'd have to cancel the card and get replacements or risk getting popped for not having ID.

"What now?" Billy asked.

"Lost my wallet," he mumbled, wondering if he should venture back out to the pool. He looked out the window, patting himself down again just to be sure. As he considered his options, two cop cars raced up the street, full lights and sirens. Kyle's hand went in to slow motion, touching his back pockets and the front of his jacket, all the while gazing out to the street.

"You're lying."

"Are you crazy? My wallet *is* gone."

"No," Billy said calmly, staring him in the eye. "Not about that. Whatever's going on isn't about your wallet and it's not about hunger." Kyle kept touching his jacket, going through the motions, ignoring Billy. "Know how I know that? You aren't doing the one thing that you'd normally do when cop cars come screaming."

Kyle stopped his actions. "What's that?"

Billy leaned close. "You'd be the first one running down the street to see what was going on, because you're an adrenaline junkie."

He patted himself down one last time and then gave up. "It is possible I have more on my mind than chasing lights."

Billy observed him. "Add to the fact that you're sweaty in the middle of a snow storm, and you never sweat, not when you have three seconds on the clock, you're at center court, the game is in overtime and the score is tied."

"If you've ever seen a game, you know I sweat a ton."

"Not like this. This is a pale sweat. Not a face-flushed-with-energy sweat."

"I'm hot. So what?"

"And you've lost your wallet, which you have probably never done in your life because you're so stinking responsible." Billy leaned closer still, eyes steady. "The topper is that cops are zooming right by us and you're acting like a deer in the headlights getting ready to take a full-body hit. It all tells me that you're most likely in the middle of some deep shit." Billy had whispered the last comment, requiring Kyle to involuntarily move closer to catch the last words. He'd felt his eyes widening at Billy's theory, and he forced them lower so as not to look surprised.

"Wow. The golden boy's in trouble," Billy said smugly, and Kyle knew he'd given himself up by remaining silent. "Let me ponder the implications of this turn of events while I get you a Coke and some potato skins. I'm suddenly hungry."

Billy stood up, then bent to Kyle's ear. "That'll teach you never to go against a female's intuition," she said, leaving Kyle without an adequate response.

CHAPTER 04

Kyle's heart raced faster than it had since running down the mountain. The only difference was he now had a cold chill instead of hot sweat dripping down the middle of his back. One piece of evidence was out there in the snow. The wallet could be anywhere; on the trail, near the Bailey place. It would be a blessing if it was on the floor at the pool.

Kyle forced his eyes west, watching the activity on the street while Billy placed the order. At least she'll get fast service, and it would be on the house. He got on fine with her dad Ty, the owner of the bar, who was a solid basketball fan and knew Kyle's stats better than he did himself. Ty never missed a game, scooting out of the bar just before tip-off then racing back before the crowd hit for after game drinks.

Billy spoke with her dad as she waited for the food. She was laughing, looking up at the screen, acting as if she was unaware of his predicament. Callous. That's how he'd describe her, but she'd always been that way. She'd practically grown up inside these darkened walls, no mother around, her dad a barman. When she wasn't here, Billy was into her books or computers, and in the winter, shredding down the mountain on her snowboard. She put the guys to shame on the slopes, not that she cared. Rumor had it she didn't prefer guys all that much, though it couldn't be proven, and in five months, she'd graduate along with him and the rest of the seniors. Other than fighting it out for the valedictorian spot, Kyle sensed she wanted to get out of town as badly as he did, neither likely to return except to visit family. No one worked that hard for good grades just to graduate and work at the local bar.

A cop car did a U-turn and parked opposite the bar on the other side of the street. Kyle recognized the man. Deputy Mark Hancock, a stout guy five years older than himself. His other job was security and personal bodyguard to Ralph Lauren's family, since the fashion designer's 3,000-acre ranch was twenty minutes from Ouray.

As Officer Hancock crossed the street, Kyle noticed his sour face. *Not good.*

Hancock came straight in and glanced at Kyle without a word. He surveyed the room, zeroing in on the strangers opposite Kyle's table. He approached the men and in seconds, they were removing their wallets and presenting IDs. Hancock carefully inspected each one, holding the documents up to the dim lights that hung from the ceiling. The men at the bar caught the energy and the tone of the conversation and immediately down shifted a level quieter. Something was going on. This was a friendly tourist town, not a Patrol zone in the inner city.

As Kyle waited for Billy's return, he considered Hancock. Since high school, he'd gained thirty pounds, but it seemed to be equally proportioned from his shoulders to his hips, making him a block of a man. His round face was accented by a scar on his chin that sliced it in half, the indent permanent, courtesy of taking a hockey puck his junior year of high school while wearing a half-face mask.

Government issued faces developed normally with age but didn't protect against scrapes or burns or the odd hockey puck. Still, the combination on Hancock's face intimidated the weak and comforted the strong, as though he was a nice guy but knew what it was like to take a beating.

Kyle glanced back out to the street. Sheriff Deardon's car was parked by the library, mid-town, not far from the Stagecoach Hotel. They seemed to be going door-to-door, starting with the obvious places first, as though someone who'd broken into a top-secret facility was going to stop and have a beer afterward.

"Potato skins and a coke," Billy announced, startling him. He took the drink from her outstretched hand. "Looks like Mark is actually doing something for a change," she added under her breath. She sat down and plunged the potato skin deep into the sour cream. "Here he comes," she said just before she took a bite. "So, anyway," she said in a louder voice, "the fridge is down and Dad wants to know if you can come over tonight and fix it."

"Tonight?" Kyle said, not having to feign surprise. "I'd like to go over but it's curfew. I don't know…" and he let the statement hang.

"You getting ready to break curfew again?" asked Officer Hancock behind him. Kyle looked over his left shoulder.

"Blame it on her," he responded, jerking his head to Billy. She shrugged innocence.

"It's the fridge's fault," Billy countered. "Dad wants him to fix it before the food goes bad. He can take the alley home, can't he?" Kyle had a moment of admiration for the girl. She was completely straight-faced, no frills or fancy words to entice the man. Where Ashley would have cocked her head and done something with her hair, making the request with the innocence of a nun, Billy told it like it was, regardless of the consequences.

"You two are already breaking the law, but you know that." He scrutinized them but not in an entirely unpleasant way. It was a look that said the unspoken truth: the three of them had grown up together, liked one another, and even though one was a cop and the other two underage kids in a bar, nothing was going to happen. Still, appearances had to be kept up.

"If it's really bad, I'll load up the food and take Kyle back to the place now," Billy said, cocking an eyebrow. "Want me to?"

"Don't go being all polite to me Billy," Hancock said. "Now isn't the time."

Billy smirked and put her hands up. "I'm just being respectful. Can't I be nice once without causing an uproar?"

"No. Not really," Hancock replied. Kyle smirked, because it was funny, and received a mock scowl from Billy. She wasn't known for her gregarious personality.

Officer Hancock took in Billy's spread on the table. "Standard Friday night studying?" She nodded. The police department knew the routines of everyone in town.

"Pretty much. My dad is convinced my hands are getting early-age arthritis from working on the computer. I'm trying to mix it up with a pencil and paper tonight."

Hancock ignored the sarcasm and looked out the window. Billy's eyes went to the food in front of her, but Kyle knew it would be unnatural if he didn't look out the window too. As Billy said, he was a guy and would be the first to run after the action in town.

"No game tonight Kyle. What have you been up to?"

"Got done working out, then checked on the new guy over at the pool, made sure the fish weren't dead. Barrett was with me and invited me up. Never say no to the boss." He paused to take a bite before jerking his thumb over his finger at Barrett. "Seriously, you going to tell us what's going on? Someone rob a bank?"

Hancock looked back at him. "Police business."

"We've heard that before," Billy drawled, her disinterest clear.

"Not even a hint?" Kyle pushed, doing his best to sound like a typical, curious teenager.

"Can't tell you what I don't know," Hancock said turning his back to the bar and adjusting himself so he stood between the two of them. "Just...watch it," he continued in a lower voice. "We are likely to be having someone else in law enforcement from out of town, maybe as early as tomorrow. I'd strongly advise both of you to be absent from the bar. And follow curfew. You, especially," he said to Kyle. "Saw the scouts at your last game. Don't go blowing your ride out of here." Hancock gave them a curt nod and walked down the sidewalk, crossed the street and headed to Ashley's house.

"You want to tell me what Mark didn't?" Billy asked him.

Kyle swallowed his food and took a drink. How could he possibly risk getting her involved in something that he couldn't anticipate or control? Taking a deep breath, he said, "Yes. And I am also going to ask for your help."

CHAPTER 05

Billy wiped her mouth with her napkin and shut down her computer.

"I've known you since fourth grade. In that time, you've asked for my help exactly twice. Once, in eighth grade, for the sludge experiment. The other time when you asked me to review our paper in 10th grade, but then promptly ignored what I'd written, submitting it as you'd written---"

"And got a B-."

"Exactly. So, needing *me* for something related to school? Don't think so. Winter formal? I presume you have a date, so that's out. And even if you did ask, I don't have a dress. That leaves one possibility." Billy deposited the computer and her papers in the backpack, zipped it up and folding her arms on the top. "I don't have anything you desire other than a computer and my brains. That means you can't do whatever it is you need done yourself. Plus, you lost your wallet, are sweating and are afraid of the cops. Whatever has happened involves you, and now me."

Kyle pressed his lips together, fighting off the urge to rip her a comeback that would wipe away the accuracy of her summation, but couldn't.

"That's pretty much it," he unwillingly admitted. He needed her. Badly. And this one time, her social-outcast status was a layer of protection against being a target if he got caught.

She frowned in concentration. "Let's get on it then," she said, motioning for him to look out the front window. "Looks like Mark's done at your girlfriend's house. He looks pissed." Sure enough, Mark was walking up the road, stomping would be a better word, his eyebrows a dark line that would make Frida Kahlo proud, the scowl accentuating his jowls.

Kyle followed Billy through the human corridor that led to the back of the bar. Instead of turning left to the bathrooms, she went straight and right, into a hallway connecting the grocery store on the north side. Through the door they went, then took a hard left where she unlocked what she called her front door.

"Try not to be overwhelmed by the glamour you're about to encounter." Kyle set his expectations suitably low. He walked through the door and stopped, stunned. "That's you not being overwhelmed?"

"Sorry," Kyle stuttered, "I guess, I..." and he just stopped talking, knowing his brain wasn't operating the way it should after the events of the evening, and now this.

"Grab a seat and I'll be right back," she told him. The home was a small-scale replica of a lodge, the pine-lined walls stained a warm chestnut, a river-rock fireplace on the far wall extended to the ceiling and above the coffee table in the center was a round, western-styled light fixture of metal covered with antlers.

"Nice," he said out loud. The coat hook was a horse hoof, dented and worn. Real, not faux. When he sat back down, he examined the antler chandelier closer. The horns didn't match. The white wasn't even all over. Some of the tips were broken. The thing was real. Only faux antler chandeliers were perfect.

Kyle took a seat in a faded, extremely comfortable, rust-colored leather arm chair. It matched the adjacent couch, its bullet-like buttons serving as the trim along the bottom and arms. *Bullets, not standard brass rivets,* touching one with his forefinger. The metal was warm, just like the feeling in the room. He wondered if it was Ty's doing, or Billy, or Billy's long-gone mother.

Billy returned with the Coke in one hand, a remote in the other. Suddenly music filled the room, hidden speakers blasting the sounds of country Christmas.

"Country? Really?" Kyle questioned.

"Consider it cowboy Christmas. You're not opposed to horses and cows, are you?"

He grunted. "Cow-tipping has never been at the top of my bucket list," he replied. Billy laughed, a lyrical jingle of sounds that caught him off guard. He'd never heard her laugh before, and he expected a deeper, rough sound.

"Come on," she said, motioning for him to follow her. He got up and they entered a smaller, wood-paneled room with floor to ceiling built-in bookshelves. He ran a finger across one of the hardwood panels. This wasn't even a normal North American hardwood. He heard the clinking of ice in a glass.

"Brazilian cumaru," he said, still admiring the material. Only his dad's celebrity clients over in Telluride could get the licenses required to import this stuff and his father had always been required to sign a confidentiality agreement. They didn't want him sharing secrets or taking pictures of the insides of their homes.

Billy stood beside him, holding out his drink. "Took Dad a while to find what he wanted, but eventually the right customer came in and replaced the existing stuff with newer wood. We got the leftovers."

"This place is pretty cool."

"Look behind you."

It was a tree adorned with cowboy ornaments. Cowboy Santas made out of iron, boots in metal and glass, a miniature guitar, metal spurs, turquoise stars with mirrors on the inside, lassos for garland, and of course, plenty of cows. "I hope you didn't take offense at my cow-tipping comment."

"No. You just confirmed you need to broaden your mind."

Billy took a seat in a dark armchair. She curled her feet up underneath her legs, sipping from a mug. It smelled like hot chocolate. Opposite her was a two-person love seat, at one time embroidered with a picture-like pattern, but it was now faded into oblivion. Kyle sat, admiring a metal floor lamp featuring molded cowboys and horses, the soft light within the tan cowhide showing an intricately stitched fighting scene. To his left was a substantial desk, not notable for its exotic wood, but because it looked quite old, from another age where the carving was done in a style he hadn't seen around here.

Billy pulled off her cap, revealing a mop of platinum-dyed hair which was wedge cut to the side. One part flopped over her left eye, the look avant garde and sexy, more New York hipster than Rocky Mountain snowboarder. The sides were close cut and dark, matching her eyebrows. At once, her greenish-hazel eyes popped out, her dark lashes contrasting even more.

"Since you're wondering, I'll put you out of my misery." Kyle felt heat in his neck and he wondered if he was so transparent in his examination. "My relatives were immigrants from Germany and settled in Minnesota before coming to Durango. My great-grandfather got lucky in the hills and started a mine, made a bucket of money and went back home, returning with some family pieces."

"This is pretty cool," Kyle complimented, grateful she had gone to her history and not her looks. "Didn't know you were German and in the mining business. Does Stu know?"

"I doubt it, but it wouldn't matter much if he did. My dad got disinherited by marrying a woman with Indian blood. Then Grandfather died and his wife sold off the mine. It's up there," she finished, absently gesturing up the mountain.

"The Durango Mine?" Kyle asked incredulously.

"The very one." No one in this town had a clue as to what Ty and his daughter Billy were all about, including himself, and he got the feeling he was just scratching the surface.

"So? I'm waiting." Kyle had a moment of paranoid hesitation. "If you're worried about someone eavesdropping, we have Santa Claus is Coming to Town covering us. It's a favorite." Billy raised her eyes to the speakers in the ceiling. "See those red dots in the corners of the moldings? Infa-red radar that blocks listening devices. Someone can be standing right outside our house and only pick up the music, because the speakers are above the radar. The voices are below."

"Billy…" he stopped, unable to continue.

"Just spit it out, already," she said, losing her patience.

"I think I've got the deepest secret the U.S. government has ever tried to hide. If it's what I think it is, and they find out, they—whoever tracks me down—won't let me live to tell about it."

"That's pretty dramatic," she deadpanned, waiting expectantly. Kyle didn't laugh. When she saw he was serious, her lashes dropped. "And you think I'm going to want to help you?"

"When you hear the story, you're either going to want to help me, or I'll be going to jail and you'll get the valedictorian award you've always wanted."

CHAPTER 06

Ouray county Sheriff Jack Deardon squinted against the pelting snow and pulled up his thick, police-issue belt. It was late, and he should have been on his couch at home, his belt loosened a notch, a Bud Light in one hand, watching basketball. Instead, he was going door-to-door, starting at the top of Main Street, asking questions of the locals; searching out the tourists, checking the locks, all done with the urgency given to the scenario of an escaped convict, not an inactive mine that had set off alarms.

When he was asked what the fuss was about, he answered it was nothing more than some thrill-seekers making trouble. That was the party line, but he felt inclined to imply that it was the owners of the mine who were overreacting, not his department. Heck, it would be just like that uptight ass Stu to get the alarm notice and call in the SWAT team. What a waste of manpower. There were real criminals around—not so much in Ouray, thank God—but elsewhere that needed actual attention.

To his surprise, it seemed that Stu had been ignorant of what happened until he'd gotten a call from State, who had been downstream from the feds in D.C. By now, Deputy Hancock had already visited Stu, getting his own butt chewed off for interrupting dinner and Stu being irritated he wasn't the first one told about the mine. Hancock had to remind Stu he was the police. That in turn, inspired Stu to get on the phone and go back upstream, like a salmon in the fall. All the way to Maury O'Connell, Colorado's head of police. The tide pool of pain had continued and was still swirling, and he and his deputy were like fish caught in the current.

He pulled the collar up on his waterproof, police-issued coat and kept walking. This was the sleepiest town in this corner of the state, and he was happy for it. Sure, it had the odd meth lab on the outskirts, but those were quickly discovered and almost always set up by some big-city vagrant from a bordering county. Big news in his town was the basketball team getting its butt whipped, but with Kyle Smith as Captain, that hadn't happened in four years. Next year, when the kid was gone, the town would be rioting over the losses, but would eventually drink down their depression at Ty's bar before heading home.

Deardon passed Hancock on the other side of the street.

"Anything?" Hancock shook his head and raised his hands. Deardon kept walking, replaying the conversation he had with the head of the state's police department, Maury O'Connell.

"Was there anything in the mine worth stealing?" Deardon had asked the number one guy.

"It's being investigated," O'Connell had answered, his Boston accent still thick, even though he'd been in Denver a decade.

That was a non-answer, and it meant that the guy, or guys, probably weren't armed and dangerous. It wasn't like the mine had produced gold for years. All it had in it were mice and dust.

"Shouldn't we be heading back up there to see if the person who set off the alarm has fallen down a shaft?" Deardon asked. "Whoever tripped the alarm could still be there."

"Whoever it was made it inside," O'Connell had told him with authority. *They knew that?*

"If you have cameras then you have to have a description."

O'Connell hesitated ever so slightly. "No footage. It has pads on the floor."

Pads on the floor? Deardon's analytical mind kicked in. The floor was supposed to be dirt—it was a mine, after all.

Pads meant cement, a walkway. Metal. Sophisticated sensors that gave alerts.

"Did the sensors have a weight?" he asked without hesitation. "We can use it for a description of the guy."

"The data suggests that whoever penetrated the facility was running fast and hard based upon the space between the steps and the pound per square inch."

Deardon listened for more than the content. Something else was here. This was getting interesting.

"So, you don't know the weight, but the person was athletic enough to get away and you think he's still in town."

"Without a doubt." And by getting involved, the government was admitting—at least to him—that whatever might have been removed from within the mine was so important, it required a door to door search.

Deardon wondered if Stu knew what was in the mine. Deardon thought not. When it got cleaned up, it was sold to the government. It was their property now.

"Tell me this. Are we searching for something dangerous?" He could just see some dime-sized nuclear reactor go off in his hands without warning.

"Not dangerous in a *physical* sense," O'Connell answered, the cadence of his words spread out, like Peter walking out on the water towards Jesus, one step at a time, unsure if the next step was going to be solid or not.

In the physical sense. A bit of tension released from Deardon's shoulders. No nuclear weapons, that was comforting. Gold reserves? That wasn't dangerous to anyone but the financial community who continually feared the renegade anarchists who wanted to topple what financial stability remained in the country.

"So, more important than the person, is an item that's small or large, believed to be on that person. Is that the net of it?" After O'Connell gave him an affirmative, Deardon had only one more question. The most important, which he'd saved for last.

"Do we consider this suspect armed and dangerous?" It should have been an immediate and emphatic yes. Terrorists are by definition, extremely dangerous, and invariably armed.

"Armed, we don't know. Dangerous? Extremely."

"At all costs then," Deardon affirmed, an awareness of the situation sinking in. To use the phrase at all costs meant dead or alive. In the case of taking a person down was the license to kill at will, without hesitation.

"Yes. Bring that person—or persons—in, at all costs."

CHAPTER 07

Billy's face was immobile. No movement save for her eyes that roved over his face, absorbing his words and expressions at the same time. Kyle had told a story of impossibilities, and Billy was reconciling his monologue with what she knew to be possible. She would either call him a liar or laugh. She did neither.

"It's too crazy to make up, and why would you?" she asked rhetorically, shaking her head, the hair flipping across her forehead. "What in the world was old D thinking when he told you? I mean, did he have some sort of come-to-the-alter moment with himself, fearing he was going to die in the near future so he had to tell someone?" Kyle had asked himself the same question.

"Doesn't matter," he answered. "He's back at the nursing home, the last place I'm going right now."

Billy stood, stretching her arms above, then over each side, like a tree swaying in the wind. Her shirt pulled up just far enough for her belly button to show, right in the middle of a ripped six-pack. It struck him that he'd never once seen her at the pool, not in the summer, nor in the winter. She didn't work out at the pool's gym, the only one in town. *At least not when I'm there.*

She shook her head, as if dismissing a thought.

"What?" he inquired.

"The mountains. The Saints. They took their idea."

"Not following."

Billy tilted her head back to the ceiling, raising her arms overhead and bending back, lifting her shirt an inch higher, the pose a yoga stretch. The girl didn't have a stitch of extra fat on her. Her skin coloring was also warmer due to her Indian blood. Unlike Ashley, whose light skin easily burned in the summer, he could see Billy becoming luxuriously dark.

Billy caught him looking at her stomach and mocked him. "What? You think I don't get out?" She dropped her arms, and lifted her leg, crossing one ankle over her opposite knee, sitting in a human chair.

"I've never seen evidence otherwise. What was your comment about?"

"The government copied the hole-in-the-mountain thing. Decades ago, the Saints in Utah dug out miles of tunnels straight into the Wasatch mountains. Locked it up like Fort Knox, concrete doors and all."

"What for?"

"Geneology. Records of people's ancestors. I just think it's funny the government did the same thing here."

She sat, placing her hands together in prayer position. "You said you're on shift tomorrow? And you said by the turtles?" He clarified where. "Then here's the plan. Get the cubes from Fred, put them in a bag and I'll come get it and the clothes you wore at the pool. Just leave it in a sack by the stool next to the floaties. People put their stuff there all the time. I'll get it and go." It could work, Kyle thought. Nothing out of the ordinary.

Suddenly he glanced around, unconsciously searching for a window that wasn't there.

"Don't do it," she said to Kyle, and he refocused on her eyes. "You're delusional if you think you can go up out and find your wallet in the middle of a blizzard. You're good but not that good." Kyle started to defend himself and she waived him off, just as she'd done in chemistry class when he gave a less-than-superior answer.

"By tomorrow, I'll figure out what's on the cubes. But what if D is wrong and they are useless? I mean, do you really think the government of the United States would store information so valuable it could change the face of the country—literally—here, in our town?" It was pretty far-fetched, but D had been so convincing…so sure of what he was saying.

"Old minds wander," Billy continued, the first hint of compassion in her voice he'd ever heard. "I'm not doubting what you've told me, it's just that he was a drunk, and already half-senile."

Part of Kyle wished it were all a hoax. What would the world look like with different faces? Would his good looks be stripped, along with his ego? And what was he going to do if the cubes turned out to be full of the secrets to go backwards? Would anyone want to go back? It might create an anarchy worse than the one the government had stopped thirty-seven years before.

"Look at this as our first group project," she said.

"And if it turns out to be nothing, we go back to what we were before; academic competitors who have very little say to one another?"

"Pretty much."

He doubted it. Either way, they'd have a forged a bond, albeit one on a very unstable platform.

That raised another topic and he shifted in his chair.

"What's got you now?" she asked bluntly. One thing about Billy. This girl observed everything.

"At school, we…us…"

Billy gave him a condescending head shake. "Are you kidding? We're going to be no different than we are now. If I need you, I'll figure out some secret handshake or gang wave in the hallway. Besides, we have nearly two weeks before school starts again. Christmas and New Year's," she continued, her words lightening his mood. "This whole thing might be over and done with."

"When you see Ashley—"

"Please. She's dense to anything but attention anyway. As long as she gets that, you have no reason to worry. You better get going. It's almost ten."

Kyle placed the bottle down and followed her through the home. He noticed the back door. From the alley, it was a non-descript, dark brown piece of wood. On the inside, it was an ornately carved.

Just like Billy. She was not at all on the inside what she appeared to be on the outside.

"See you tomorrow," she said.

"Yeah. See you."

Kyle jogged down the alley and two minutes later he was at his own back door. Hancock's car was still out front, but Kyle didn't see the officer on the street.

He kicked the snow off his shoes and turned the nob. It was unlocked as always. One of the few benefits of living in a small town in a remote corner of the state. Burglary was practically non-existent. He hung his jacket on the metal post, calling to his mom. He took one step through the kitchen, another in to the hallway and the third he was in his mom's office.

"How's it going?" he asked, giving her a hug from behind.

"Good." He looked over her shoulder to the workspace. She was in the middle of placing a piece of blue glass into the outline of a bird. Moments later, she picked up the soldering iron and expertly lined the glass, adhering it in place.

"Nice," he complimented, glancing out the large bay window. The snow wasn't falling as hard now, but it was still coming down. He thought he saw a figure over at the pool, walking around the outside. It was too far away to identify the individual, but he guessed it was Barrett, checking the gates one last time.

A gut check gave him an uncomfortable pang. His wallet could be anywhere. But then Billy's words came to him. She was probably right. No-one was going to be searching the mountain trails in the dark for him or anyone else.

The cubes were hidden. Relax. Get some rest. Tomorrow his shift started at 10. He'd get there on time 9 a.m. and retrieve them. Feeling a lot better than he had in the last hour, he told his Mom he was going to watch a movie then hit it.

He took five steps down the hall to his tiny bedroom, located at the northern end of the house. He dropped the blind, turned on the tv and crashed on the couch, not bothering to open up the bed. He flipped off the lights, feeling his muscles release. First his back, then his shoulders, then legs, which became like the dead weight of a tree sinking into soft ground. In five minutes, he was snoring softly, oblivious to the world outside his home.

From across the street, the entrance into the Smith home was clearly visible for anyone to see. Stuart Fine had been standing at the window of his living room, a snifter full of brandy in his hand, contemplating the unforeseen events of the evening when he saw Kyle approach his mother and give her a hug.

Friday night, home on time, as usual, he thought approvingly. The boy was as clean as they came in this town. Didn't drink. Didn't smoke. Didn't fool around. Stu was confident the kid would be a straight-arrow without the subtle encouragement he'd offered, but it didn't hurt to provide the added incentive. He knew Kyle didn't have a basketball game so he'd probably been up at Ty's, drinking his standard Coke and eating either potato skins or chicken wings.

"Hey, Dad, what are you doing all alone in here?" It was Ashley, the second love of his life. She simply had it all. The looks. The personality. She had a perfect life and he was going to do all he could to ensure it didn't change.

"Just making certain all is right in the world," he told her, turning away from the window. Her eyes sparkled. She knew better.

"He's home?"

"Yep. Nothing to worry about." He draped his arm around her shoulder, careful not to squash the curls of her hair. He'd phone O'Connell in the morning for an update. Why the government hadn't called to notify him the mine alarm had tripped was beyond reason. It was an empty shell, like a snail that had been eaten alive, but it had once been under his control. Washington had asked for a lease and paid a handsome price for a closed version, where Daimonte couldn't access it without permission and the presence of the lessee. He hadn't been inside for over two years, and wouldn't mind seeing how they'd kept it up.

"What did Deputy Hancock want?"

Stu turned off the light and led her from the room. "Someone was up poking around the mine is all. Word got out and it's been blown out of proportion."

"Why does anyone care about that place?"

"My thoughts exactly," he said. Stu shut the door behind him, closing the subject as easily. "Let's get back to the party."

CHAPTER 08

FBI Deputy Director Forland used the eraser end of the pencil to call the White House. He got the NSA director on the line, gave her the update and made his recommendation. "We send in Cox." A single affirmative on the other end gave him the go ahead. The next call was to his senior operative in Denver, Colorado, Brayden Cox. It was just after ten p.m. mountain time.

"Cox here." Forland heard the noise of a game in the background and the cheering and swearing that went along with it.

"Director Forland. Can we talk?"

"Give me a moment." Seconds passed and the sounds gradually faded. He heard the clicking and shutting of a door, and then complete silence. "I'm in my car, and the blocker is on. What can I do for you, sir?"

Forland explained the details.

"The team will need time---"

"No team," Forland interrupted. "Just you. This is a small town wary of the Patrol and the FBI won't be far behind on their list. The residents will close ranks."

"You're suggesting someone who did this was local?"

"Yes, or had help from one. The majority of people who worked at and closed up that mine were employed by Daimonte and hired by Stuart Fine. I'd bet most are still residents. I've got Desoto already pulling the files on every employee from the security firm the government hired, and we already have the names of the Daimonte employees."

"Could it be a new group of naturalists not on our radar?"

"That's one scenario. Another is that they had help from someone on the inside, over at NSA, the only group associated with this project. That investigation has already started. You are to discover who they tapped, where they got the entry information and what's missing."

"Missing, sir?"

Forland took a deep breath. "Brayden, what's stored in that shaft are the DNA records of every man, woman and child for the past thirty-seven years."

"A backup for the national medical records? Sir, I don't mean to be disrespectful, but we already have duplicates of that, along with the Social Security data in the retired nuclear shafts in Arizona."

"This is entirely different. I've been told the data are unique identifiers of the individuals in this country. The data is stored on metal cubes the size of your thumb. You have to get there and determine what's missing, if anything. It will decide the direction we take."

A pause followed his statement. "Got it." Investigating was one thing. Search and destroy another, but that was the Patrol's job, not his.

"One other thing," Forland continued. "The local executive I mentioned, Stuart Fine, may get in your way. He's with Daimonte and used to run the place, but he still lives there."

"Dangerous?" asked Brayden.

"Not that we know of. Just irritating. Let me know if you need help and we'll manage it."

Brayden called his wife at the hospital and was told she was in surgery. He sent her a text with the barest of information: he would be gone for a few days on assignment to Ouray. By eleven, he was driving out of Denver. With any luck, he'd arrive around six a.m., get a couple hours of sleep and be on the streets by nine.

Kyle woke at eight the next morning and immediately looked out the window, half-expecting to see cops staked outside his house. The snow plow operator had been at work; chest-high piles of grey edged the sidewalks. As he watched, one of the noisy machines made a turn at the corner past the pool, ready to come back again this direction. The adjacent baseball field was pristine white, no tracks of animal or man.

As he took his shower, he told himself today would be like any other. *Like any other day*, he mentally repeated, hearing Billy's voice in his ears. She was right; the cubes might not turn out to be anything other than social security numbers. Better to stay busy and focused. He had his job, his basketball scholarship to get and his girlfriend, in that order.

"Hey kid," greeted his dad from the kitchen. He was sitting at the small table, drinking his coffee, and Kyle knew he'd already been out on his walk and returned.

"How's the trail this morning?"

"Couldn't make it. Snow's too deep. Went up the road instead. Saw Deardon. He was making another round, on the look-out for a stranger who might have broken into the mine. Looked tired. Food on the stove if you want some. Made extra."

Kyle saw the sausage patties and forked two. "Sounds like he was searching for work."

"Well, he has help now. Someone arrived from Denver this morning and Deardon's none too happy about it. I told him to take it easy. No-one's been up to the Daimonte mine for any reason since Stu and his team formally closed it." Kyle pulled out the orange juice. "You do the usual last night?"

"Yep. Ty's then home. Pretty non-exciting."

"You see Ashley at all?"

"Dad. It was Friday. No game. What do you think?" His father drank his coffee and shrugged.

"Just makin' sure. Don't want you getting in trouble with only a few months left." Kyle loaded the food on his plate and sat down across from his father. *You and everybody else in this no-light town,* thought Kyle without resentment. It wasn't that he minded the attention, or even the expectation of success. It was just so apparent that no one born or raised here had ever amounted to much more than a grown-up version of themselves. The hopes of a local boy done good rested heavily on his shoulders.

"You need a haircut, Dad." His father glanced at his shoulder, then gave his head a shake like a dog. His hair was a yellow-ish gray, hanging nearly down to his shoulders with his front cut in bangs too long. Between the 7,000 foot elevation of the town and more than 300 days of sun a year, his dad's beach-blond look counterbalanced by his heavily-lined, tan face, which was a testament to time spent outdoors.

"Yeah, maybe today I'll go uptown when the dust has settled."

Kyle finished off the last of the sausage. "*Maybe* the Sheriff will tell you what's really going on," his intonation a suggestion.

"Unlikely. Usually he's a talker but this morning, he didn't say much other than to ask if I saw anything strange on my walk. I couldn't tell if he was really concerned or covering his butt."

"Same thing happened at Ty's. Mark came in and made some guys from Telluride pull out their ID before he told me and Billy to be in by curfew."

"Billy? Ty's girl?" his father took another drink. "That's different."

Kyle played it cool. "The guys from Telluride were sitting in my usual place. She commands the only other table in front as we all know."

"I do. Just don't want Stu blackballing you for stepping out on his daughter."

Kyle was done and stood up, deciding it was better not to dignify the insinuation with a response.

"Heading to the pool, Dad. Catch you later."

"Later," drawled his father. Kyle went out the front door and glanced both ways a millisecond before he jogged across the packed snow. The sidewalk was two feet of crud, so he kept to the road, zeroing in on the fish pond. No tracks, nothing out of place.

"What a mess," he said out loud. He went inside, got the water testing container and walked directly to the pond. He was going to get the cubes at the same time, easily done when the place was empty. He lifted the tubes out of the container and set it on the ground, his hand already fishing for the rock when he saw a jeep drive down Main Street. It was a deep blue metallic, unusual enough to be noticed.

He kept his head down, eyes up, watching it stop right in front of his parent's home. A customer? No, the guy wasn't going up the pathway. He was now walking across the street toward him.

Kyle took the tube and dunked it in the water, lifted it up, put in a few drops of chemical, swirled it then dipped the piece of paper into the mixture. Over the rim, he saw the man approaching. His hair was sandy colored and cropped short, the buzz cut around the sides the obvious sign of a government employee. His shoulders barely moved but his arms swayed loosely. He was most definitely part of a tactical or security unit. Must be the guy Mark mentioned last night and Deardon confirmed this morning to his dad. *That was fast.*

"Early morning?"

Kyle looked up and nodded. "Not for the pool." He pulled out the strip. It was normal, and he had nothing else to do with the fish pond or Fred. Putting the testing equipment back into the bucket he stood. "You visiting?"

"You could say that. You live here?"

"Right across the street, where you parked."

The man turned back around. "Window to the World," he said. "A business?"

"Stained glass." If Kyle were ignorant of the situation, and this guy were a visitor from out of town, he would normally offer assistance. "You need directions or something?"

The man looked up at the mountain behind Kyle. "Sure. You know about the mine?"

"I worked in the reclamation over the summers for the past few years. I know all about it."

"I mean the break in."

Kyle smirked. "It's a small town."

The man laughed. "Fair enough. Since you worked on reclamation, have you ever been up there in the winter?"

"We did all the reclamation work in the summer, when you can see the shafts in order to string the nets. The whole point being---"

"That you don't have a snow skier going down them in the winter."

"Exactly," Kyle agreed.

"I've come to town to make a trip up there and check things out. Do you have any idea who could get me up there? I don't know if my jeep will make it."

"I don't know how much snow is on the road. If your jeep can't make, a snowmobile might do the trick." He glanced at the doors to the pool. "I don't mean to be rude, but I've got to finish testing and get the place ready for the Gerry—I mean the older crowd. They are ready and waiting at 10, the minute the doors open."

"Sure thing. Do you have any idea where I might be able to find Sheriff Deardon?"

"My dad saw him on his walk this morning and told me he was up at the Stagecoach hotel, having a coffee. Just up the street, two blocks from my house."

Brayden went back to his car and watched the young man test the water at each pool, then start to clear the path inside the perimeter of the fence. He looked up the mountain, behind the pool. It was directly below the mine.

He started the car and made a U-turn, driving up Main Street.

CHAPTER 09

It took Kyle thirty minutes to clear the snow from within the chained link fence, a task that normally would have taken forty-five. His encounter with the government guy had created an anxiety-laced adrenaline surge that he channeled for the good of the geriatric crowd who would soon be arriving. Kyle kept his mind off his conversation with the man by envisioning Barrett's most important customers and their bright swim caps and parka-like bathing suits, stepping down from the busses who picked them up from nursing homes in Montrose. They were prone to loud complaints if the soap dispensers were half-full or the pool was too cold at a mere 101, as opposed to its regular temperature of 105. Government regulations on heat were ignored in the small town, those with pacemakers knowing they were taking their chances.

By the time the first bus arrived, Amanda, a twenty-two-year-old San Francisco transplant, had opened up the front office and clicked on the music while Kyle turned the manual metal lever on the pool covering. His shoulders ached and burned with each turn. He thanked God the rocks hadn't cut his clothes or his skin. That would be hard to explain. Within minutes of the last turn, the patrons were discarding their robes and wading into the hot water.

When to remove the cubes? He was required to be on lifeguard duty until Matt showed up in another hour. For the time being, he sat on the pedestal above the water, a warm blanket around him.

Matt arrived on time, but the cashier's computer broke, so Matt took over life guard duties while Kyle sprinted to the bank for cash. A man complained about the airdry machine in the men's room, requiring Kyle to take it off, examine the back, attempt to fix it then reattach the metal box. It was two before he was done, and by then, Matt needed his break, putting Kyle back on duty.

At 2:40, he was still up on the pedestal, his eyes wandering the pool area, replaying every aspect of the conversation with the stranger. Kyle thought of his answers and his responses, the inflections he used and if he came off as a typical teenager. He realized he hadn't given a direct answer to the question about being up on the mountain in the winter. But they'd been talking about reclamation, and so his response did make sense…

I'm being paranoid, he told himself. *And you should be*! His mind shouted back. D, the old miner who confided in him, was in a nursing home. What if he opened his mouth to anyone else—someone far more important or less discrete than Kyle?

That would be bad.

Kyle's attention was diverted when he saw a lone figure coming down the path by the baseball diamond. He couldn't discern the face, but the head band was unmistakable. It was a strip of lime green, and the hoody was black. Billy had come. As she got closer, he saw that she had a pack draped on her shoulder and a lunch sack of some sort in her hand.

This is the first time she's ever been here when I've been on duty.

When Billy came out of the women's changing room a few minutes later, Kyle was grateful he had his cap on and his eyes were already squinted. Her body was…unbelievable. Whereas Ashley was long and skinny, a flat butt and stomach, Billy was lean and hard, but still had curves, up top and bottom. From her manner, it was obvious Billy wasn't conscious of her good figure, or it wasn't a priority to her. That was probably it. What good did a figure do up here in the middle of the mountains when there was no one to date?

Besides me of course.

Billy stepped in the cool lap area and swam for the next forty minutes straight. Over the years he'd lifeguarded, not many swimmers could maintain a good speed for more than ten. She had endurance.

Matt relieved him, and Kyle passed through the office, getting his lunch sack from the locker.

"Kyle, this was left for you," said Mandy, handing him a brown sack. "One of your older female fans I'm sure."

"Don't dismiss the geri-hotties," he said, winking. Mandy made a sound of disgust, and he went upstairs to the closet-sized lunch room. The sack had two plastic containers, and he opened both. One contained potato skins and meatballs he recognized from Ty's. The other had Doritos and at the bottom, a note.

Take your clothes from yesterday and cubes and put them in this sack. Wipe down the inside of the locker really good. I'll wait for about ten minutes after I see you leave.

Kyle had one potato skin and a chip before he went back downstairs and opened his locker. He folded the items as tight as possible, placing them in the sack, then put it back inside the locker. Returning to the cleaning supply area, he removed the yellow bucket containing the temperature gauges and the box for checking the water quality, another bucket for waste. He put his coat back on and headed out for the fish pond, saying friendly hellos to some of the swimmers.

He knelt beside the concrete-lined pond, checking the filters for debris as normal, removing the waste and placing it in the bucket. His back was to the pool, giving him a perfect view of the road and either side. No blue jeep or person on the sidewalk. The light at his own home was on, and he knew his father was in the front room, continuing the work where his mother had left off. What a team they'd been, all these years, creating works of art to display in other people's homes, not their own.

Kyle moved positions, using his chemical set to check the water quality, which he was required to do at several locations around the pond. He finished the first set of testing, then went to Fred's domain.

Kyle placed the chemical set by his leg, removed a vial and dipped it under the water. He inserted the slip of paper into the vial and put it on the ground, waiting for the reaction. Casually but quickly, he placed his hand back under the water, pushed the rock to the side and felt for the blocks. With one final glance under his shoulder and towards the street, he removed the bag and brought it to his side. No was paying him any attention.

His chest felt microscopically looser as he inspected the vial, verified it was normal and placed both it and the cubes in the container with the testing materials. He had one last water test to finish, and after that was completed, he took his buckets inside, dumped the first in the trash bin outside the facilities and returned to the cleaning supply with the other. Inside, he locked the door, removed the Ziploc and placed it inside his pocket.

Next stop, the locker. He put the cubes under the Dorito chips and turned down the top on the sack. As he walked to the front office, he hesitated outside the door, wondering what he was going to tell Mandy. If Billy had gotten some woman to drop it off for her, then wouldn't that same person want to pick it back up? He didn't want to second guess her, but he wasn't about to put it out where Mandy might snoop through it.

He went back to the men's changing room, sack in hand, and stood in the doorway. Billy saw him, caught his eye for a split second and looked at the bench to his left, under the hanging floaties. He took the hint without so much as a glance, put in the bag on the bench and walked away. After a few moments he went back out to the pool, walking the perimeter as he did while on duty.

Billy waited another five minutes, casually taking in the other swimmers and Matt. They were equally oblivious, and when Billy wrapped her towel around her, she did so in front of the bench, picking up the sack and then disappearing in the women's room. When she walked out of the back of the building, it was just after four.

Now it was a waiting game. As he stood guard over the swimmers for the next two hours, he wondered what she'd uncover and how she'd give him the update. They didn't even have one another's cell phone numbers and wouldn't use them even if they did. The Internet wasn't safe, and here again, they didn't have each other's contact information. Plus, tonight he had a date with Ashley.

Kyle debated the merits of feigning illness, but that would be the most obvious signal something was up. In four years of high school, he'd not had one sick day, a point of pride for his parents but regular for him. He just never got ill.

Once again, he coached himself not to worry about the details. Billy would find him.

After his shift, he hit the gym upstairs, lifting weights on his legs before running three miles on the treadmill. Coach would have liked him shooting hoops because they had the final game next weekend, right after Christmas, then playoffs starting in January. But his arm was becoming increasingly sore from his slide down the mountain and he wanted to make sure he didn't make it worse.

When he returned home, his mom was in the front room, helping a couple pick out small glass Christmas ornaments and the sound of metal crunching emerged from the basement. His dad must be in the kiln firing up glass for a project. Kyle made a bee-line for the bathroom and showered, all the while, wondering if Billy had been able to access the cubes and what that government guy had discovered.

CHAPTER 10

Kyle rang the doorbell and straightened his fingers, twitching them before forcing them limp. Not that he aspired to emulate a gorilla, but his arms were long and his palms wide, perfect for playing basketball but not helpful when he was easing nervous tension.

"Good evening Kyle."

"Hello, Sir." Stuart Fine shook his hand as usual, stepping back, closing the door after him. It was only bowling and a movie, but Ashley's dad always treated every date like it was the prom. "She's still upstairs." Kyle nodded, wondering for the hundredth time if this was Ashley's ploy to make him wait, in order to increase his level of desire for her, or her father's choice, to sweat out any nervous tension. After a year of dating, he'd moved beyond both.

"Ready for the game this Friday?" Stuart asked with the tone of an executive requesting a quarterly report.

"Yes, sir. Worked out this afternoon."

"Coach Harrison has you doing daily doubles over the holidays, I hear."

Kyle nodded. "Only one formal practice during the weekdays. The other stuff is on my own time."

"Keeping in shape is a good thing."

"Yes, Sir." Kyle smiled, glancing at the foyer. Instead of seeing Ashley, he took in the round, oriental rug, a waist-height credenza under a mirror and faux plants in a porcelain vase.

"How are you managing all that with work?"

"Barrett has been really great."

Stuart gave Kyle a mock scowl. "He should. A winning team brings in more business to his pool, so it behooves him to treat the star player well. How are the college acceptance letters coming along?"

Kyle shrugged modestly. "Good. Three basketball scholarship offers so far. All small, midwestern universities, nothing top ten in any region."

Stuart frowned. "I'm surprised you haven't received more."

"We knew my athletic career was limited when I capped out at 6'2. But the bright side is the colleges have stellar engineering departments."

"You set your sights higher than basketball. Good man."

"He is a good man," drawled Ashley from the foyer. Kyle stood and smiled, keeping his eyes locked on her face. She closed her eyes and turned her head lightly when Kyle leaned in to give her a kiss on her cheek, her shoulder-length blond hair tickling his cheek. It was about as far as he was going to ever get with the girl before he left for college.

"Hi Ashley," he said softly, feeling a twinge of guilt. He envisioned a college far away from her, one where he could date anyone without worrying about what he did, who he did it with and when. Graduation would be the natural separation point, where no hard feelings would be involved.

"Dad, you know where we are going."

"And I know what you are going to put on over that thin shirt." He pulled a heavy coat with fur trim on the collar out of the closet, unmoved as she pushed out her lips. She slipped her arms into the jacket and he zipped it up. Kyle used to think the father-daughter act was cute, her pouting when she didn't get her way, her father's quiet scolding and periodically giving in.

"You ready?" Ashley asked him.

Kyle shook her father's hand again as he always did and opened the door. "9:55," he promised Stuart. "Or earlier. I'm thinking we may skip the bowling for an early showing of a movie."

"Let me guess," interjected Ashley. "It's half-price?" Kyle shrugged off the remark but her father's eyebrows bunched in critique.

"Until you start paying for the dates Ashley, learn the word compromise."

"Sorry," she said Kyle. "Let's go."

The door closed and a minute later, Stuart watched Ashley slip her arm through Kyle's, slowing him down. Ashley put one hand on Kyle's face and pulled him close, aggressively. Kyle was stiff, unwilling to bend to his daughter's will. Stuart watched this interaction with satisfaction, thinking that if it had been any other boy than Kyle, his daughter would already be pregnant. If Ashley had been like her older sister Ruth, he'd never even have such a thought. Where Ruth was directed, focused and purposeful, Ashley was random, desire driven and undisciplined.

Stuart watched as Kyle took her hand and brought it down, looping it through his arm. They turned and walked up Main Street, the perfect picture of the perfect couple.

"Good man," Stuart repeated to himself. Ashley always wanted the unattainable, and she'd found it in Kyle. His aloofness kept her working for his attention.

You didn't find many young men around like Kyle Smith, that was for sure. Stuart made a mental note to learn which schools had offered Kyle a scholarship and make sure Ashley was accepted to all of them. If she was going to make it through college and graduate unscathed, she was going to need

Kyle, who served the same purpose as bumpers on a bowling lane; to keep his daughter on the straight and narrow.

"Are we going the long way for a reason?" Ashley asked, the flirtatious insinuation the furthest thing from Kyle's mind.

"Yessss," he drawled, thinking up a response. "We are going around the back of the block to see the Christmas lights that you can't see from Main Street."

"Hmm, romantic," she purred, giving him a hug. *Hardly*, thought Kyle, smiling through his thoughts. He wanted to see if his wallet was behind the Bailey home. They rounded the corner and saw two men standing on the sidewalk. Kyle's heart stopped, but he forced his legs to keep going.

"Hey, Kyle. Hi, Ashley."

"Deputy Hancock," Ashley greeted, before Kyle had the chance. "Are you still looking for the bad guys?"

"Standard rounds in the neighborhood," he replied. "Let me guess. Bowling and a movie?" His question was directed at Kyle, but Ashley responded for them both.

"Just a movie. I changed our plans."

Thanks for telling me, Ash.

Mark threw him a glance of validation, and Kyle caught the man's look of sympathy. It wasn't cool being minimized, no matter how good looking the girl on your arm.

"And you are?" Ashley said to the other man.

"My apologies," he said, extending his hand to her. "Special agent Brayden Cox, FBI, Denver office."

"Oh, you must be the one dad was talking to this morning. Ashley Fine. Stuart Fine is my father."

"The executive at Daimonte Mines isn't it?" He focused on Kyle. "I didn't realize I was talking to the local basketball star earlier this morning." His hand was out and Kyle shook it. His hand was thick, and he gripped Kyle's hand firmly. "Call me Brayden."

The moment he recognized him, Kyle thought of Billy and what she would do. She'd be a bit full of herself, not shy and demure. Strong versus weak. "I was in disguise."

"Are you going to stay long?" Ashley asked Brayden.

"Unsure, but I've been told the Friday night basketball games are entertaining and the hot springs is the must do in the area."

"Yep and when Kyle's there, he'll keep you from drowning." Kyle refrained from rolling his eyes.

After they were out of earshot, Brayden asked Mark if he thought Kyle could possibly be involved in the events at the mine. Mark scoffed.

"Not a chance. Kyle's the cleanest kid in town, male or female. Top grades, all-state basketball player and drug free, despite complete hippie parents."

Brayden thought about alternative lifestyles and the effect on kids. "Sometimes they can be the most dangerous."

"Not in this case." They watched the kids turn the corner and disappear. "Let me tell you a story about Kyle. When he was eleven, he told his parents to stop smoking in front of him—substances of any kind. If they didn't, he was going to pack up and leave. They called his bluff, and that night he moved in with his best friend Mario. He stays there four days, and on the fifth, his parents agree to his demands."

"How do you know this?"

"The whole town knew it. Besides the fact that they live on Main Street and you can see his parents working through the windows and just about everything else that goes on in that house, Ed, his father, told the entire Elks club about the ordeal over beers. To be honest, the town sided with Kyle, but that's no surprise."

"High school boy scout."

"Every bit of it. And let me tell you something else. He's never so much as touched Stuart Fine's daughter. If he did, he'd be the walking eunuch."

"I thought Fine was more annoying that dangerous."

At this, Mark turned and looked towards the Fine home.

"Danger comes in many forms."

CHAPTER 11

Ten minutes later, Kyle and Ashley were in the theatre. It was the earlier showing, which meant getting home before curfew.

Kyle barely noticed Ashley pouring the peanut M & M's into the bucket of popcorn. His mind was on Special Deputy Cox. He'd been here only one day and if he was by the Bailey home, it was in the realm of possibility that he'd found the location where he'd come down the mountain. He'd been sure the heavy snow would have covered the tracks from the top of the trail, although anyone who'd been up at the mine knew where it was. Mark, being a local, had used it himself over the years.

Don't act surprised. Anticipate and keep reacting calmly.

His internal coaching lasted through the credits, until Ashley attempted to hold his hand. Instead, he looped it over the back of her shoulder, making sure his elbow draped behind the chair, not touching her back.

So fatiguing. Wanting to touch Ashley, and not being able to, at least in the early days, had been tough. Initially, it had been out of fear of her dad, then it switched to worry she was going to take advantage of the situation. Ashley was like a Catholic schoolgirl, wanting more because she was given less.

The movie began and he thought back to the likely discussions Mark and Brayden were having. It didn't take a rocket scientist to think that a person might either run through the neighborhood or straight to the pool, and the only people with pool keys were the employees of the pool itself. Six total, including Barrett.

He thought of the gloves in the trash dumpster, sitting at the edge of the parking lot. Monday at five a.m. the gloves would be gone for good. He thought of the only other element that could loosely tie him to the mine.

Ashley nudged him out his thoughts. "Aren't you so looking forward to going to college, where we can do anything we want, whenever?"

"Dare to dream," he said, keeping his eyes on the screen.

"Okay," she said, rising to his challenge. "Let's daydream about having our first experience at college."

First experience, for Ashley? He'd never asked directly, but with her…zest for life…he would be surprised if he'd be her first anything.

"I'm daydreaming and watching the movie simultaneously," he told her, knowing any minute her attention would shift from him to the screen.

Sure enough, as soon as the dialogue started, he was invisible. His mind wandered. When exactly had Ashley's attractive mannerisms begun to wear off?

When I began filling out the college applications. That was when he'd started thinking about life beyond his senior year, beyond Ouray. One that included designing buildings, bridges and roads, or maybe going into the biochemical field. His scores in each aptitude test had been almost identical, with biochem slightly higher. Enough for the academic scholarships, but he'd kept that to himself. The entire town might riot if they thought he was choosing engineering over playing ball. Ideally, he could do both, but if it came down to it, there wasn't a question which one he'd pursue.

His arm never moved from its position during the movie, and the night ended with a kiss on Ashley's lips, too short for her but almost too long for him.

"Dad is asleep, I'm sure," she whispered.

"You've always been a bad poker player Ashley." Her response was a giggle, the acknowledgement of being caught but still wanting her way. They both knew her dad was likely up and waiting in the living room, and, for all either one of them knew, had a camera stationed outside the door. "Just be happy Rick is already at college or he'd be out here waiting for you too. See you Monday."

"You aren't coming for dinner tomorrow?"

"Can't. Helping my parents on a project in our basement." It was true, in a sense. His dad had been meaning to change the lines on the kiln and it took four hands—for about ten minutes. The fact was, he had Billy on his mind.

When it became clear that no amount of pouting was going to change Kyle's mind, she gave him a final kiss and said goodnight.

He could see his mom clearly through the window, her head down, working. She lifted a cup to her mouth, full of steaming coffee or highly caffeinated tea, her food group of choice after nine p.m. She said it was when she got her best work done.

Nearing, he assessed her in the way so many townspeople had done over the years. His high cheekbones and square jaw; her narrow, oval face and slight features. His broad shoulders and height, her slip of a frame, and not even a hundred pounds dripping wet. About the only thing they shared was the color of their honey blond hair, but even that was off. Whereas his was thick and had a wave when it grew past his ears, hers was pin straight.

His father Ed, wasn't even considered in the equation of genetics. Everyone knew his mother had gotten pregnant by a foreign exchange student in high school, having Kyle when she was just eighteen. Ed had come into the picture when Kyle was five and had raised him like his own. To Kyle, the other guy had been nothing more than a sperm donor, and Ed was his dad. Period.

"Hey Mom," Kyle called, hugging her from behind. Then he went around her large desk and pulled the blinds down.

"You know I hate it when you do that," she grumped, her voice raspy from years of smoking.

"And you know I hate it that the entire world sees our business." She started to get up and change it back, when he put his hand on her arm. "Compromise. Open during the day, closed at night, okay? I can basically see the zit on your face from Ashley's house and I hate it."

"I have a zit?" she asked, touching her face, momentarily distracted. Kyle laughed for the first time in twenty-four hours.

"No, but you get my point."

She smacked his butt. "Before I forget, Billy brought by some food for you. Said it was payback for work you did on the fridge."

His chest immediately constricted and he faked a yawn to get the air back in. "She does owe me," he muttered, heading into the kitchen. In the brown paper sack was an order of chicken wings and two sides of ranch. He lifted the sack upside down, turning it inside out. Nothing. Bewildered, he considered it a possibility she was grateful for something, but certainly not the fictitious broken fridge.

He ate the wings, dipping the sauce into the ranch, one after another, until he scraped something. It caught on something. Scratching again, he saw she'd taped something to the bottom. Clever.

Washing the cup out, he carefully removed her note, peeling off the Saran wrap. He read her microscopic writing twice, took the other ranch cup and repeated the process. When he'd absorbed the contents, he shredded the notes, dropped the pieces in the sink, turned on the water and the disposal, and waited until the sound of grinding stopped.

He sat down, feeling a sensation move up his legs. It wasn't adrenaline or tension or anxiety. Those he could deal with. This was hollow and cold, his body's way of telling him the situation was grave, whether his mind was going to acknowledge it or not.

It was the feeling of fear.

CHAPTER 12

"Sir, what I have for you isn't much." Brayden was sitting at the desk in his small room of the Stagecoach Hotel, looking over the snow-covered roads. He told his boss about the inability to get up to the mine due to the avalanche threat, along with the Deputy's conjecture about how a person might have gotten down so quickly without being caught. "One trail in particular is a straight shot from the mine, but it was covered with several feet of snow. The local deputy thinks it's unlikely anyone but a local would know where it began and ended, which proves your theory of the person being from town. Tomorrow, an outdoors company is going to bring up snowmobiles. But from what you've said, the mine is big and the files many. Sir, if I may ask, why don't I get a team up here with me? We could do a lot more in less time. They could be up in a half a day, tops. And if the level of sensitivity is what you suggest, this isn't the time to be worrying about budgets and overtime."

"One word Brayden. Containment."

"Yes, sir. We'll talk tomorrow."

Forland set down his pencil and took the phone off speaker. Sitting in front of him was Janet Reese, the country's national security advisor.

"You still agree with this approach?" he asked her. The woman's skin was spot free and unlined, even though she was in her seventies. One of the beautiful side effects of a genetically created face. If kept up, they tended to have better skin elasticity than the natural versions.

"Yes. Until we find out what's happened within the mine, we keep the circle finite."

"Brayden's going to figure it out at some point you know, and I'm not going to support you eliminating my best field agent to keep this quiet."

The woman's expression barely changed. "Then we'll have to wait and see how he handles the information and make a judgement call then, won't we?"

The woman's manner put him off. They all had a job to do, but Brayden Cox wasn't an expendable person. "What are you expecting from him?"

"To find out who was recruited locally. We can handle it from there."

Forland leaned back, twirling his pencil.

"You are credited with single handedly saving the population of the United States from being faceless horrors after the viral attack of the Chinese. But it's not clear to me why anyone would want to go back to the way it was—before the apocalypse. I mean, even if someone takes a DNA thread for a particular year or region, it doesn't make sense as to why anyone would want to use it. The virus is still out there, living and breathing, waiting to mutate the natural face." The pregnant silence was long and heavy.

The stately woman crossed her legs and interlaced her fingers. "Don't call me any names just yet," she said cautiously. "The truth is, we aren't sure."

Forland blinked. "Not sure? How can you say those words with a straight face?"

The woman shrugged her shoulders with all the calm of a person who had the codes to the country's nuclear arsenal. "It took two decades and a full generation to bring the population to the point of acceptance. Would you risk unrest on a mass scale to test out if the virus was eradicated in full? And let me ask you another question. You were a kid just after virus occurred. You were old enough to remember it happening but young enough to adapt. Was there ever a time you regretted what you didn't know? And if you say yes, do you really think you could or would want to change your face?"

Forland contemplated her words. It was a conjecture he and all his friends and discussed over the years. What would they do if given the chance?

"Today, we are living with an incarnation of ourselves," she continued. "The government's incarnation. My incarnation, if you want me to be blunt. By most people's assessment, this is a better version than nature gave us. How do you believe three quarters of the population will feel if they are the ones to be stripped of a nice-looking face and replaced with an average or homely one?" It was another question debated among every person he knew…until the subject got exhausted. It wasn't in the realm of reality.

Hadn't been, until now.

"I don't know."

"Exactly, and every president I've served under hasn't been willing to answer the question." She unlaced her fingers and looped her hands around her knee, leaning forward. "The DNA strands on the storage cubes mean that we, or someone smart enough, can dissect the information and recreate the natural face, the one they were meant to have, not the one we gave them."

"The act of terrorism–the virus—could be reversed," Forland said. Janet nodded. "I think you're right. It would be anarchy. Some for it, others against it."

"And those who have the code right in the middle."

"Hunted down by both sides," finished Forland.

Deputy Director Forland ran his fingers along his salt and pepper hair, contemplating the scenario, the faces of peers at the agency, his neighbors and relatives, all passing in front of his mind's eye like a fast-frame photo.

"What if you, FBI Director Gary Forland, were to suddenly be a pock-marked man with saggy skin. Is that something you really want to see?"

"Not particularly." He was considered a handsome black man. From his youth, he'd enjoyed appreciative looks from everyone, men and women alike, regardless of race. He was tall and well-built, and he worked out daily, wanting his body to match his appearance.

Janet hadn't relegated beauty just to the privileged. Her agency had dispensed it equally among all classes of society, thereby ensuring general satisfaction. It had long been thought that better looking people made more money, were likelier to have a better sex life and live longer. Confidence, attitude and happiness were intertwined like the threads in a rug.

That had been the theory.

But looks hadn't been a panacea. People still had their issues and hang-ups, strengths or skills. Heck, he sure did. Over the years and decades since the virus, nature had taken its course. A good sales person rose to the top based upon acumen, not a strong-jawline. Others worked in trade and were happy to drink a lot of beer and gain weight.

That had begat the movement by the Naturalists. Return to how life had intended, was the battle cry. They were the brave ones. *Or the ones with nothing to lose.*

"To find out what you really look like," he said to himself. It was a reality—could be a reality.

His counterpart nodded gravely.

"Gary, what do you think that will do to people? How will most react?"

"I would start with depression," he offered.

"Which leads to suicide, which would eventually lead to other, more desperate actions. Gary, the minority are like the pregnant women of today who still insist on a natural birth. They want to experience life as it was meant to be; naturally, without drugs. The face is no different.

"Trust me. We've considered every scenario. But each time a president has gotten close to giving the order to trying it on a small group, giving them their real faces back, it's been pulled at the last minute. We couldn't risk trying and failing, only to have the subject run around and tell everyone, forcing us to call in the Patrol."

"But you have no idea if it would work."

"Exactly. Perhaps they'd be susceptible to the original virus and die. Who knows?"

"So, the end game is to keep to the status quo, forever, as in, all eternity," he concluded.

"That's what the current president has requested and I agree."

Forland understood the President's position. Looks equaled appeal and he had a lot of it.

"And if we can't find the person responsible for the break-in, assuming items are gone?" he asked her.

"We bring in the Patrol."

It took a millisecond before Forland nodded his head. The Patrol had one way of operating: to destroy. They would go into that idyllic town and annihilate it.

"Gary, there's one other thing. We blamed it on the Chinese."

Gary stopped twirling the pencil, starting again when he sifted through what she hadn't said. In six words, she'd confirmed another conspiracy theory that had also circulated for the last three decades. The virus wasn't let loose on American soil by foreign invaders. They had arrived with the timing of its release.

"Now that I know it was all from within," he began. "I'm going to set aside my emotional reaction and go straight to pragmatism. Was it intentional, or was it the screw up of the millennium?"

"I can't answer that, not because I don't want to. But because I truly don't know."

"Your team worked on the fix."

She nodded. "Not on the cause."

Gary wasn't so sure, but he wasn't going to get into a world of knowledge that could only do him harm in the future. Brayden Cox wasn't the only person in his organization that could lose his life over this…situation.

"Back to Brayden and my original question," he said, focusing on his field man.

"If it comes right down to it, we learn where his loyalties lie, with the government and his current face, or on the other end of a barrel."

"How could you possibly think he of all people, would side with the naturalists?"

"Because he's already lost almost everyone dear to him over this very issue. A third time might break him."

CHAPTER 13

Kyle slept restlessly that night and at four he finally gave it up and made sausage and eggs. Over breakfast, he flipped through his pre-college biochem book, the sun rising behind the mountains, burning off the thin layer of fog shrouding the jagged tips.

He went to the chapters on gene splicing. He was especially interested in validating what Billy had communicated. The book included the basics of gene replication and cloning, but nothing about alternative mutations of DNA swapping or reversion, all things Billy had mentioned in her notes.

Wanting to find the information for himself, he was typing in the search query when he paused. Computer forensics could pull up every search ever made, and although he knew it was possible to delete records, his forte wasn't the machine in front of him. That was Billy's domain. For the time being, he was relegated to letting Billy conduct the searches, not him. If he wanted to get more information, he'd have to see her at practice as she'd said in her note. This time, she was going to be delivering food, courtesy of her father. All under the guise of keeping the team healthy and fed.

Kyle was drinking a glass of orange juice in the kitchen when he saw a truck pulling two snow mobiles drive by. Following behind was a blue Jeep driven by Brayden. He knew exactly where the driver was going to stop: at the turn off to highway 95, up the dirt road that led to the mine.

Putting on his coat, he went out the back door and crossed over to the park leading down to the pool. He walked the fence line, around the north end, near a row of new condos, behind the waterslides and then to the overflow parking area.

He heard the sound of snowmobiles firing up and visualized the scene. Brayden had gone up the narrow road, almost too thin for a dump truck to handle, through a rock overhang and then along another mile of uneven gravel, with plunging ravines that he'd canvassed with the ropes on one side. They'd arrive, get out, Brayden would use the codes and down he'd go into the cavern. How long would it take him to open the file drawers and identify what cubes were missing?

Without thinking, Kyle turned around and went to the upstairs gym. He changed into his gear and got on the treadmill. He had to confront what Billy had written in the note and figure out what he was going to. He honestly had no idea, short of going to the press, which would only get him killed.

"Talk to me, Brayden."

"I've been through every drawer, and Sir, I want to state right now and for the record, that while this place is Fort Knox on the outside, it's a kids candy store on the inside. And by that, I mean the file drawers were all unlocked, every last one."

"What?"

"And further," Brayden continued, "the storage cubes were in simple clear envelopes, within the file drawers. Not a safe in site or lock box. Nothing. Whoever set this up thought minimalism was the way to go, or were ego-filled enough to dismiss any relevant precautions employed at even low-security facilities."

"You have more bad news to deliver, I take it."

"Yes. Files from California, New York and Colorado are missing, no apparent pattern. Also, the blocks in the Master is gone. It's unclear how many were in each, because the clear slip covers have no information, only the year. The intruder used latex gloves, used in everything from dental offices to cleaning. No clues there.

"As to how the person got away, it had to be going down the side of the mountain like the local Deputy hypothesized.

The pilot of the chopper unit said he was here within ten minutes. Now that I've come up here by snowmobile, I know that wasn't enough time to get in, search and get down in any typical capacity." Brayden described the shoot-like path. "Skis are a possibility or even a toboggin. Whatever form was used, the person had real nerve. From the top this path looks littered with boulders the size of my head."

"Could a person have survived without injury?"

"Unclear." Brayden hadn't seen anyone with visible signs of injury on his initial rounds. "I'll ask the deputies and Sheriff to keep an eye for that though, because unless I get a warrant to strip search every person in this town, it's going to remain a mystery. What now, Sir?"

"I get on the phone with NSA and coordinate with O'Connell, Colorado's Chief of Police to give him the update. How has your interaction with the locals been?"

Brayden told him about Deputy Hancock and taking a tour of the town.

"For now, stay put. I'm going to send out Saachi." Brayden agreed. A single strand of hair could provide the DNA to lock away a person for life, and the footprint traceable to a particular type of shoe. No detail was too small.

"How soon?"

"Figure Tuesday night at the latest."

Time enough for Brayden to start on the list of the individuals he'd been given who used to work at the mine, some of whom lived in remote, rural towns. He had learned a few were in nursing homes and others had died. It would consume his Monday and most of Tuesday.

But in the evening, he'd be able to take a soak in the hot pool, maybe pay a stop at the Window to the World. Deputy Hancock could think what he wanted, but no-one was a boy scout anymore.

Not even me.

CHAPTER 14

Kyle was about to knock on the door when it opened. "Come on in," Billy invited, standing back to let him through.

"It's weird, you being civil to me."

"Good news for you. It's going to get weirder." She handed him a Coke and they walked into the room with the cool furniture. "Saw your dad today on his ritual walk. He told me you worked hard this morning."

"Moving big parts on that ancient kiln is hard work, actually." He raised his hand. The back of it was scraped across the top, pinpoints of red where the rough surface had slipped as he'd lifted.

"You're looking for sympathy points?" Kyle couldn't help himself and smiled. She was so tough and yet so funny at the same time.

"Will it help with what we're going to talk about?"

She grabbed her laptop computer and sat on the couch. "No, but it was fun saying it. Sit here," she directed, next to her. "You will want to see this."

"For what it's worth, it did take the afternoon to deconstruct that thing and put it back together."

"You don't need to apologize for coming over late. I had things to do."

The Christmas music was already playing, and he heard the television from the other room.

"Is that the Grinch?" he asked.

She didn't look up from her laptop, but nodded. "With Jim Carrey. My favorite."

Kyle set down his drink and took off his coat. "You didn't ask me to take off my boots, and this rug looks expensive." A lot more than the rug in Ashley's foyer, actually. This one was worn, but the colors were rich and the edges were thick and plush. It was just a gut feeling, but he guessed the one in the Fine's house was faux and this was the real deal. Billy's home felt authentic.

She turned to him abruptly. "Jacket off, shoes on. Then sit." Kyle automatically did what he was told. Her eyes didn't leave his for a moment. They were hard, but that wasn't what put Kyle off balance. It was the determination of her glare, as though she could divine all she wanted by watching his every move.

"I feel like I'm being interrogated and you haven't even asked a question."

"I don't have to. I'm watching you because I'm a skeptic by nature, and I want to believe the here and now, what I see in front of me, then make decisions. Get things done, like finishing high school and leaving this micro town. But now I'm screwed. You are screwed and we, then by definition, are going to be screwed together." Kyle blinked. "And don't mistake my words. I'm not being sexual, I'm talking prison at best and the Patrol at worst."

Kyle wanted to laugh or make a witty comment, but the gravity of her body language told him now wasn't the time. In truth, he knew his life was at a crossroads, just as she was implying. The difference was that he could tell she had already figured out the options and had already made a decision.

"Closer," she said, noting the distance between them.

"I want you to know I'm sorry."

She raised an eyebrow at him. "That you have potentially ruined the course of my life? I've already accepted that reality and moved on. Everything else is pretty small stuff."

"Billy, I never meant to bring you harm or potentially ruin your life. If I could take it back, I would, or do things differently, had there been any other option…" he trailed off and she finished his thought for him.

"But you knew there wasn't."

He nodded. He had spoken softly and sincerely, in a tone that he'd never once used with Ashley. It was too…vulnerable. "I had my life planned out too, you know?" he said. "Go to college, get out of here, away from all this and live by myself, for the first time ever."

Billy cocked her head. "And be without the benefit of the Fine family?" Her sarcastic comment broke his mood and he leaned back, staring at the ceiling.

"If you only knew." He expected another smart remark, one that he would be ill equipped to handle at the moment. He wasn't feeling strong and secure, but naked and scared, emotions he'd never felt before, not even when he was repelling over a ravine five-hundred feet deep.

"My turn to be sorry."

Kyle turned his head to her. "What for?"

"Making you feel bad." Their eyes held for a moment, enough time to see the dark spots of blue in her mostly hazel-colored eyes.

"You're uncommonly intuitive."

She broke her gaze and leaned back. With her left hand, she picked up her drink from the end table and swallowed, waiting until she set it down again to speak. "Yeah, I know," she replied, staring straight ahead, her voice flat. "It's a blessing and a curse."

In that moment, Kyle admired her profile. Her angular haircut dropped over the side, touching her cheek, partially hiding her eye. Long lashes peeked out, naturally dark, contrasting with her platinum top. Her face was absent skin damage or self-inflicted marks the government-issued face couldn't prevent. Even Ashley had a half-inch scar on her jawline, the result of a fall into a glass table as a kid. Billy's lips were evenly full and wider than Ashley's as well.

Highly kissable.

"Are you going to keep staring at me or look at the screen?" Kyle thought she'd meant to come across as annoyed, but he caught an inflection of something else.

His gaze didn't change as he spoke. "I have to be honest Billy, totally and completely. From the first minute D told me about the mine to the time I saw the cubes I'd been thinking of you. You are the one person in this school I admire. You are brilliant and I know it. What you choose to hide under your clothes or how you push people away is probably all done because you were, and are, so bloody smart it makes people uncomfortable."

"It even makes you uncomfortable," she said softly, her eyes still at the screen.

"Yes, and competitive, and insecure," he admitted. "All those things that everyone else feels when they are around you. Can you blame me? You are more self-assured than the entire population of this town. I mean, who does this?" he asked, pointing a finger at her platinum hair. "And pulls it off? It's unsettling, even for me."

"I figure why not?" she said, her voice absent its hard edge. "Nobody likes me anyway."

"Dislike because of insecurity is human nature. I'm not going to apologize for trying to spare your feelings."

Her eyes narrowed a little. "I like it, actually. Even if I am surprised at the emotion."

It was Kyle's turn to feel unsettled. "So, the truth table goes to you now. You really do think I'm that shallow." She said nothing to contradict his statement. "You can correctly nail me for that. I'm a guy. Ashley is good looking. I worked for her dad. It was all easy and natural." Thoughts of his girlfriend brought him down instantly, like anchor thrown over a canoe that had been gliding over crystal clear, motionless water. Billy looked like she was going to speak again. "No, and you don't need to apologize for reading me right. You can probably tell all my feelings about the subject anyway, as you've recently proven to be more perceptive than I imagined."

Billy pushed her hair away from her eyes, a graceful motion allowing him to see her eyes. "So, what was the final part of your shallow comment, because it looked you had more to say."

Kyle shifted and forged ahead. "When I said I wanted to get out of here, I was really saying to get away from Ashley and her family, all the pressures and anticipation of an event and a life that will never be mine—that I never wanted to be mine. You don't think I've heard the girls talk about Ashley's plans to go to college with me and get married? That's beyond my universe of reality and emotions."

She turned to him. "Then why do you continue with it all? It's such a charade, although I think it has most people fooled."

"But not you."

"No. Not me."

Kyle felt a sensation moving from his knees, through his legs and up to his chest, a pulsing, tingling feeling that carried with it nerves, excitement and a knowledge that what he was experiencing now was new, and he liked it.

"I didn't think anything else would be better."

"What do you think now?"

His eyes flitted between hers. "I think I was wrong."

Billy drew her lips inward and resolutely looked at the screen. When she spoke, her voice and manner had altered completely. "That's good, because we are in this deep, and for the foreseeable future, locked at the hip."

I'm not entirely opposed to that idea.

"I'm watching," he replied.

Billy rapidly moved her fingers on the keyboard, the tapping made quicker because she had no nails to speak of and the tips never slipped. "I've had access to the University of Colorado's computer science lab since we were sophomores. I've been auditing courses, and a few of my geekier, male friends showed me the ins and outs of the dark web."

"Illegal sites?" he asked.

"Sure, some are. But half the dark web is comprised of a sub category where the groups are closed, meaning they are private and encrypted at every level. It's anonymous and impossible to discover who, or where, a user resides, so it's really popular with illegal and legal groups alike, from conspiracy theorists to researches and gun traders. You name it, it exists."

"But it's safe," he surmised.

"It's anonymous, but that's different from being safe. I got on line, anonymized myself and asked about the storage blocks."

"Your note said you got a hit on what it meant."

She nodded. "Huge amounts of data is stored on solid state technology. It's accessed magnetically." She closed her computer and opened a drawer, pulling out three cubes. She put the first on the coffee table, and then slowly, put the second on top. A hologram of data pushed out from all four quadrants of the top cube. "Now this." She added the third, and the data multiplied, included both the top and bottom cubes."

"Whoa."

"No kidding." The images were multi-dimensional. "I spent half the night entering private chat rooms with people who probably worked for the company that invented this. In the 1990's, an engineer from Microsoft displayed the cubes at a tech forum, then it was never heard about again. Word is that the government purchased the technology and went underground. One conspiracy theory proven true."

"Everyone always says the Enquirer has it right every time." He slowly sliced his hand through the green imagery, the figures, symbols and codes momentarily appearing on his skin.

"How do you make sense of it?"

"That took the other part of the night."

"And that's when you went full undercover in the digital darkness?" She glanced at him. "I like the codename Sunsetmoon by the way. Very happy. Does it mean anything?"

"I *am* happy, when I'm not annoyed with everyone in this town. And yes, it does. When I was a kid, I was with my…anyway, we were visiting Idaho. The sun was going down on the water, and the moon was in the sky at the same time. My…I was told that it was a sunset moon. I like the thought."

Her momentary look of remembrance abruptly changed. "Look here. What do you see?"

"My name, which is weird. And DNA threading."

She pointed. "Yes. These chains carry the genetic instructions for the development of the body. All the living organism, animals, plants, bacteria, viruses, all carry DNA."

"I like how you are completely dumbing this down for me. And no, I'm not offended, but I do know it's a double helix. We covered that in eighth grade, remember?"

"I do. I got an 97 and you a 96 on the final."

"But who's keeping score?"

"Both of us. Now, skipping over all the details like proteins, lipids and the rest, DNA consists of two biopolymer strands or chains coiled around each other, like a spiral staircase."

"This," he said, pointing to what he assumed was his own DNA strand.

"Yes," she confirmed. "Mutations in DNA can occur, some spontaneous, others environmental or planned. For some, the body can actually remove and replace bad components."

"Still with you."

"Now look at this." Billy used the tip of her forefinger to scroll through the digital directory on the screen until she found her own name. "Next to my name, they label me as

MGST. I found out that means multiple gene successful transduction."

Kyle looked up and down the other names on the screen. "They all have it."

"Yes. You don't, but I'll come back to that in a minute. Transduction is what I had to look up. I think they mentioned it once in class." Kyle said nothing. "Not ringing a bell? Basically, you can infect an organism with a virus, and it makes that person incorporate the viral DNA into their own."

"Oh, man," he said, immediately understanding what that implied.

"An understatement. That's what conspiracy theorists call intentional." A slight smile played at her lips. "I messed around with the cubes, focusing on the Colorado one. Most, but not all of the records came up with these unique DNA threads."

She sat back and he adjusted his position to face her, his left knee parallel her hip, his elbow resting on the back of the couch. His breathing had gone shallow, the pressure from his ribs closing in, feeling tighter with each word she spoke.

For the first time in their discussion, she looked uncomfortable. "Watch this." Her fingers swiped through more electronic pages. "I'm bringing up yours again. The note about transduction is missing." Kyle had a hard time concentrating. "It means this," she patted her cheek, "is fake. It's what the government calls the government-issued face.

Yours," she said, her voice a notch lower, touching his jaw briefly, "is real. It's what you were born with."

His hand had unconsciously gone to his cheek. His whole life, nearly eighteen years, he'd believed it wasn't his. It had a been a shield in some ways, because he was like everyone else he knew. Despite those on the fringes, who believed the government was behind the virus, he held on to the notion it couldn't be…those in leadership wouldn't do this to their own citizens.

"Why would someone do that?"

"Well, DNA codes our appearance, but it also codes all the chemicals and proteins throughout our body. Sorry, I'll speed this up."

"No, no," he said, "This is critical stuff and I'm not the one who's been up all night. Keep going." In truth, it was fascinating.

"Okay. If you want the body to make more of something, you can create a gene that makes whatever you want, then insert it into the body through a virus."

"Like uploading the virus that blows the space ship apart in Independence Day."

She tilted her head. "A really old, really odd reference, but yes. You got it. It's pretty common for people who have had gene mutations or even cancers. This has become a major way to create individualized medical treatment."

"The human genome project, right? Where they coded out the entire DNA of a person."

"Exactly. They traced all sorts of genes in DNA to figure out where stuff was on our chromosomes."

"Then began to replace the bad with the good."

She nodded. "And now, it appears some of the good, with bad. Maybe it wasn't even intentional, it just happened," Billy said more to herself.

"You just lost me."

"Well, we know mutations happen all the time, gazillions to count in the human body every day. The body actually has a way to remove and replace bad sections of DNA strands itself, without outside intervention. That's not always 100% successful, so over time, small mutations can occur. Statistically, it doesn't cause any problems, but occasionally, according to what I read, the mutation can occur in a very important part and lead to big problems, like cancers or deficiencies of a key chemical."

"I get it," Kyle said with sudden understanding. "So, it's possible a virus might have existed, unleashed on the country by the enemy, just as the government said. They figured out a way to combat the virus, which was to implant us with a DNA that was resistant to the effects, and this affected our appearance."

"That's been the party line for thirty-seven years."

"But," he continued, "the naturalists have always said no virus existed. That this was created by the government and purposefully done to pacify the people. Who do you believe?"

She leaned forward, earnestly. "Kyle, it doesn't matter—the who or the why. I think—and it's only a thought—that these are vital because perhaps it could be changed back."

He used his fingers to scroll through the names on the screen. "You thinking what I am? They were storing the code in case they wanted to reverse it."

"Exactly. Take out the inserted DNA code and you are left with what the person could or should look like." They looked at each other in silence. The idea had been talked about for years, but there was always one stumbling block.

"Even if a person has the code, which is what appears to be on the cubes, the face is gone. You can't just go skin grafting…" he stopped as she pursed her lips, shaking her head in disagreement.

"Skin is grown in labs for burn victims," she reminded him. "Get the DNA, grow the skin, put it on. The first partial face transplant to be a success was done in 2005. Five years later in Spain, was the first full facial. All those were done using cadavers. People still have accidents and face transplants are performed regularly."

"But these people—I'm sorry," he broke in, not sure how to refer to her.

"No," she said, dismissing the need for an apology. "Keep going. I know what you mean."

"Well, you came out with this face. It wasn't like they slapped it on you at three years old."

"Correct. The anonymous resources said it that human development begins at the embryonic stage, within the uterus."

"That's impossible," Kyle disputed. "The virus had to be in your mom, then."

"It *is* possible," she countered. "I'm not going to pretend I know the conjecture from truth, but I heard enough theories last night that a few rang true. One in particular. Back in the early 2000's, some states started requiring girls who reached puberty, roughly eleven, to get shots to prevent against certain sexually transmitted diseases. It was for the human papilloma virus or HPV. Some thought it was a scare tactic, but the majority of the population thought it was a good preventative measure for cervical cancer. Pretty soon, most of the countries' pre-pubescent females had received the shot. All except for the outliers, the non-conformists."

Kyle could barely get out the words. "Like my mom."

Billy nodded. "She was a hippy. A classic non-conformist, I'd imagine. Anyway, the theory goes that this new thread was inside the girls. When they got pregnant, the mutated DNA strand was genetically modified. Already in place. Another theory was when this worked, the government started including the virus in things like flu shots when given to females, so women who might have missed the HPV shot in puberty got it later."

"And then they got pregnant."

"Right."

Had his mother not been a hippy, and also been against western medicine and things like flu shots, she still might have gotten the virus and he'd be like everyone else.

Kyle leaned over, breathing warm air onto his cold fingers. He glanced at the cubes on the table, a different kind of tingling went through his arms. This was uneven and came in waves, like his blood cells had physically reacted with the truth.

"Perhaps the government has had the ability to reverse the DNA all these years, but chose not to," he finally said.

"That's what I believe, and what D guessed, or was told."

"With this information, and help from the right people, we could change it back." Billy nodded. "Knowing what you know now, would you?"

CHAPTER 15

As he waited for Billy's answer, he kept thinking of all he'd learned. It now clicked what the naturalists had been putting out as conspiracy theory. Fighting all these years, hiding from the Patrol, getting caught and executed. When he spoke, his voice sounded weary, like he was at the start of an ultramarathon and was tired before he began.

"The government had to keep saying the virus was active," he hypothesized. "We've seen pictures that prove the virus ate and ravaged the skin, making people monsters. Faced with the reality of the virus, everyone willingly and gratefully accepted what they were born with, all the while knowing it was unnatural.

"But Billy, what if the government is right?" he asked intently. "That the natural face *is* less immune and can't withstand the virus? The whole point was that the man-made version was better, stronger and all that."

"I'd have gone along with that 100% if it weren't for one person," she said, pausing. "You. Your face hasn't fallen off, mutated, gotten eaten away or anything. You're clear-skinned, zero wrinkles, perfect complexion. You're as handsome as they come, plus, it's all real, which makes it even more incredible. But the real point here is that you seem to be like the rest of us—healthy and normal."

"And able to withstand the effects of a virus."

"That's what I'm thinking got D so riled up," Billy continued. "Somehow he learned or suspected enough. Heck, maybe he's a lot smarter than we gave him credit for. Or someone told him outright."

"That's possible as well," Kyle conceded. "He spent time up in the mines, always coming across as the town drunk. Perhaps he put the cubes together himself, but knew he wasn't young enough to carry out change."

Kyle changed positions. This time, his elbows were on his knees and he was rubbing his face in his hands. He knitted his fingers together, a basketball player ready to make the call of his life. He cocked his head to her.

"Can you believe that way back when, before this happened, people got elective surgery? Purposefully changing their nose or eyes, getting a chin reduction or cheek implant?"

"They didn't know how good they had it. Their natural face was enough. Something I'll never have."

"Why would you want to change a thing? Especially this." He'd intended to flip a piece of her hair away from her eyes, but when he touched it, his manner changed.

"To see what I look like," she answered simply. "The real me." His fingertips brushed her skin as he tucked the hair behind her ear.

"Your eyes will never change," he said softly.

"But the rest of me will."

Kyle didn't plan it out. He acted on his desire, a word that before this moment hadn't even been in his vocabulary. He ran his fingers down her neck, the smooth surface drawing him in. She watched him observe her, the wariness that used to be in her eyes gone. Curiosity filled those hazel orbs now, the lashes moving down the clear signal of promise.

He cautiously leaned in, watching her eyes close. The touch of her lips was a lightning rod for all the energy that had been growing within him. He unconsciously opened his mouth, brushing his lips against hers, feeling every sensation, his desire increasing as she responded. Billy had all the brains and maturity of someone ten years older, a woman in body and mind.

"Do you want me to stop?" he murmured. The warmth of her hand on his neck, pushing up into his hair caused him to involuntarily exhale. "We are so much alike," he murmured, happy at the thought. Billy's lips raised in response, tickling his own. It encouraged him further.

He kept his hand in place as he relaxed back on the leather couch, the motion drawing her body on him. It was her turn to lead, and his craving hit another level. He'd always had to exercise control with Ashley, pushing his feelings down or away—if he'd had any at all. Now, all he wanted was to be on the receiving end.

Her smile turned to a grin, a though she'd just heard a joke and liked it.

"Really?" she quipped. "Me and you? Two arch rivals since the seventh grade?"

He grinned, his hands on her hips. "No. But then I never imagined myself a soon to be criminal."

"Soon to be?" she queried, her eyebrow raised.

"Okay. Already guilty. And you didn't say it, but I suspect you are going to tell me next that we have to find the people who can help us decipher this information and set the world right." He closed his eyes as he enjoyed the sensation of her roving above him, but gradually closed his eyes as she moved down to him, her open lips running along his skin, first his cheek then his jaw, over his nose then finally to his lips.

"No. I'm not going to say another word for a few moments, if that's all right with you."

Kyle's eyes remained shut as he nodded. Her soft caresses continued, evolving into presses that he would have called kisses, but they were so much more than he'd ever experienced. Where had this girl learned her skills, or was this her first time, like it felt with him?

His arms moved up her back, embracing her, pulling her tighter into him. He didn't know where this was going or how long it would last, but it felt right, and it felt real, neither emotion he'd experienced before Billy.

Kyle took his time going home. The three-block walk on the back roads barely long enough to replay all that he'd learned at Billy's, and what had happened between them. The kissing had eventually stopped, both sensing that to go further would be a wedge, not a glue. It was that same, unspoken connection, the near ability to understand what the other was thinking that surprised him the most. One moment, his arms were on her back and she was covering him with kisses, and the next, she had placed her cheek against his, gave him a final kiss near his ear, then removed herself. It wasn't awkward, just the end. They both had to get back to reality.

To Ashley, he thought to himself.

No. Not to Ashley. Although he'd been with her a year, after this he knew he'd feel guilty, and unfaithful.

To Billy. In a single hour, he'd given more to her, emotionally, intellectually and physically, than he'd ever given to Ashley.

Kyle took his shoes off in the mud room and greeted his mom.

"Honey, you have a visitor." Kyle walked around the corner and saw Brayden Cox in his living room.

"How are you this evening?" Brayden asked, standing, his hand out again. Kyle shook it and felt the discomfort that comes with a member of the FBI in his home. "I came to give you something."

"A basketball I hope," Kyle quipped as he sat down. Brayden sat at the edge of the couch, closest to Kyle. A call rang on the business line in the office, and his mom left to answer. She had on the oldies she preferred, Led Zeppelin Kyle guessed, but couldn't make it out clearly. The small, open window was half-closed.

"This." Brayden extended his hand. It was his wallet, the leather dark from being in the snow.

"Wow, thanks," Kyle replied, pushing down the surge of adrenaline he felt, hoping his voice didn't shake and his face wasn't red. "I lost it Friday."

Brayden nodded. "The evening of the break in up at the mine?"

"The same night when all the police cars lit up and we all got interrogated? The very one."

"Aren't you going to open it up?"

Kyle smirked. "I guess I should, but it's a small town and I only had a ten or something in it anyway. School ID cards are easy to come by." He paused for a moment. "Oh, do I need to give you something?" He opened it then, thinking he'd give him a five. That's what a non-guilty teenager would do.

Brayden laughed. "I didn't come here for a reward, but it's a nice thought. Just doing my civic duty." He stood. "I'll be going then."

Kyle could barely get air into his lungs, the reprieve from being handcuffed felt like the firing squad being told to put down their guns. He must not have found a thing, and Kyle was off the hook. "You still going to try for a soak in the hot tub, this week?"

"Yeah. That's on the agenda."

"Come by. You can get a first-time's freebie pass. By the way, where'd you find my wallet? I assume somewhere near the pool?"

Brayden's hand was on the screen glass door. He paused to look out at the road. It was clear, and Kyle's mom was still in her workshop, the sounds of cutting audible.

"No. It was about twenty feet down from the top of the mine. The same place we found some blood. Looks like someone got knocked up pretty bad." It wasn't his imagination. Kyle felt a spike of pain in the base of his skull, just where he'd cracked it. "This town has become a lot more dangerous in the last few days, kid. Might want to hold onto that thing a little better."

Kyle could only nod. Why wasn't he being arrested or pushed for information? Why wasn't the Patrol already at his home?

He shut the door behind Special Agent Cox and walked to his room. Mechanically, he turned on the television set. All he could think about was Billy. He wanted her opinion on what just happened. Most of all, he wondered why Brayden was letting him off the hook.

Brayden walked up Main Street, reaching the Stagecoach Hotel but then he turned around and went back down to Ty's. He sat at the bar, ordered the chicken wings and watched the basketball game as he sipped a beer. It had been his intention to push the kid, but on instinct, changed his mind. If he broke the kid now, he'd have to tell Central, they'd take him in, and it would be left up to the Patrol. The young man was just getting started. Senior year. Girlfriend. Small town basketball player. Brayden could see it in his eyes. He was itching to get out of here. All of it would end with a single phone call. His dreams, aspirations, and likely, his life.

The chicken wings came and after he took a bite, the bartender asked him how he liked the food. "Superb," was his one-word reply.

"They are, in my humble opinion. Ty, the owner," greeted the man, wiping his hands. Brayden reached over the counter and shook it. Brayden knew he should ask Ty if Kyle was in the restaurant Friday night, had food and how he paid for it, but suddenly, he didn't want to know. It would identify who Kyle was relying on to cover his tracks, and that in turn would give him the name of a person he needed to find.

Kyle's not the big fish anyway. A kid like that didn't come upon insider information on his own. Someone told him. Someone wanted the kid to do the dirty work and get caught.

Ty left him and Brayden glanced around the bar. It was empty, save for a teenage girl sitting in the front part of the bar.

"Is she legal?" Brayden asked Ty when he returned.

"No, but the locals let me get away with it. She's my daughter. That's her usual spot." Brayden turned back to his food. She undoubtedly went to school with Kyle.

Hancock's report came to mind. He'd checked out Ty's. Out of towners from Telluride had been there.

"Was she here Friday night?"

"As always," Ty answered, giving him a glass of water. "Sitting right there with Kyle. You going to be here to catch a local basketball game?"

"Not sure." Brayden took another wing in his fingers. "This sauce is to die for."

"It better be or my dead mother will come back from the grave and shoot me herself." Brayden gave the man a genuine smile. Humor wasn't a common emotion for him anymore. It had been, right up until twenty-four months ago. Then his world had mostly fallen apart. Again.

"You going to get visitors?" The question stopped him from going down a dark, mental road.

"Yeah." By now, he assumed the entire town knew of the mine and were conjecturing about the enemy in their midst. The enemy being him, of course.

"Got any good suspects yet?"

Brayden smiled wider, shaking his head. He loved the direct approach of small-town folks. "Nope. You want to help me out on that?"

The bartended raised an eyebrow, jerking his head to the television. "The only thing the entire town cares about is the basketball team and the playoff game this Friday. Who cares about a retired mine anyway? I'll get you more of my spectacular sauce."

Brayden was watching the screen when a ping hit his phone. On Monday he'd be finding former mine workers, then the forensics specialist would be in town.

Waste of time. I already know who entered the mine. That wasn't what worried him. He had to learn what Kyle knew before the forensics specialist put it together. Because if that happened, Kyle would be on his own.

CHAPTER 16

"Open!"

Kyle passed the ball to Mario, who dribbled ten feet, shot it to Dwaine, laying the ball up for the score. Monday morning practice, coach's orders.

Up and down the court, passing, shooting and scoring, the players used their skills, but it was hard to improve upon great, and that was no false modesty. The Ouray Trojans had been the number one team in the state for three years, and Kyle relished the fact. What he hated was being in the triple A category, not the coveted four A. Whole legions of scouts didn't know he existed, and the few who had showed up last year at the state championships had been underwhelmed by his performance. The night before, he'd gotten food poisoning. Up all night puking, he'd played like crap. Any chance at elite college recruitment ended then and there.

Fate's intervention hadn't propelled him towards bitterness, but pragmatism. Before his senior year, his mind had already pivoted towards his career, and with it, his intent to graduate top of the class.

Billy, his only competitor, was now his ally. How the world changes.

"Hey, buddy!" shouted Mario. He'd almost missed the pass, barely touching it with his fingertips, directing back into his other hand. He drove forward, spun and made the shot, the whoosh a sign of success.

He purposefully avoided looking into the stands. He'd already caught the vision of a green hat and the peekaboo lock of platinum blond. The entire gym smelled of food; Billy making good on her excuse to show up.

At the break, Ben came close. "She trying to buy you out of the valedictorian spot?'

Kyle grunted and stole the ball from his loose hands. Coach Elliott barked orders, told Mario to switch places with a guard on the other team. Now Kyle was facing his best friend. Kyle had the ball, and at the next opening, he took the three-pointer.

"What'd you do this weekend?" asked Mario as he crouched low, opposite Kyle. "You got two girls showing up to watch you?"

"What?" Kyle asked, distracted. Mario stole the ball and passed it off before Kyle reacted. "Showing off isn't going to make Ashley want you anymore than she already does," mumbled Mario as they ran down the court. "Send her to me. You don't need both."

Ashley was sitting in stands, just above homecourt center. Unfortunate. Her presence nullified any ability to talk with Billy. The clock wound down, and with two minutes before the period, Billy got up from her bench, spoke with the assistant coach and left.

Kyle was already running in the direction of the door, parallel his new friend.

"Thanks for the food," he said as he ran. She lifted her left hand in a response, a cool wave that was barely an acknowledgment. Exactly what he and everyone else would expect of the girl.

The bell rang and the guys went for the food. Kyle was certain Billy showing up at the gym was a part of her plan to become more of a regular fixture in public; a hermit crab branching out of its shell for longer periods of time. Ashley was already walking crossing the gym floor and touched his sweaty arm.

"Can I walk you home?" she asked sweetly.

Kyle caught the smirk on Mario's face.

"Absolutely," interjected Mario. "He needs protection from himself and you can be the bodyguard."

"Funny, Mario," Ashley responded, unamused.

"Your right shoulder sore?" asked his coach, coming beside him.

Ashley's fingers were immediately on it. "Did you pull a muscle?' He caught another look from Mario, who smirked.

"No coach. Weights got sideways on a bench press. At least it didn't hit my face." The guys walked around him, heading towards the food while Ashley wanted to play nurse. "It's nothing Ash, barely even feel it."

It was a complete and utter lie. His shoulder hurt like a thousand fire ants eating his arm and his coach could see it had been affecting his playing. At least it wasn't coloring up.

The food did look great but he'd lost his appetite. The only place he wanted to be was with Billy and figure out a plan. So far, he had three options, each a level of bad.

Ashley was on her phone when he emerged from the locker, and they began the short walk down Main Street to his home.

Five minutes. I can make small talk with Ashley for five minutes.

Kyle asked if her sister was ever going to marry Greg, the farmer she'd treated at the hospital one Saturday afternoon. He listened, nodding at intervals, because he really did think Ruth was in love with the guy. As Ashley spoke of her father's unhappiness at the prospect, Kyle kept an eye out for Deputy Hancock, the Sheriff and Brayden. Every store and doorway along the mundane street were now of interest.

Ashley hooked her arm through his elbow.

"That feel okay?" she asked, her concern genuine.

"Really Ash, it's fine. It was just a shoulder bump, and I'm probably low on my iron."

"Tell your mom to start putting meat into your diet and you wouldn't bruise so easy."

"Sure." If Ash only knew. Kyle could be a vampire for the all the red meat he consumed, but his mother's reputation for being a hippy-love child who ate only greens served him well at the moment. "You sound like your sister," he remarked, "dispensing medical advice."

She smiled, taking it as a compliment. "It's accurate, isn't it?"

"Of course, it is. And you, like Ruth, are rarely wrong."

She hugged him close as they passed Duckett's, the largest supermarket. He thought more about Ashley's older sister. Ruth was more introspective and not so quick to be the center of the conversation. When she spoke, her words meant more. Ruth had paid her own way through college, lived independently and while respectful of her family, wasn't bound by the umbilical cord of dependence Ashley seemed to have. Whereas Ashley wanted to graduate and move back to Ouray, Ruth viewed Montrose as the first step of emancipation, placing more space between her and her family.

"What was Billy doing at the gym? I can't imagine she's dating someone."

"Billy, dating?" Kyle had responded with the same incredulous tone Ashley had used. "She was there delivering food for the guys, courtesy of her dad. He doesn't want us missing any meals so we can win the playoffs."

Ashley talked over his last words. He got the impression she just wanted validation that Kyle thought Billy was still the smart, self-imposed oddball.

"So, what was the occasion to come by to today?" he asked when she paused.

Ashley groaned. "We ate early, and Dad wanted it short. He's been grumping in his study, mad about what's going on with the mine."

"I didn't think anything was going on, other than the rumors of a break-in."

"That's what I keep telling him. He's been on the phone, back and forth with the head of the state's police, telling him he wants to be involved, even though it's no longer even his business."

"Daimonte turned that over to the government a while back."

"I know, right?" she signed in exasperation, looking to her house at the end of the street. "Anyway, mom is frustrated watching him pace the house, and he kept asking about my college applications and acceptance letters. I just couldn't take it anymore. So," she said brightly, "I came to see you. If I hear one more conversation between my dad and those guys, I'm going to lose it."

They were now in front of Dan Robbins' house, a modern, metal and cedar two-story chalet three doors up from his own home. It was sleek and modern, representing the new face of Ouray, a stark contrast to his parent's own egg-shell blue house. Past and present, coming together within fifty feet of one another.

"Do you want to know a secret?" Ashley had a light in her eyes. "Dad told me special agent Cox is being made to stay here until another person from the FBI shows up to go through the mine. Dad is furious he can't go in, and Sheriff is annoyed someone else lurking around his town."

"They finally have something in common." They both laughed at that. Sheriff Deardon was overweight, drank a little too much on the weekends and chewed tobacco. Her father was a refined and trim East-coast transplant, who abhorred tobacco of any kind and only sniffed a brandy once a week.

"Then it seems like a wise plan to avoid both of them, don't you think?"

"Totally."

"Did your dad know the person they are sending to help Cox?"

"All I know is that it's a woman, which I think is pretty cool for forensics."

Kyle grunted. "Do me a favor, Ash. If anyone else is going to show up, would you mind telling me? That way I can be prepared if people are going to start being at the games. I'd get all hyped up, thinking their scouts and they turn out to be cops. I don't want any distractions before the playoff game."

"Other than me, you mean."

He squeezed her arm in lieu of a verbal answer. "You know Ash, your dad is brilliant. Maybe he retired too young and should go run another big company."

"That's what my mom has been hinting."

"Does your mom know how to hint?"

Ashley laughed. "No. It's been causing a lot of fights recently, which makes it all worse."

"It could be the tipping point. One day your dad will say you're out of here."

"No way. Not until graduation, and even if he did say that, it wouldn't matter to me anyway."

"Why's that?"

"Because I'll be where ever you are."

Her smile was sweet, and Kyle felt all the affection and guilt of being on the receiving end. It was high school, they were the classic sweethearts, in every sense of the word, because their relationship was about as wholesome as anyone could imagine—weirdly so.

"Why the silence?" she asked.

"Just thinking about the prospect of moving on from this town, into college, the great beyond." He said the last word with exaggeration, taking his free hand and drawing a rainbow around the mountains. She laughed at his silliness.

As they walked up the path to her home, he did feel a pang of regret. For the sadness he was going to cause when they ultimately broke up. Yes, she was a little self-absorbed and liked to be the center of attention, but it wasn't even really her fault. It would be like asking the sun stop being the center of the universe. It couldn't change what it was.

"What are you thinking about now?" she asked him, this time with a slight annoyance in her voice.

He turned her directly facing him and put his hands on her shoulders. "I was just then thinking about how you are like the sun in the universe, shining bright, and we all swirl around you."

Her eyes grew wide, a smile making the curl of her lips meeting her cheeks. "Really?"

Kyle raised his right hand off her shoulder. "On the Bible."

"You don't go to church."

"It doesn't mean I don't believe I won't end up in the bad place if I lie. Give me a hug and get inside. It's cold."

She looped her arms under his shoulders and squeezed hard. He involuntarily made a sound of pain. "You hurt here, too?"

"Yeah, a love pain." She pinched him in response. She looked up for a kiss and he gave it to her. It was light, brief and completely insincere on his part. Not that it hurt, he told himself as he walked across the street to his home. As Mario often put it, having Ashley Fine as his girlfriend didn't suck. It just wasn't what he wanted anymore.

It took him less than sixty seconds to cross the street and hang his coat up.

"Hey kid, glad your home early. You are wanted."

Kyle groaned in agony. "Such a burden." His dad gave him a piece of paper.

Fridge died again. If you can it would be appreciated. Billy

"Just another girl needing my attention."

His dad grunted. "Some of the men in this town would dispute Billy's female persuasion."

Kyle checked his watch. "I'll be back before 10."

"Don't you need some tools?"

"Nah. He's got everything but the knowledge. Oh, and Dad," he paused, his hand on the door, "I just got a look at her body yesterday at the pool, first time ever. I can say on a stack of Bibles, if you ever saw her in a bathing suit, you'd never doubt her female-ness."

His dad raised an eyebrow. "That good?"

"Better than that. Catch you later."

CHAPTER 17

Kyle had always known Stu kept track of his coming and going's. From the moment he began dating Ashley, her father would make a point of standing in the living room, opening the curtains, making sure Kyle saw him. There were no secrets, Kyle thought, and he'd never minded, until now.

It's the first time I have something to hide.

He took the back door out of the house, jogging up to Billy's. Snow was falling, the flakes small, barely covering the ground. No tracks, no traces…yet.

He knocked, brushing the snow from his shoulders as the door opened. "I heard your fridge is down again?"

"Yeah, thanks for coming over. Dad doesn't want the food to go bad." She stepped back and he wiped his shoes off. When the door shut, he turned, catching the brush of her angled hair hit the tip of her chin. A spike of interest went up his inner thighs, as strong as he'd felt last night.

Just seeing her did does this to me.

"Yes?" she asked.

"I, uh…" he stammered, looking down.

"Really?" She laughed, laying her palms on his chest. Without asking, she pressed herself into him, her fingers moving to his neck, the smile still on her lips when she kissed him. The scratching of her short nails was like lightening on a dry field, whipping up a heat that he'd never experienced. His hands automatically went to her lower back, gripping, pulling her up and into him. Just as suddenly, she pulled back, releasing her palms, keeping only the touch of her fingertips on his skin.

"There. Now we have that out of the way." She cocked an eyebrow and laughed again. "Here, let me help you with that." Billy used her right hand to push up his mouth, which had fallen slightly.

"Really?" he half-whispered, sure he was feeling symptoms of withdrawal.

She nodded, her mouth closed, but still wide with delight. "I've found more on the cubes that we need to talk about."

"I have news myself. It's not good and I need your advice."

"That's what I'm here for."

That's what I used to think. Not anymore.

Kyle followed her, wanting to reach forward and touch her hand, to continue the contact they'd had at any level.

"I feel your eyes on my back," she said, her voice the standard, smug Billy.

"Just on your back?" he quipped. She looked over her shoulder, her hair almost concealing her arched eyebrow. He sat down beside her on the worn, leather couch and she pivoted, turning to him, her knee touching his thigh, leaning forward.

"What's your news?" she asked, all romance gone from her eyes. It was the antidote he required.

"Last night, after I came home, Brayden Cox was waiting for me…" As he described what happened, Billy's eyes were level and concentrated, just as they'd been when he first revealed the information about the mine.

"Anything today?"

Kyle ran his fingers through his hair. "Nothing. No sign of him. I can't figure out why he hasn't arrested me." Billy's eyes moved up, past his head and to the wall behind, staring.

"I'll see what the dark web has on him."

"Maybe he's waiting because someone else is showing up tomorrow." He told her what Ashley had revealed about the female forensics agent. "I could see him wanting evidence before he takes me in."

Billy's eyes grew darker. "What are you going to do about that?" she asked.

"The woman? I can't do a thing—"

"No. I mean Ashley." Kyle stopped breathing for a moment, catching all that was in her words. It was strange, thought Kyle, looking into her eyes, how she knew him, and all that he was, emotionally and mentally, without him saying a word.

"End it."

"No way. You absolutely can *not* do that."

"Are you serious?" he asked, incredulous.

"Completely and utterly. Too many things will be happening at once. The mine. Your hurt arm. You breaking up with her."

"No one is going to put those things together," Kyle argued.

"Someone will. You can't take the chance."

Kyle was stupefied. "You can't be asking me to continue with her as though nothing has changed? I don't even want to be with her now. And to imagine…" he trailed off, thinking of kissing her. Tonight it had been torture.

"Just be Machiavellian about it. She's a means to an end."

"Billy, I've already left her behind. I'm with you."

"I know that."

He blinked. "How can you be so emotionally detached about it all? The thought of kissing her is revolting."

"What you do with your lips is completely separate from your heart."

"Wow. Aren't most girls supposed to be jealous and angry?"

The corner of her curled, at first playful, then resigned. "I'm not most girls. I am secure in how you feel about me. Lastly, when my mom left us, she took a big part of my innocence with her."

Kyle didn't have a quick comeback. It had always occurred to him that Billy's tough demeanor was a front to distance herself from people. A barrier against the rumors and lack of friends, her own personal safety net which allowed her to accept being alone. Her statement broke that illusion. It wasn't fake. Billy's loss had hardened her from the inside.

"The difference between you and me is that until now, you've had your innocence," she continued. "Your parents are together. You are good-looking, smart, popular, a superior athlete, and dating the hottest girl in town. You know, this might break you."

She'd said it with such conviction, Kyle's eyes popped and then he laughed. "I'm not that pathetic!"

"Pathetic is the wrong word. You're naïve."

"Billy, if naïve means that I care more than you can imagine, then I'm ok with that."

"How can you be sure? Maybe it's the temporary fascination with something new?"

A short, frustrated sigh escaped before he spoke. "I miss you when we aren't together. Visualizing your smile makes me happy, and remembering your funny comments make me laugh out loud when no one else is in the room. You're the last person I think of at night and the first person in the morning. Does that sound temporary?"

"Not really."

"You know what else? Today, when Ashley asked me to walk her home I felt guilty, like I was being disloyal to you because I was with her."

The moment he stopped talking, his hands were on her cheeks, pulling her into him. This time, he didn't limit his kisses to her lips, but traversed to her cheek, holding her close. Somehow, their skin touching felt far more emotionally intimate.

"Does that tell you what I'm going to do?"

"She's going to be mean," Billy whispered. "But I think Mario will be happy."

He released her, sitting back against the couch, head resting on the back. He faced her. "I don't care about either one of them. It's her father I worry about. Doesn't matter though." In his mind, they were more than partners trying to solve a riddle. They were together. "Now, what else did you find on the cubes?"

Her lips parted and she blew out a thin slice of air. "Well…I spent more time going through files of people we know, just to see if I missed anything. The records seem to have been updated every year. New babies, deaths, that sort of thing. I looked up Mario for instance. Did you know his parents had a child who died at six months old?" Kyle shook his head. "That means that even if the government weren't alerted the cubes were missing now, if they do an update once a year, they would have discovered the cubes then."

"Have you thought about copying the data?"

"There is a way, but I don't have the devices to do it, nor do I have the software. I think one or two of my new anonymous friends can help me out with that, but I don't know if I can trust them. In the meantime, we have bigger issues. D." She leaned forward, her eyes intense. "Brayden would be an idiot not to track down every person who had access to the mine and is still living. He might have left you alone, but he will be forced to report back. You know what that means."

"He'll find D. Make him talk."

"Then the Patrol. They'll kill you first Kyle. Then me." She tapped his arm confidently. "But I've already thought of what to do."

"Of course, you have," he said with a slight smile. It faded as he listened to her plan. She'd looked up D's family on the cube and learned of a granddaughter living in Grand Junction.

"It's Christmas Eve tomorrow. I'll get a wig, change my outfit and visit him in the nursing home."

"And say what? We have to get you out of there?"

"Why not? We'll go for a walk. I'll see if he'll get on a one-way bus to visit his brother in Mexico. He'll never go back to the nursing home and it will take a while for them to track him down, if they can."

"I didn't think it was possible for you to make a mistake, Billy, but this one's it. They'll find him eventually. I'll be done for, and then they'll get you." He stared up at the ceiling again and found inspiration. "I got it," he said, sitting straight up. "The naturalists."

"As in, the group?"

"Sure. They could hide him. They're underground and everywhere."

"Everywhere and nowhere," she affirmed, using the government propaganda.

"Billy," he said, his voice picking up speed. "You found the people who helped you decipher what was on the cubes.

There has to be a way to reach out to them. To get them to…hide him. And then…"

"Then what? You're going to disappear too?"

Kyle blinked. He hadn't thought that far ahead but already sensed the inevitable. "The minute I took them, heard the choppers and you verified what was on the cubes, we knew it was only a matter of time. I have to leave so they can't find you. I'd never want you to give up your life."

Billy stood, hands interlaced behind her back. She bent over, her shoulders cracking as they dropped over her head. She stood back up.

"What life? I told you before. My plans are gone."

"But they might still be fulfilled."

"We'll see what happens after I visit D."

CHAPTER 18

"Mom, it's time to get the tree up," Kyle yelled. She hollered back from her workshop that his father could help out if he wanted to wait. "No, I got it."

Kyle's feet tickled on the cold, cement steps leading down to the basement. He flipped on the light, illuminating the car-sized kiln. It smelled of dust, metal and grinding, the entire area covered with the fine particles that lifted from the hot cylinder when it was in use. For his entire life, this kiln had been the source of his parent's income; without it, his parents would be forced to go into another town and pay extra for an inferior product.

"It's old, ugly and works," Kyle muttered to himself, repeating his father's favorite phrase.

He rounded it, gliding his fingers along the top of the curved, metal rim, his skin catching on a divet. "That will leave a mark." He put his finger in his mouth, sucking the blood. Just one more wound on his list of injuries.

He entered the storage room, lifting the fake Christmas tree from the back wall, along with a small box of ornaments. He made two trips, up and down the stairs to the living room. He moved the worn couch and corner pine hutch to the left, placing the four-pronged tree pedestal on top of the inset window. He slid the metal post into the holder, tightened the screws and adjusted the top. The three-foot fake blue spruce filled the inset window perfectly.

"Hey Mom, put on the Christmas music will you?" He shook his head, smiling. "Led Zeppelin isn't in the same category as Handel."

"And you're too young to know or appreciate either!" she retorted, her raspy cough starting on the final words.

"Can we at least compromise?" Soon enough, a rap version of Here Comes Santa Clause was playing. "Killing me Mom," he wailed, smiling as her laughter mixed with the music.

Kyle concentrated on the garland which he threaded between the branches. After that were the two strings of lights, one white, the other one colored. It was a complete mish-mash of colors without a theme. Exactly the way he liked it.

He fixed the ugly, little ornaments he'd created as a kid on the tree. They were happy times, happy memories. All the years he'd had with his parents in this little town, closed off from the rest of the country, protected from all that was evil. Exactly what his parents had wanted. Now, he'd brought that evil to town in the form of federal agents.

No, D brought it to me.

When he plugged in the lights, he sat back, wishing he could do it all over again. Christmas memories gave way to the reality of today. He thought of Billy and what she was preparing to do tomorrow.

Stu watched through the window as Kyle put up the Christmas tree by himself. He wondered why Kyle hadn't asked Ashley to help him.

"Ashley, honey, what are you doing right now?"

"Wrapping presents," she answered. It didn't take long until she was beside him, looking out the window. "That's really sad."

"That's what I was thinking." He placed his arm around her shoulder, hugging her close. "Maybe tomorrow being Christmas Eve, you could do something special for him."

"Like what?"

"I don't know. What's his favorite dessert?"

"I have no idea."

Stu turned to her. "You have been dating him for a year, plan to go to college with him and you don't know his favorite dessert?"

Ashley nudged him playfully with her elbow. "For all I know, he prefers oatmeal granola bars. Look at his parents!"

Stu leaned in, his gentle whispering causing her to squeal. "Go over and ask him. A homemade pie is the best gift a person can get. Trust me." She gave him a peck on the cheek and went to the hallway. "Don't be long," he counseled. "There's the curfew, but you should also respect their family time during the holidays, whatever that means."

"Sure, Dad."

She gave him another kiss before she left and then was out the door, pulling her hood up over her head as she walked. He stayed at the window, watching her until the door opened and Kyle invited her in. The boy took a moment, looked across the street and waved at him. He waved back.

They had an understanding, Kyle and himself. He was a good young man, Stu thought to himself for the millionth time. The best his daughter was ever going to find.

When the door shut, Stu let the curtains drop. Sometimes, he wondered if Kyle was too good for his daughter.

CHAPTER 19

Brayden listened to the evening's events within the Smith residence from the comfort of his hotel room. He'd received permission from Sheriff Deardon to keep his jeep parked in the vacant lot across from a former horse stable, and within his vehicle, he placed a small antenna on the front dashboard aimed at Kyle's home. He didn't need permission to eavesdrop or wiretap. When Director Forland told him to do what was necessary, that meant up to, and including, killing.

It won't come to that. Not with Kyle Smith.

It hadn't taken much to learn Ty's girl, Billy, and Kyle were together Friday night. It was Kyle's alibi. Today, he knew Kyle went to Billy's house to fix the fridge, then returned home and put up the Christmas tree. Ashley showed up, and from what Brayden heard, Kyle was a perfectly polite young man, exactly what any normal teenage boy was not.

If he'd been in love, the kid would act differently. Irrational and excited, emoting some level of interest for Christmas and gift-giving. Kyle spoke like his every word was being monitored. Brayden recalled Officer Hancock's words about Stu's penchant for a gun when it came to his daughter, and had taken note of the position of Kyle's house and bedroom in relation to the Fine residence. They probably knew his comings and goings to the minute.

Ashley had left shortly after learning Kyle didn't have much interest in sweets. She'd told him her mother had a great recipe for cherry pie, and Kyle had responded his dad would love that.

"I heard I'm going to be having a cherry pie all to myself," Kyle's father said, his words sliding into one another, like he'd enjoyed his evening cocktail.

"She wasn't taking no for an answer," said Kyle. "Standard Ashley operating procedure."

"You're going to take care of that before you head to college, right?"

"Way before." Kyle sounded like he was stretching. The Christmas music was the only noise in the house. Brayden kept the listening device on until the music switched to classic rock. He assumed Kyle was in bed, and he called Forland.

"No news on identifying the perpetrator," he informed the Deputy Director. "But I'll be tracking down the remaining employees tomorrow as planned."

"Wait. I changed Saachi's flight. You'll pick her up at the airport and take her with you."

"With all due respect sir, that will use up hours from my schedule. She could get her own car and meet me in in town."

"Reese wants her with you." As in, Janet Reese, the head of National Security.

"Yes, sir," he responded professionally. If Reese wanted him to have a babysitter, he'd go along with it. Brayden was off the call and received the flight information for his counterpart seconds later.

Just as well, he thought. It simply put more time between the event and the potential for others to track Kyle down.

CHAPTER 20

"Kyle, remember to thank Ty for the food if you're going his way," said Kyle's coach. His mouth was full, so he nodded. "Two days in a row."

"Glad somebody thought of feeding us," said Mario, causing the group to vigorously nod their heads. "Bet no one else is having practice on Christmas Eve."

"Because no one else is going to win the game this Friday," retorted the coach. "They'll be in a carb coma and you'll actually remember your plays."

Kyle had kept his focus when he'd caught a glimpse of Billy walking through the side door, depositing the food, then leaving. Her expression was as surly as ever, just what one would expect from being made an errand girl the day before a holiday.

"You got Ashley anything special?" Mario asked, his voice low and mischievous.

"As special as what my mom can make," he answered. Mario's dad owned a construction company, which meant he wasn't on the same social level as Stu, but Kyle was sure the money was nearly as good.

"Oh, come on!" his friend pleaded. "A year and nothing! These are big deals, Christmas, Valentine's. You *must* have it covered."

Kyle retied the laces on his shoe, then paused, elbows on his knees. "Mario, what I have covered is going to college, getting my degree and moving on with life, and it all starts with the game this Friday."

"Fine," his friend grumbled. "I was just looking…"

"For juice. I know."

But it's not there.

Two hours later, Kyle was at the pool for his 2 p.m. shift. Holidays were the busiest time of year, Christmas Eve being no exception. Out of towners filled the two local hotels, their first and usually only stop before hitting the hot springs. It was a clear night, not a cloud in the sky, which made it breathtakingly cold. He was fully clothed, the waterproof, thick parka and blanket wrapped around him as he sat in the life guard chair. All he could do was think about Billy.

He thought about her schedule. She'd dropped the food off at 11 a.m., which meant she could have made it to D's retirement center before noon. If her plan played out, D would be on a bus headed across the country before anyone had a chance to find him. What he and Billy didn't discuss was the police protocol for tracking down a missing person. It would be a country-wide all-points bulletin, with every bus stop and airport on alert.

Kyle concentrated on the men and women shivering their way to the hot pools, stripping off their towels before easing themselves into the water. He looked over the heads of the swimmers to the road leading into town. It curved around the north end of the pool, then right in front of his parent's home that officially started Main Street.

Not a cop car in sight all day, nor Brayden's blue jeep. The sheriff and Deputy Hancock had stopped going door to door, but everyone knew Brayden was still here, and that Stu was still mad. The teller at the grocery store had helped Ashley's mom, who mentioned she was making Stu a decadent dessert. The same transaction had included her purchasing cherries for Ashley's boyfriend, the head lifeguard, so they could make a pie. The clerk had replayed the conversation to everyone else who'd come in that day, including the out-of-towners.

"Are you the one getting the cherry pie today?" asked one woman who looked like a withered old grape. It was the fourth time he'd heard a variation of the question.

"That's the rumor," he answered through a smile. It faded when he saw the blue jeep on the street. Thankfully, it continued up Main.

Kyle pulled the covering closer. Had they spoken with D? Was the forensics woman with him? Was the pool going to be surrounded by Patrol, coming for him and then Billy?

His stomach was clenched tight, a ball of pain uncomfortable and uncommon until last Friday. He'd spent his whole life staying out of trouble and living anxiety free. That existence was a memory now.

Kyle motioned to the other lifeguard on duty who replaced him. He checked on Fred, testing the chemicals and water, feeding the group a treat, anything to delay getting back on the pedestal for another hour.

His phone buzzed and he read the text.

It's done

The words caused his chest to throb, but then he saw it was from his mother. She included a picture. It was a photo of the intricate glass hummingbird feeder Kyle had asked her to make for Ashley's Christmas present. Hummingbirds were Ashley's favorite, and this gift was one of a kind.

Those were the words I was going to use, Kyle thought to himself. And they sounded so good, too. He thought about still using them, because it was still true. She was one of a kind. Just not *his* kind.

"How's Fred?"

Kyle nearly dropped his phone in the water.

"Alive," Kyle answered. He looked up to see Brayden Cox standing next to him. "Want to feed him?"

"No thanks," answered Brayden. "I just wanted to see where you were."

Kyle squinted against the sun as he spread food around. "Been working since practice finished this morning. I have a few more hours to go." Kyle looked down at the water, wondering if the forensics woman was nearby.

"Did you know an old miner named D?"

Kyle swished the water with his fingers, feeling a few of the creatures nibble at the ends. "The entire town knew D. He's down at the nursing home in Montrose, if you're looking for him."

"We found him."

This is it. My life is officially over.

Kyle put the lid back on the container and brushed off the sides. He had nothing to say that wouldn't come across as incriminating. "How is old D? As talkative as ever?"

Brayden dropped down, squatting across from him, his elbows on his knees, hands together, like a coach before a big play. "He's dead."

Kyle's jaw dropped open. "Dead, as in, old age dead? When did that happen?" A look of scrutiny from the FBI agent caused a flow of heat to move up Kyle's neck. When it hit his lower lip, he realized his mouth was still open and he closed it.

"We aren't sure exactly, but it appears as though it occurred between the time his granddaughter paid him a visit and when we showed up."

"Geeze," was all Kyle said.

"Yeah. The nurse called to D's room, but he didn't pick up. We asked for the nurse to knock on his door. No answer. She tried to open it up, but it was locked from within. She used her key and found D lying on his bed."

"Heart attack?" Kyle suggested.

"Don't think so. The pill containers in the bathroom were empty. Another agent is there now, collecting evidence."

A dozen thoughts flashed through Kyle's mind. A single piece of hair or a skin cell off Billy and she'd be tracked down. Even before the discovery of the mine and the cubes, it was common knowledge that the DNA files of every person in this country were collected and saved. It had all started with the virus.

"I can't believe he's dead," said Kyle, more to himself. That wasn't the plan Billy had outlined. Had the man taken his life after she left? Kyle had a hard time imagining she'd encourage him to end it all. He wondered if Billy even knew what had happened.

"You think he had a reason?" Brayden asked him.

"He was going senile," Kyle said, the sympathy he felt real.

"Perhaps." Brayden said, his voice low. "It's also possible he had something to tell, got it off his chest and then made the decision to end his life rather than divulge the identity of who he told."

Kyle couldn't help himself. He stared the FBI agent in the eye, his desire to run and hide in direct conflict with a need for honesty.

"Kyle, things were taken from the mine. More people will come and search until they find out what happened to them."

Kyle stood up with Brayden, nearly eye to eye with the man. He looked over the agent's shoulder, nodding at the lifeguard. "What if the items missing were returned to you? Would that make you all leave and let the town go back to normal?"

"Unfortunately, no."

CHAPTER 21

The cold air hurt Kyle's lungs, the pain momentarily robbing him of words. It was second time Kyle felt the noose had been placed around his neck and then removed, the reprieve momentary.

"You going to take that plunge in the water?" he asked Brayden.

"Not tonight. Maybe tomorrow. You working?"

Kyle pressed his lips, thinking. "I have it off."

Brayden pushed his hands into the pockets of his coat, hunching his shoulders against another breeze. "Might want to stay busy until the town clears out."

Kyle nodded, and the man left. He took Brayden's advice. He had the office call Matt with the good news Kyle was giving him the afternoon off and that Kyle would swap him places for Christmas starting at ten a.m.

An hour after the sun had set, a lean figure emerged from the women's locker room. Billy's platinum hair popped against the parameter lights, disappearing when she went under the water. The lap lane was empty and she proceeded to occupy it for thirty minutes. Kyle did his best to watch her no more or less than anyone else in the pool, his gaze that of an alert lifeguard.

When she finished, she put her towel around her, disappeared into the changing room and came back out, this time her towel wrapped in a ball. She appeared to search for a misplaced item around the bench underneath the life jackets. He saw the orange pads rustle once before she shook her head in frustration and left.

When the ten-minute warning bell sounded, the swimmers leisurely made their way to the edge of the pool. Feeling the cold air was to be put off until the last minute. The springs closed at six Christmas Eve, which was too early according to the grumbles he heard.

Kyle descended from the top of the lifeguard tower and walked around the smaller hot springs then the larger pool and lap area. He smiled and joked with customers, taking their gripes about the hours in stride. When he reached the life jackets, he straightened the rows. One fell off the bench and he bent down, brushing his fingers along the floor.

Kyle almost mistook the gum wrapper for trash. Billy had placed a square, flat media card in the paper. It stayed within his fingers as he put it in the pocket of his pants.

Smart. Three nights in a row to fix her fridge wasn't going to go unnoticed. He could put the media card in his car or computer, pull up the files and listen or extract whatever was on it.

After closing up the pool, Kyle walked up the path to the cross walk connecting Ashley's home to his own.

With luck, she won't see me.

His foot was just off the sidewalk when he heard a door open.

"Hey, handsome," Ashley called. "Come say hi for a minute." Kyle dutifully turned and went up the path. "Weren't you supposed to be home hours ago?" she asked.

"Yeah, but I got caught up in the Christmas spirit. Giving Matt extra time to shop."

"You're the town Santa Clause," she breathed. Had Kyle not already lost his affection for her, he would have ogled the girl. She wore a form-fitting red sweater, the scoop-neck stopping just at the top of her chest, her blond curls draped strategically on either side.

"Red is a good color on you," he complimented. Better to be honest when he could.

"Matches my lipstick," she added, purposefully pushing them out.

"Then I won't mess them up." Her mouth turned down in her pouty grump. "It's not my fault, Ash. Me and mom are wrapping presents tonight. Yours included."

That softened the rejection. "Then I'll let you go. This once. But," she paused, tilting her head. "What about coming tomorrow for Christmas dinner?"

"Sorry, Ash. We have our big, turkey dinner on Christmas Day."

"I remember," she nudged him. "I just thought this once, since it will be the last as high schoolers before we leave."

"Trust me. What works on your dad won't work on my mom."

She laughed. "What about gifts tonight?"

"Sorry, but mom closes the shop at eight and then we eat."

"Then come over after you open presents in the morning, around noon. Mom likes to make these horrible nut covered cheese balls and talk with everyone while she makes the big dinner."

"I like those things," he said.

"You would!" she laughed at him.

"Unfortunately, I'm covering for Matt most of the day tomorrow until we close at six."

"Are you kidding me? I won't be able to see you at all on Christmas?" Kyle shrugged, letting his shoulders droop.

"Okay, fine. But then for sure you have to come over the following night. At least one special meal."

A last supper.

"Ash," he said with false patience. "You live in a world where you don't have to work, play sports, and are not responsible for paying for college. I'm working every day. The only time I have off is for practice. We have the big game on Friday, but my schedule continues through New Year's, then we are back to school."

"True, but it won't be long before we graduate and have the summer."

"No," he corrected. "*You* have the summer to play and travel, while I will be working full time, hopefully two jobs to make the money I need."

"Oh, Kyle," she said, her tone dismissing the reality of his comment. "My dad could help you get into any college you want and probably even help with the money."

"Not on my life," he said with a grin, but meant every word. "I appreciate the thought though."

"It's not a thought, Kyle," she said earnestly. "I was being serious. You have no idea what my dad can do."

"Actually, I have a pretty good idea. Look, I need to get home and help Mom."

He brushed her cheek with a barely-there pass of his lips and said goodbye.

"You aren't walking me to the door?" Kyle rolled his lips together. Don't act frustrated. Do not get angry. Do not walk away. Do what Billy advised. Don't make it obvious anything has changed.

"Sure."

When Ashley was at the door, she gave him a peck on the cheek, snuffing in irritation when he didn't kiss her back.

"My nose is frozen and I'd rather not get an icicle on you."

"Gross," she laughed, pushing him away. "Next time."

I don't want a next time.

CHAPTER 22

Kyle saw his father through the window, talking to his mother. He walked around the side of the house, going through the back entrance. Only visitors and customers used the front door.

"Mom, you need to put out the sign that you're closed."

"Wrong," she rasped back, a smokers coughing fit taking over. "You know some of our best business comes through that door on Christmas Eve with people desperate for a last minute gift."

He got a Coke out of the fridge. "Yeah, and we never have the night as a family because of it."

"Not true. We always have our gift exchange."

Kyle sat on the couch in the living room, thinking of Billy. The mixed lights dotted his jeans, the random pattern a galaxy of stars. Billy had her cowboy Christmas ornaments, music and hot chocolate. What did she do on Christmas Eve? he wondered. Ty kept the bar open until eleven, catering to the crowd who had family dinners then went to Ty's to have hot toffees. Maybe she'd be at the bar.

"Hey mom, you mind if I go out later?"

"To where?" his father asked, coming into the living room. "Weren't you just whining we aren't together as a family?"

"I wasn't whining," Kyle countered. "I was advocating for mom to stop letting strangers in the house."

"Sure." His dad sat down, picking up the beer on the end table.

"Isn't that warm?"

His dad smiled and drank. "It's always good, grumpy."

"I'm not grumpy."

"Whiny and grumpy."

Theirs had never been a relationship full of deep conversation. It wasn't a negative, Kyle thought, watching his father tip back the beer. Prior to now, neither had a reason to get deep over anything, girls or school. Kyle played ball, he would be leaving for college soon, Ashley was temporary. That was it.

"Can we have our gift exchange no later than seven please?" Kyle half yelled to his mom. "Then I can go up town."

"Nope," came her response. "Not until eight."

Kyle felt something in the pocket of his jeans. He'd totally forgotten about the media card when Ashley called out to him.

"Sure," he said suddenly, sitting up. "Going to take a shower."

He felt his father's eyes on him but he was already imagining his evening. Reading what Billy had found. Going up to Ty's, slipping through the back to see Billy. Kyle imagined the music playing in the background, his arm around her, pressing against him.

"When are you going to give Ashley the gift I made?" asked his mother as he walked by.

"I don't know. I shifted with Matt tomorrow because I knew you and Dad were working."

She swiveled in her chair. "Kyle, we are never open on Christmas, you know that."

"But we don't do anything after we open presents and our dinner is late because one of you will be sleeping."

"Kyle, today we work. Tomorrow we are together, just like you wanted. That's our routine."

"Sorry, mom. The routine has to change. I've got to work."

It was still quiet when Kyle closed the door to the bathroom. He imagined his mother talking with his father. His towel was still around him when his dad came into his room after he finished with is shower.

"Pretty abrupt with your mother in there."

"Yeah. Sorry."

His father lingered at the door. "You want to talk about what's really going on?"

Kyle slipped on a hoodie. "Nope."

"Never had much of a reason to pry into your life before, and I don't want to start. But it's obvious, to me anyway, that something is up with you."

Kyle looked up. His father wouldn't have pried into his belongings, and even if he had, Kyle had nothing to hide. The media card was in his pants, and his father was a complete luddite. Mom had to operate the computer because he couldn't.

The towel dropped and Kyle finished dressing in his sweats. "Dad. It's the holidays. I'm tired."

"Uh-huh. That bull crap may work with Mario but not me. I'm not forcing you to talk, but you be respectful to your mother. She does nothing that's not for you."

Kyle was still looking down when his father left, the sting of his words going deep, where it would remain, buried, until he apologized. He tussled his mop of sandy blond hair, pushing it to one side and went into his mother's workspace. He checked she wasn't inserting a piece of glass into a form and put his arm around her.

"Hey. Sorry for my tone and what I said. You don't deserve that."

She kept working. "No, I don't."

He kissed the top of her head. "I'm really sorry, Mom."

His mother grunted. "I'm the one who's sorry. I spent a lot of time making that hummingbird for Ashley, who is going to smash it into a thousand pieces."

Kyle's chest compressed. "Where did that come from?"

"My eyes," she said, looking up at him. Her hair and skin tone were lighter than his, a pure northern European background, given to freckles instead of a tan.

"And you have started seeing things?"

"Yes, from right here," she said, lifting up her head. He followed her gaze, across the street to the Fine residence. The heavy drapes in the front living room were open, revealing the double doors leading into the dining room. Kyle watched Ashley and her mother bring in food to the table while others took their seats.

"I have to agree with your father. It might be better if you come right out and break up with her. This inching back bit by bit is painful to watch."

Kyle stepped back, a half-grin already on his face. "You watch me?"

"Only half as much as Ashley's father does," interjected his father from behind him. Kyle took in both parents.

"Huh," was all Kyle said. He ran his palm along the right side of his hair, interlacing both hands behind his neck, pulling it down. His right shoulder spasmed and he dropped it, rolling the muscle. "Okay, since you both see it coming, let me state the obvious. There is no good time to ditch Ashley, and I don't want to be mean about it. I just…we don't want the same things. We aren't the same people, never were."

"That's an understatement," muttered his dad.

"Hon, a girl never wants to be dumped during the holidays," said his mom.

"But you just said it was painful to watch."

"It is. But I'm not saying do it now. Wait until after New Year's and you're back to school. Hopefully she will be occupied with other things and you will be too busy to care if she gets snippy."

Kyle glanced back over at Ashley's home. "You think she'll get snippy?"

"Mmm-hmm," answered his mother, now refocused on the glasswork before her.

"Be optimistic, Son. Maybe Stu will buy her a fancy something to take her mind off you."

"Like a sharp set of knives to kill you with," said his mom. Kyle looked down, she started laughing and his father patted his back.

"Not to worry. It will be over quick, one way or the other."

Kyle sure hoped so.

CHAPTER 23

It was after nine when Forland got the call he'd been expecting. When he'd finished asking his questions, he disconnected then hit speed dial.

"Janet, it's Forland. The first forensics are back. Good news and bad. Which do you want first?"

"The bad."

"Brayden reports the death of an old man who used to work at the mine, who coincidentally took a bottle full of tablets about an hour just before they showed up to interview him. This happened right after a visit from a granddaughter."

"Interesting."

"I'll say. A half-dozen DNA strands found in his room matched others in town, and Brayden has already identified a few commonalities, one being that most frequent the same bar. All adults, all male, sans the nurses in the facility. One match is underage, but that's due to her being the bar owner's daughter."

"The circle may be getting smaller."

"And we might have gotten real lucky up front. About an hour before Brayden showed up, a young woman signed in as the man's granddaughter. Brayden traced the woman to a nearby city and gave her a call. She says was never there. Also," he paused for effect, "Saachi found several strands of brown hair from a wig. The granddaughter's hair is blond."

The head of NSA verbalized the hypothesis shared by Brayden. "She could have been a naturalist and killed him, or he passed along something else he didn't want anyone to know and killed himself."

"Brayden says the man was a known drunk who spent a lot of time talking up at the local bar he referenced."

"Conclusion?"

"The facts don't support a conclusion as yet. It is possible an old timer who worked on the mine was around when the security systems were put in, a naturalist got to him and he spilled the beans."

"And that person injected him with any variety of psychoactive medication, then made it look like a suicide."

"That's Brayden's hunch," Forland conceded. "The body has already been transported to the morgue. The autopsy will be performed there unless you deem it a security risk."

"Brayden's hunches are usually right," Janet said. "Does he have any others?"

"He believes focusing on the townspeople further is a waste. He suspects this was initiated by someone who used the miner and someone else for the entry."

"A naturalist?"

"Not necessarily. Someone with an agenda, and it could be anything—government disruption or internal wars with the Patrol. Too early to say. He just doesn't feel that a town comprised of less than five hundred people, all who grew up there and half who worked at the mine, suddenly decided to get curious and break into the local mountain. He's thinking someone from within the NSA, or a person who helped construct it. Speaking of which, how did your internal investigation turn out?"

"Clean." Forland thought about the definition of clean. That only meant no unlawful acts or strange behavior conducted by the person investigated. "We started with a total of 43. Thirty-eight remain on the payroll. One died of a heart attack and four retired, two still consult with the government."

"If not within the construction and design sector, then medical."

"Unlikely. Medical personnel weren't told what was going to be done with the data, where it was to be stored or how."

"Does that mean you didn't run the checks?"

"Of course, we did. Once again, all clean. Tell me about your forensics person."

Forland tapped his pencil. "Nothing new from her personnel file," he answered, ready to end the call. She thought her staff was above board, so did he. Their trust only need extend to their keyboards to verify the other's staff, as the computer systems shared the same data.

"I'm looking at her file now," said Reese. "Still single. Never married. No debt. Looks clean on the surface."

"Yep."

"And Brayden? He's operating to standard?" Janet had already insinuated Brayden's fiber of loyalty might have a tear.

Forland stopped tapping the pencil, placing his thumb on the pointed edge. He pushed down, channeling his increasing annoyance at the woman. "Brayden operates above standard, which is why he's there now."

"His wife has been increasing her loads at the hospital lately."

"Normal when her husband is on the road."

"It started before he left."

"Janet, we keep tabs on our own people and their issues for our mutual purposes of national security. It appears you are doing redundant duty. For the sake of operating at maximum efficiency, let's limit the unnecessary discussions until such time you tell me to pull Brayden."

"Fair enough."

Off the call, Forland thought about his best agent. He didn't blame Janet for being paranoid. It was a common emotion to anyone in the higher echelons of the government; no one was immune to having a drone flying overhead for additional monitoring. But Brayden Cox?

Forland typed out a query on Cox's wife, refreshing what he knew. Laura Cox was a surgeon at Denver General. Their only daughter had died at age three, the mutation in her DNA causing a rare disorder. She'd slipped into a coma, and life support had been terminated. Ten years later, their oldest son had taken his life by a gunshot wound the day before his seventeenth birthday using one of Brayden's government-issued pieces. Each time, his wife took a two-week leave of absence with Brayden by her side. Both eventually returned to their lives and work, which became one and the same.

A broken, anguish-filled marriage. Unfulfilled men tended to look outside their marriage. That led to compromising positions and pictures, costing even the most talented men their jobs. Brayden wouldn't have been the first with a top-security clearance to go to a low-end motel with a prostitute. Extortion wasn't a concern, but the loss of state secrets was, especially when Janet told him the real cause of his son's death.

Forland had assigned a tail to monitor Brayden's whereabouts for six months after his son died just to be sure. Reese requested another six months, coming out of her budget. The woman was only satisfied when the officer assigned to tail him wrote in his report it was unnecessary. Brayden Cox was steady, stable and had adjusted to the second tragedy in his life with the characteristic calm Forland expected.

In truth, Forland wished he had a team of Brayden's. He simply couldn't find guys like him anymore.

CHAPTER 24

Kyle's head was still in the dark clouds when he sat down in front of his laptop in the small dining nook beside the kitchen. It was in the back of the home, the blinds always up, giving a clear view of the man-sized boulders, which had rolled down from the mountain about a million years prior. They formed a jagged line thirty feet from their home, shielding billy goats and rams in the winter and deer in the summer. Kyle visualized himself like a boulder, strong and immobile, impervious to the actions of others.

He glanced through the kitchen, seeing his parents hunched over the work table. He slid Billy's media card in the side of the computer, scanning the file folders that automatically appeared. One was a word document, the other files were letters strung together, indecipherable.

Kyle read the letter twice. His left finger shook as he popped out the flat, square data holder. Taking Billy's advice, he found a drill, punctured the memory card in the center until it turned to dust. Then he flushed the remaining bits down the toilet, knowing it was going into the processing center miles away, never to be recovered.

"Mom, can I start getting dinner ready?" He'd lost his desire for food, the anxiety from what he'd read constricting his stomach. She told him where she'd put the sweet potatoes and what recipe she wanted and he got to work. He walked into her office minutes later.

"I don't want to be a downer by taking the fun out of making food, but can we make it easy this year? You want sweet sauce for the sweet potatoes, and to make them right, it will take two hours. Ty has sweet potato mashers permanently on the menu."

"He has turkey every day of the year too," added his dad, not looking up.

"You men," she rasped. "Next you're going to suggest you stop by the store and pick up a pie."

"Well…" Kyle said, "Look at you two. If you actually want a homemade meal, we won't eat until midnight." Which might not be a bad idea, he thought to himself.

The door opened and the ding of a visitor stepping through the infrared on the floor confirmed someone was in the living room.

"See?" he whispered, then turned. "Hi, can I help you?"

Kyle's mother came out and took over sales person duties.

"Do I have your approval?" he muttered in her ear.

"Oh, go on."

Kyle felt the pains in his stomach merge with other sensations, eagerness and worry, the excitement of seeing Billy on Christmas Eve conflicting with his concern over her welfare. She'd crossed over the line from safety into possible danger and hadn't asked for Kyle's approval before she did it.

Exactly what he'd expect of Billy. She was confident in her approach, that the precautions she'd taken were sufficient and what she'd done wasn't up for debate. He'd live with it, just as she had.

He went out the back door, then paused. Brayden told him to stay visible, but to walk up the street risked Ashley seeing him, opening the door for a grenade of questions that might blow up in his face. To go up the side street wasn't much of a help, since he had to go through the front door of the bar to order food.

Kyle compromised by taking the back streets until 6th Street, then onto Main.

"Hey Kyle," greeted Ty. An older couple sat at the far side of the bar and a full table occupied the corner nearest the back screen.

Kyle waved. "Can I get some takeout?" he asked, heading to the bar. Ty pointed to a seat at the end, nearest the big screen but also giving a view of the street. Kyle took off his coat and leaned on the counter, scanning a menu. "Where's Billy? Making you a big dinner?"

The man grunted. "Scotty quit this morning, so my dear, beloved daughter is back washing dishes and none too happy about it."

"I expect not. Then who's cooking?"

"That would be her as well." Kyle chuckled, his humor genuine. Billy had to be irate.

"Can I use your phone for a sec?" Kyle placed the call to his home, speaking with his father who picked up. When he hung up, Ty caught his eye. "The least I could do for all the great food you've been giving our team this last week."

"Anything to help you win, kid."

Kyle grabbed his coat and went to the back, turning right at the end of the corridor. He hung his coat up and said hello.

"Hey," said Billy, her voice flat. "What are you doing here?"

"Paying your dad back for his free food," Kyle said blandly. He found an apron on far wall and offered to take over dishwashing while she cooked.

"My mom is helping customers, dad is working and I realized we'd starve if I didn't get some help. You okay?"

Billy shook her head, taking her place behind the stove. Two dishes were simmering, and a pot with pasta was boiling.

She reached above her, turning up the music slightly, checking the food.

"You hear about D?"

"Dad told me," she answered, turning off a timer then emptying the pasta into a sieve. "Brayden came into the bar and was asking my dad about him."

Kyle couldn't help glancing over his shoulder. The hallway was as quiet as his paranoia was high.

Kyle rinsed dishes and loaded the machine. She pointed to the plates and he handed them to her, their quiet choreography seamless.

"Read the disk," he said, his voice covered by the country music. "I'm worried for you."

Billy removed the garlic bread from the oven. "Don't be. I got this. Here. Load me up with the parmesan, there." Kyle found the grater, and soon Billy had two full plates of food in her hands and left. After filling the washer, he found the broom and swept near the back of the door, Brayden's words of keeping busy ringing in his ears. What were Brayden and his partner up to? He hypothesized the woman was in her hotel room, probably set up with some sort of portable forensics equipment.

Kyle jumped when he felt hands around his waist, a flat surface leaning against his shoulder blades. Billy was hugging him, holding him tight, like he was the tree in the middle of a storm and she was hanging on for dear life. He put his warm palms on her cold hands. "You always surprise me. I like it." He felt her nudge closer, as though she were removing the last bit of air and space between them.

A bell went off and she dropped her arms, turning to the sink. "Be busy. And normal," she whispered.

Kyle immediately picked up the broom and began sweeping again, his back to the kitchen as he moved towards the back door.

"Ty said I'd find you here." Kyle looked over his shoulder, turning.

"Hey Ash," he said. "What are you doing here?" He kept sweeping, making it clear his conversation wasn't going to interrupt his activity.

"I should ask you that. It's Billy, isn't it?"

"Yep," Billy answered without turning. Kyle heard dishes moving, and figured she was preparing another order.

"I'm here because Mom and Dad are helping customers, don't have food ready and so in desperation I came up here, but Ty only has Billy tonight. Now I'm trading some kitchen help for food."

"We could have given you some."

Kyle bent to the dustpan. "Be right back." He went out the door and emptied the pan into the trashcan, getting hit with a slap of cold wind from the alley. "I wasn't going to interrupt your family to beg for food, Ash. I'd rather work for it. How long do you think it will take, Billy?"

"You ordered a lot," she said, reaching for the potatoes. "Twenty minutes. More with dessert. You can speed things up by peeling."

"Sure."

Kyle pointedly ignored Ashley as he lifted the peeler off the magnetic plate attached to the steel backsplash and went to the sink.

"Are you paying for this?" she asked, incredulous. "I mean, you're working for your food."

Billy said nothing, but Kyle guessed she had a whole lot going through her mind.

"I can help and get something in return, or do nothing and starve. You want to join in?" He turned to her, a half-smile on his face, although he felt an inward challenge rising within him. She'd never touched a dish, broom or mop in her life. She didn't know the word paycheck, but she certainly knew allowance and credit card.

"You don't know what you're missing," Kyle said dryly.

"I'm sure she doesn't," muttered Billy. In the silence that followed, Kyle kept peeling, unsure if Ashley heard the comment or not.

"You're as classy as everyone says you are," said Ashley, using a tone Kyle hadn't heard before.

Kyle glanced to his right, watching Billy turn.

"And you're not half as classy as you pretend to be." The two girls stared at one another. "What are you waiting for? Oh, an invitation to leave. I invite you to leave now."

"Nice," Ashley said.

"My apologies. I meant to be rude."

Ashley turned to him, her look one of shock. Did she expect something from him?

"Well?" she asked.

"Well what? I need to eat, Ashley. I'm going to be here until the food is done, then I'm going home to be with my parents."

"Seriously?"

Kyle looked at her. "What?"

"Unreal."

When she'd left, another ding sounded. "I'll be back," Billy told him, wiping her hands. A few minutes later, she came back and picked up the potato peeler. "Sorry."

"Don't be. I liked it. I've never had a girl stand up for me."

She caught his eye. "You've never had a real girl."

CHAPTER 25

Deputy Hancock was on the corner of Main and Fourth when he saw an unusual sight: Ashley Fine walking towards him, alone. Hands in her pocket and a scowl on her face, she resembled her father.

"You out for a stroll?" he asked as she approached.

"No," she said, her usual coy smile missing.

"On your way home?"

"Yes," she answered, eyes straight as she passed.

"Hey, you alright?"

"No, but I haven't been physically harmed, if that's what you want to know."

"Just checking," he called to her back. "Always need to be on the alert for strange people in town."

The girl stopped and turned abruptly. "You're wrong Deputy Hancock. We don't have to be on alert. We have strange people in this town, like a certain bar owner and his weird daughter."

Mark let the comment slide. Billy and Ty were good people.

"Kyle could be protecting you about now. Where is he?"

"With the weird family as we speak."

"Kyle? At their home?" he asked, unable to hide his surprise.

"No," she grumbled, as if even that were over the top. "Getting food from them. Take out."

She turned and kept walking. Mark smiled to himself, pressing his hands deeper into his coat pocket.

Mark had made the final walk along the road at his boss's request. Deardon had eased up on the rounds, but O'Connell at State still required once a night walking patrols while Brayden and his partner were in town. After that, Deardon said life could go back to normal.

He went up the east side of the road, made a U at Stagecoach Hotel and saw Brayden inside, speaking with a woman at the bar. On a whim, he went inside. He hadn't met a female FBI forensics specialist before and this might be his only shot.

"Merry Christmas Eve, Brayden," Hancock greeted, stepping up to the restaurant counter.

The FBI agent extended his hand, turning to his companion. "Have you met Saachi Gupta?"

Mark smiled, instantly glad he'd come in. "Deputy Mark Hancock," he said. Her hand was warm and soft.

"Hello, Mark." Brayden gestured for him to take a seat but he remained standing.

"How are you two enjoying our little town on Christmas Eve?" They smiled in unison. "The joys of working in law, huh?"

"You still on duty?" Brayden asked.

"For another half a block."

"Come back and join us," Saachi offered. "Unless you have to go wrap presents for your kids."

He shook his head. "No kids, no family. Just me."

"Then join us," Brayden seconded.

"Sure. We'll have a three-way law enforcement party. Oh," Hancock said immediately. "Didn't meant it that way."

Saachi laughed heartily. "Sure you did. Go. We've just got our menus."

Mark's face was still warm as he walked through the cold, asking himself what in the world had possessed him to make an innuendo of such grand proportions, and with two members of the FBI no less.

Instant attraction, that's what. Saachi was an exotic beauty of pint-sized proportions with an edgy vibe and fiercely intelligent eyes. He hadn't seen that in a while. If ever.

And law enforcement to boot.

He walked briskly down the road, turning around at the Smith family home. He saw Kyle's father bent over, soldering a piece of glass into a frame and his mother in the front helping a fifty-something man pick out hanging ornaments. Ashley had said Kyle was up at Ty's grabbing food.

All checked and accounted for, he thought, turning uptown and back to the hotel. Brayden and Saachi were still at the bar and Hancock took the stool by Brayden, who pushed a half-full plate of bacon-wrapped jalapeño peppers towards him. "Saved you some."

"You can have mine," he said, pushing them back. "But thanks. The cream cheese makes my tongue break out."

Saachi laughed. "You would not believe how many people have that same reaction."

"Are they dead when you find this out?" Brayden caught himself from choking on his food, and Mark banged his back once. "Don't die on me buddy. My Heimlich maneuver is rusty."

"Sorry," croaked Brayden, clearing his throat with a drink. "Her job doesn't always involve dead people."

"He's right," Saachi confirmed, "and I wasn't kidding. Tons of people break out over cream cheese."

"Seriously?" Mark asked. She nodded, putting a whole pepper in her mouth. A woman not afraid to eat. He liked that.

"Here, let's get a table," Brayden suggested. Gesturing to the bartender, he pointed and got the nod to take an empty table against the wall. "You're now officially off duty?" Brayden asked him once they'd sat and he'd taken off his coat.

"It's a small town in the center of some weird happenings," Mark replied. "I'm always on duty. But technically, yes. I'm off," he said a bit louder. "The bright spot is I'm missing my aunt's stuffed cannoli, which has never seemed all that festive to me. What are you two missing this evening?"

"My cat," Saachi offered. "Who is likely tearing my couch apart even as we speak." Mark laughed, looking to Brayden.

"My wife is on call and if history is any predictor of the future, she'll be really busy in about twelve hours."

"Why's that?" Mark asked.

"Let me guess," Saachi offered. "Diabetic attacks," she said as she lifted another jalapeno popper. Brayden nodded, but Mark was baffled. "Too many carbs and drinking," she added.

"Eight to ten hours after the big blowout meal, the kidneys start collapsing and the hospital is a zoo," Brayen explained.

"Being up here is nice change from being home alone, which is guaranteed on holidays."

"No kids for you then?" Mark asked.

"Or pets either."

Mark caught a look between Saachi and Brayden, who had his eyes on his glass as he took a drink. Sore subject.

"Never been to a mountain town like this," Saachi remarked. "It's as beautiful as a postcard."

Mark nodded. "It's as untouched as it looks."

"We'll try to leave before we can screw it up," Brayden said.

"I'd appreciate that," Mark replied seriously. "You should see it in the summer time." The FBI agents took the hint, asking about the area, and Mark gave them a verbal tourist's guide description that would make the chamber of commerce president proud.

He wanted to ask about what they'd learned so far, but figured if he kept them talking long enough, they'd eventually talk. Law enforcement officers working a case couldn't help themselves; they wanted new information as badly as anyone, otherwise, they'd already be gone.

Mark glanced around the room, taking in the group. The dimly lit hotel restaurant was only semi-crowded, full of visitors he recognized.

"You looking for someone?" Saachi asked.

"Nope. I already know most of these people."

"They from around here?"

"Everyone but those two at the far end of the bar, are either from Montrose, Durango or Telluride."

"Why do they come here?" asked Saachi.

Mark smiled. "The warm, friendly atmosphere." He knew that would get a laugh from the two. "You guys being treated okay?"

Brayden and Saachi shared a glance. "Like we always are. A bit worse as the news from today got around. You didn't hear?"

Mark turned serious. "If it's bad, then no."

"It will be in the paper tomorrow anyway," Saachi said to Brayden.

"David Sherman was found dead today at the rest home."

"Old D passed on, huh? That's too bad. A nice man. Why'd that hit anybody's radar?" The silence between the two FBI agents sparked a moment of enlightenment. "You think he had something to do with the mine break-in because he worked there?" Mark's belly moved with his chuckle. "The man was full of lots of stories for sure. Don't go believing everything you hear."

Brayden leaned forward, stopping Mark's warning short. "He took a year's worth of sleeping pills after he was paid a visit by someone posing as his granddaughter. The female wore a wig, got access, and then the old man died right before we showed up."

Mark cocked an eyebrow, feeling relief the news wasn't worse. "Maybe he stole a few too many gold nuggets back in the day and somebody wanted them back?" The agents didn't catch his humor. "What? Stranger things could happen, but I'm just a small town police officer who grew up with most of these people. What do I know?"

"Okay," Saachi bounced back. "What do you know?"

"That those who are here need the living this small community provides. Newcomers want to get away from the big cities, but they tend towards Durango and the richies go to Telluride. That leaves the kids in town who want to leave."

"Like Kyle Smith," Brayden suggested.

"Like the entire basketball team."

"Why only basketball?" Saachi asked.

"That's all the school has," Mark explained. "Not enough kids for any other sports." Questions were stalled when the server came by, and Mark ordered an elk burger, rare with onions.

"You are clearly sleeping alone tonight," Saachi observed.

"As I do every night. Once you hit eleventh grade, you've dated everyone in town." The two FBI agents laughed.

"So other than Kyle," Brayden began once the waiter left, "any other teens of interest?"

That caught Mark up short. "Does that mean Kyle is actually on your radar? Of all the kids in this town, I already told you he's the cleanest. No drinking or smoking, straight As and dying to leave on a scholarship. I'd sooner point you to his best friend Mario, who wishes he had Kyle's athletic ability and girlfriend, and doesn't have half the intelligence. I could see that kid doing all kinds of mischief." He paused, lowering his voice. "In addition to what he's already done."

"You think he had something to do with the mine?" asked Saachi.

"Mario? Heck no," he scoffed. "He doesn't have the balls or the brains to what? Break in and steal something of national value, is what we were told. I mean, who would risk that, and what would they have to gain?"

"Maybe David Sherman's money," offered Brayden.

Mark sat back, slowly putting together the pieces before him. "Let me get this right. You two are thinking that someone, presumably male and athletic enough to make it up and down the hill, would be stupid enough to take a chance getting in there for money?"

Saachi tipped her head to the side. "Living in this town is a pretty modest existence. Most of these kids would have the motivation to do something stupid, even on a dare."

Mark exhaled. "If money were a motivation, just check out the marijuana labs that spring up every few months. A lot easier, safe and legal."

"And that's why it doesn't pay very well," added Saachi.

Brayden eyed him. "If you don't think our line of thought has merit, what about someone else like the old miner who had a grievance and lured a local to do the dirty work?"

"Then you are right back to the person or persons who could pull off the break in." Brayden nodded at his comment. "I'm sorry, but I still don't see it," Mark argued. "I can't think of a single person living in this town who isn't mostly content. We don't have any burglaries from one year to the next. Never had a single incident of violent crime since I've been on the job, and before that, when I was in junior high school, we only had one real scandal, and that was when Ty's wife left him and their young daughter behind."

"Billy?" asked Brayden. Then turning to Saachi, he added, "She's in the same grade as Kyle."

"Brilliant girl," complimented Mark. "Complete tomboy. Been giving Kyle a real run for his money on the valedictorian for years now."

"You think she could have gotten into the mine?" asked Saachi.

"Wouldn't matter. A dozen people including me saw her in the bar studying all Friday afternoon and evening as she always does. Takes out her computer and works non-stop."

Saachi turned to Brayden. "Didn't you say Kyle was also at the bar that night?"

"Yes." He turned to Mark. "How long had he been there?"

Mark shrugged. "I didn't even think to ask that question. He was there when I arrived, sitting with Billy, both of them working and eating. He'd come over from the pool with his boss."

"It's a bar, though," pointed out Saachi.

"Which to a small town, means nothing when the kids are in the front, drinking Coke. That night was no different than any other for the last few years, except it was Friday and no game."

Saachi spoke between bites. "Is Kyle Smith from a poor family?"

"Very," said Mark.

"Did he know the miner?"

"Everyone knew D. Kyle knew him a bit better because he'd worked at the mine since he was about fourteen or fifteen, hanging himself like a bat over the thousand foot shafts left behind by the mining operations." Sensing that Saachi was starting to focus on Kyle as a suspect, Mark cautioned her.

"Look, I'm telling you, Kyle is not your guy."

"How can you be so sure?" asked Saachi. "He sounds like he could have the motivation and possess the physical skills."

"Everyone, and I do mean everyone, in this town likes and respects Kyle Smith. He's the only kid in the last decade who has stayed clean, his head above water and is going to go somewhere. Weirdly, Billy Rowe, Ty's daughter, is equally smart and gifted, but she's rude, distant and disliked by as many people as admire Kyle. Too oddballs in a small town."

"Who were together Friday night," Saachi said thoughtfully. "Have those two always been good friends?"

Mark laughed. "Good friends?" he repeated. "They've been rivals since middle school." His elkburger came and the conversation turned to local hunting restrictions and the skill it took to kill an elk during bow season. "Nearly impossible," Mark contended, "but worth it."

"Mark," said Saachi. "I know you think this theory has no merit, but speaking from a pure, probability perspective, what are the odds of Billy and Kyle being together for any reason, but especially on a Friday night?"

For the first time, Mark was without a quick comeback. At the time, it had struck him as out of the ordinary, but he'd had an immediate crisis on his hands that evening. The fact they were grabbing chicken wings hadn't been priority for him.

"Is Kyle as smart as Billy?" Saachi asked.

"I'm not sure anyone is as smart as Billy," he conceded. "But we all just root for Kyle---"

"Because he's more likable," she finished for him.

"I guess."

"Mark, where do you think we can find Billy tonight?"

"I just learned that she's making food at the restaurant. Ty usually gives his help holidays off, and she gets enlisted to help out."

"Did you see Kyle at his home tonight when you did your rounds?"

He thought about Ashley's comment. "His girlfriend passed me on my way here. She told me he was up at Ty's getting take out for this evening."

Saachi had a look of increased interest in her deep brown eyes. "Another item for the probability equation. Mark," she said. Lowering her voice, she leaned in and asked, "How tall is Billy?" Mark guessed, raising his hand above his head. "What do you think Billy would say about her whereabouts right before the miner died?"

"If you're asking me to go have a chat with the two of them, together or separate, I'm happy to do it, although I was rather enjoying our night out."

"And you still believe it's the wrong people anyway," suggested Brayden.

"Yes, but Saachi raises two interesting points: how long Kyle was at the pool prior to being the bar, and the insinuation that Billy could have been the person who spoke to D prior to his death. To take this idea further, you're then implying D killed himself because he told Billy his secrets, or she got out of him the information about a stash of gold in a mine."

Saachi blinked. "That does sound far-fetched, I will grant you."

"No, I'm all about a good conspiracy theory, and I have nothing better to do on this lovely Christmas Eve than chase down the ideas from two, equally bored officers. And you, ma'am," Mark said, giving Saachi his respectful, officer expression. "I can tell you were serious about the probability equation. So, I will prove my deputy skills and get to the bottom of both teenager's whereabouts. That good enough?"

"Sure," Saachi said. "You do the investigatory work and I'll collect more forensic evidence, then we can get together after Christmas, or whenever we gathered all our information."

"Whoa. You already have some?"

The Indian woman dipped her head. "A few strands of hair from the mine along with samples from the wig that I believe was used earlier today."

"How long before you can identify the individuals?" he asked. The two glanced at each other. "We are on the same side, right?" Mark asked rhetorically. "The more info I have the more helpful I'll be."

"Tomorrow, if we have a hit."

"That fast?" questioned Mark. "How is that possible?"

Brayden answered. "We have a lab in Montrose that covers this region."

Mark exhaled, his relief at the quick answer combined with a slight disappointment Saachi would soon be on her way. He chose to look on the bright side.

"Want to take a bet that I'm right and your wrong?" Mark challenged good-naturedly. "Five bucks says those two have nothing to do with it."

Saachi's mouth curved on one side. "Ten bucks says one of them knows something about what's going on or had a hand in it."

Brayden took a twenty out of his pocket and laid it on the table.

"That's my bet you are both wrong."

Mark started laughing while Saachi shook her head. "You mean you have no clue about the culprit here but are betting against both of us? That's comforting."

The three continued laughing, and Mark picked up the bill, intending to pay, but Brayden refused. "I'll pay, and then we are going to visit Ty's down the street and see who gets the twenty. You in?"

Once the bill was handed to the officers, an older man who had been sitting at the bar, nursing a whiskey, paid his tab and left. If he walked fast enough, he'd be at the kid's home, get what he wanted and be gone before the three arrived.

CHAPTER 26

Kyle watched Billy mashing potatoes as another order came through. She glanced at the green monitor and put another batch of onion rings in the deep fryer.

"I thought your whole strategy was to stay under the radar?" Kyle asked, a tease in his voice. "Not make waves."

"She annoyed me."

Kyle inwardly smirked, a surge of affection momentarily suppressing his worry about the future. "Nothing more?" Kyle heard the banging to the metal increase, and smiled. "I don't mind the possessiveness. It's flattering." He flipped up the lid on the dishwasher, moving behind her. Somewhere, in the span of only a few days, he felt like he'd aged, inside and out. His mouth found the warm skin on the side of her neck. "It's how I feel about you."

His lips moved along the soft hair on her neck, taking satisfaction when her hands ceased movement. When she tilted her head, he moved up, to her ear.

"I really like you, Billy."

She hummed. "Like?"

"You know how much." He felt her nod, just a bit. A ding rang and he immediately bent down and to the right, pretending to pick something off the floor.

"Billy, will you complain if I shut us down at nine tonight?"

Kyle felt the release of air in his chest, looking up. "I know I'd like that," he quipped to Billy's father.

Ty looked over his daughter's shoulder, nodding. "Looks good enough to eat. You going to stay here or take your food out?" he asked Kyle.

"Out," he replied. "My parents will eventually put up the closed sign."

"Running a small business is hard, but worth it."

"Except when unwanted people enter my kitchen," added Billy, gesturing at the Styrofoam boxes. Ty laughed, handing her a to-go container.

"She came in looking for Kyle," Ty said in his defense. "I had to tell her where he was."

"Well I so very much appreciated that," Billy said, her voice reminding Kyle of a rock pushed under the wheel of a tire, both car and rock coming to a screeching halt.

"From the way she stomped out, something interesting happened. What'd you say?" Ty asked his daughter, failing to keep the smile out of his scolding expression. "Or was it you, Kyle? You aren't going to get in a fight with your ticket out of here before your scholarship is locked down, are you?"

Kyle was offended. "You think my ride is dependent on her?"

"Hey," he said, putting up his hands. "Just suggesting caution. You've been coming up here a bit more, and…well, just saying jealousy might not help you get out of this town, is all."

"To answer your question," Kyle began, "Ashley is probably pissed at both of us. She was insulting this place, and by association Billy, who made a great cut-down. Ashley expected me to get up in arms and basically flipped when I didn't. That about right?"

Billy didn't turn around. "Yep."

Ty looked between the two of them, catching Kyle's eye. Billy's dad had finally realized there was a lot more going on than a scholastic rivalry or take-out.

Ty chuckled, his grin wide and approving. "And now you have a romantic dilemma on your hands, eh, Kyle? With my daughter?"

"No dilemma," Kyle answered. "The moment Billy and me stopped talking academics that was it. There's one girl I care about in this town, and it's not Ashley Fine."

As Billy silently assembled the boxes, he saw pink creep up from her neck to the bottom of her wedged hair. *She couldn't always keep he emotions in check*. It inwardly warmed him.

"You got anything to say to that Billy?" asked her father.

"It wasn't like Kyle cared all the much for her in the first place," muttered Billy. Ty glanced at Kyle, who nodded.

"Billy pretty much had me nailed this entire time," he conceded. "I just didn't know it."

"That makes two of us, kid."

Kyle located the plastic take-out sacks, holding one open for Billy. "It's going to be okay," he said to her.

"No, it's not," she replied. Kyle took the sack from her hand and caught her chin, lifting her eyes to meet his.

"But you'll have me," he teased. Her smirk turned into a smile. "See you tomorrow. We'll figure it out." She brushed his lips in response, then gave him a slight shove.

"I guess it's serious then," Ty remarked in a dry tone.

Kyle patted his shoulder. "Yep. Keep it to yourself okay? The town rumor mill will go crazy, and I don't want Billy taking the brunt."

Ty gave him his word and followed him out. He went behind the bar as Kyle walked into the cold night.

"Kyle Smith."

He told himself to inhale the air that had instantly stopped in his throat, the cold of the outdoors drying his lips. Purposefully casual, he stopped and turned.

"Agent Cox. Hi Deputy Hancock," Kyle greeted easily. He glanced at the female officer, knowing who she was but not her name. He hunched his shoulders, attempting to cover his exposed neck from the cold. "You all get the night off?"

"The law never gets time off," said the woman. "Saachi Gupta." She extended her hand. "Deputy Hancock was just telling us about the local basketball team and the captain."

"The night was that exciting, huh?" Kyle joked, pleased his response came across as natural. "Well, you guys have fun. I'm getting home for dinner."

"Take-out on Christmas Eve?" asked Brayden.

"Of course. My parents work until the last minute, getting any and all sales to be had, right Deputy?" The officer nodded his head. "You're all welcome to come by. I could use all the college funds possible."

"Billy in there tonight?" Hancock asked.

He raised the bag of food. "This is her work. We'll blame her if we get sick. Well, Merry Christmas." The three echoed his words and he left. He heard the door to Ty's open and assumed they were stopping for a drink, but he steeled himself from turning around. One thing he couldn't help was glancing at Ashley's home.

He wished he hadn't. A figure was standing in the living room window, the shoulders stiff and straight, the eyes black points following him as he walked. Billy had been right—again: avoiding an altercation with the Fine family would have been preferred, but Kyle was happy she'd put Ashley in her place.

Had Ash given her father a truthful replay of what had happened at Ty's or had it been mutated, just like their faces, the truth twisted like the very virus contained within them all?

Everyone but me.

What would Ashley look like without her perfect face? he wondered.

Because of Ash showing up at the bar, he hadn't been able to speak with Billy about what happened with D before he took his life. He'd wanted to stop her efforts to contact the Naturalists, but guessed it was too late. He was sure she'd gone and done it.

Kyle removed his jacket and set the take-out on the kitchen table, heading to his bedroom. He stripped off his clothes, replacing his t-shirt and sweats for a sweater and slacks. Their Christmas dinner would be at their four-seat dining room table, but he'd make it as special as he could for his mom.

It might be our last one together, he thought grimly.

He opened the small hutch and removed his grandmother's china. From inside the kitchen, he heard his mother and the man talking.

"Do you have any snowboarding ornaments?"

"Yes, I do," his mother said. Kyle watched her go into the piano room and retrieve a piece. The next moment, she was out, handing a glass ornament to the man. He quickly put down the plate in his hand.

"Oh, wait, not that one," Kyle called, knowing he sounded rude. He approached his mom, giving the man an apologetic look. "I was hoping to give that to a special person for Christmas."

"That makes two of us." Kyle made eye contact and held it. The man was not joking around. "How much do you want for it?"

"It's not for sale," Kyle interjected. "I mean, I hope it's not."

"Honey," chided his mother. "Of course, it's for sale," she told the man. "I can make another in a few hours. It's Christmas Eve, after all, and this is one of a kind. That would be twenty-five dollars."

Kyle wasn't going to cause a scene and lose the sale, but seriously? He wanted that for Billy.

"I'll tell you what," the man began, pulling out his wallet. "I'll give you fifty, since you have to make another. In fact," he said, glancing at Kyle. "I'm staying through this weekend while I'm visiting family. If you want, you can keep this one for yourself, and we can arrange a time for you to drop the new one off to me."

"No man, but thanks," Kyle said, embarrassed about his attitude. It had already occurred to him that he was giving Ashley a hanging object and doing the same thing for Billy would be completely uncool. "I just came up with another idea that's better."

The man kept his hand out with the fifty. "Take it and make me a second one for my niece. By the way, how'd you hurt your arm? That looks painful."

Kyle was caught off-guard. He followed the man's line of sight and saw the discoloration.

"Working out."

The man laughed, a line of deep wrinkles lining his olive skin. "I grew up in the desert with horses. The only time we had injuries like that was when we got thrown from a horse on to rocks. Did the barbells jump out and hit you?"

His mother joined in the man's laughter, her deep cough infectious. Despite the seriousness of what had caused his injury, he couldn't help smiling.

"Here you go," the man said to his mother. She thanked him and offered to gift wrap the ornament. When his mother left, the man casually looked around the room.

"So, seriously, how'd you get that injury?"

Kyle rubbed his arm. "It really isn't that bad. Looks worse than it is." Expecting the man to simply nod, Kyle's hand froze on his arm when the man took a step forward.

"Kid, you have one or more law enforcement officers coming down here from the bar right now. They were on their way to visit Ty's girl, Billy. They're on to you, and so am I. Get your long-sleeve shirt back on and get your story straight for where you were the evening of the break in. That FBI woman is sharp. They want to know where you were prior to being at the pool."

He glanced up as Kyle's mother came back into the room.

"Sorry this is so simple," she apologized, "but I ran out of boxes yesterday. It has a few layers of the tissue though."

The man smiled. "This is perfect," he complimented, accepting the holiday sack. "Since I'm staying through the weekend, I might get down to that pool. Is it open tomorrow?"

Kyle was numb, nodding mechanically. "I'm life guarding."

"Great. It's reputed to be pretty hot."

"It is!" confirmed his mother with a smile. "You have a Merry Christmas and come back for our after holiday sale."

Kyle was already down the hall, lifting his shirt over his head when his mother followed him into the room. "Sorry for being a jerk," he said proactively.

"That didn't bother me so much as his comment about your arm. Let me see that." She inspected it, touching lightly as he winced. "That is really bad, Kyle. I'm surprised you didn't break a bone."

"Me, too. Is there anything you can give me to make the swelling or the bruising go down?"

"Sure. Comfrey. Let me go make a compress. I don't think I have enough for your entire arm and certainly not your shoulder, but we can put it on the worst parts."

"Just the areas that will show," Kyle requested. "I don't want the coach thinking I can't play Friday."

Roy walked up the street slowly, considering his experience with Kyle Smith. The kid was a good one, he felt it in his bones. It was the reason he'd given him the heads up. His alibi was flimsy and the FBI agent knew it.

Roy also knew something else. Kyle had wanted that gift for Billy, the girl the cops had been talking about. From what he'd learned, she was a snowboarder, one of the best in town.

Could she have crept into the mine, as the forensics woman had suggested, and snowboarded down the hillside with Kyle? With a headlight, perhaps.

They'd missed that possibility. He wondered if she had more to reveal than Kyle. After all, it was Billy who had been the one who had enticed him to come to this little, out of the way town in the first place.

She knew enough about computers to get in touch with someone like himself, but she wasn't smart enough to cover her tracks.

That was his other concern. Had she contacted others and were they going to be showing up here, too? He had given Kyle a warning, but could he do the same thing with Billy? And if he did, would she listen to him?

CHAPTER 27

"Hey, mom, remember that night I told you I lost my wallet? I found it."

"No, I don't, but I'm glad you did," she said, her attention on pressing the warm washcloth on his arm.

"Yeah, I had taken the car into Montrose to do some Christmas shopping since we didn't have a game that Friday night."

"Uh-huh. How's that feel?"

"Better," he said, a bit surprised. Not that his mother was right about natural healing methods, but because it had worked so quickly. "Will the bruising fade as fast?"

"Not sure what fast means, but it will heal quicker overall now. The comfrey increases the blood circulation, reducing the swelling and the coloring goes back to normal at a faster rate. Here. Hold it there so I can get into the kitchen. If I'm hungry, you must be starving."

Kyle held the compress against his arm with one hand and used the landline to dial with the other. Calling his boss was a regular thing, and if the records were ever checked, wouldn't appear out of the ordinary.

"Hey boss, sorry to bother you…" Kyle began, "I'm hoping you can help me with something." Kyle explained the situation; he needed to do some last-minute shopping and he hoped his boss, who Kyle knew to be thrifty by nature, would have a few recommendations. He also knew something else. Barrett liked to purchase items at places where people went who wanted to be anonymous and left no traces.

"You seriously going to get Ashley a gift from a pawn shop?"

"Well, why not?" Kyle countered, "unless you're going to tell me they'll be recording me coming and going and she'll somehow find out."

His boss chuckled. "Why spend five hundred bucks when you can spend two, is my motto?"

"Do you think they will be busy?" Kyle asked.

"Pawn 1 is always busy. But if you are worried someone will tell Ashley you paid a visit…" Kyle committed the man's recommendation to memory and wished him a goodnight. He now had an alibi for the time prior to meeting up with Billy at Ty's. He'd gone to Montrose to shop, had intended to make a purchase but realized his wallet was missing. The only person who'd know he was lying was Brayden. Unless he was forced to take a lie detector test, Kyle would get away with his story. After dinner, when he was alone in his room, he'd stop and think about the man who'd come into his home, given him the warning and left.

"What did you think of that?" asked Saachi.

"That was classic Billy," answered Mark. They were on the street corner at fourth and Main. "She was likely there all afternoon studying, just as she said. You saw the cameras all about. I'm sure Ty would give us the tape if we asked, but he also said she was there. Probably half a dozen others would say the same thing."

"Effectively ruling her out," concluded Brayden.

"Only from being the one who broke in," added Saachi.

"Look, you two go back and have a Christmas," suggested Mark. "I'll go down and chat with Kyle right now, under the guise of finishing up my rounds. Sound good?"

Brayden guessed Saachi wanted to accompany Mark to the kid's house and offered up another idea. "I'd like to talk about gathering more evidence," he said to her.

Turning to Mark, she asked him if he had plans on Christmas Day.

"Nope. All yours."

"Good."

Brayden waited until he and Saachi were out of Mark's earshot before speaking. "You want to go to the high school?" he guessed.

"Where else? They have one sports team, one boy's locker room. I can get a bag full of DNA samples and have each and every one tested without prejudice. We'll see if one or more have a hit with the hairs I got from the mine."

"Or none."

"Don't count on it."

"I won't, neither will Forland. I'll call him from the hotel room."

"I thought you had authorization to do whatever you need, including anything illegal."

"I do," he confirmed, "but breaking and entering the town's only high school on Christmas Day, which may or may not have an alarm, and then trying to find the boy's locker room doesn't sound like a great way to alert the community to what we're doing."

She grunted. "Good point. You going to tell me what's up with your bet against me and Mark? You know I always win my bets."

"You do, that's why I don't make many. I think we've already missed the boat."

"How so? We're just starting."

"Sure, with tracking down who broke in. My gut is that the cubes and the information contained on them is already gone," he maintained. "And yet we're still stuck here."

Their steps made no sound as they walked in silence up the snow-covered street.

Saachi kicked a ball of snow. "And then the Patrol will come in and make a clean sweep?" He nodded, and they walked another half block without conversation. "We can prevent that, you know. We find the person who did broke in, because I think you and I both believe that person is still here. He has to be a resident who knows the mine, and we both have the gut it's a he, correct?" she asked. "It's better that one person is taken than a whole town, don't you agree?"

Brayden hedged. "Not if that one person were being used by another group like the naturalists."

She paused. "But if that person were being used, knowingly or not, we need him to get the naturalists. They've been trying to undermine the government for decades."

"You don't know what's on those cubes, do you?" Brayden asked solemnly.

She shook her head no. "And I don't need to know. That's not in my job description. I'm here to do a job, just as you are. Find the perpetrator, get him in custody and get home. Correct?"

"Correct." They reached the hotel and stopped their conversation until they were within the elevator. "I'll let you know how Forland wants to proceed tomorrow. I expect that one way or another, we'll be having our Christmas day at the school."

CHAPTER 28

"I hear what you're saying Cox, and I agree," said FBI Director Forland. "You have to get the hair samples and tomorrow is the best time for obvious reasons; everyone will be at home."

"And access, sir?"

"I'll need Maury O'Connell's direction for the local police. And you're right, it has to come from them or we risk causing a stir. I'll make the call now."

Brayden hung up. He'd wait to call Saachi until he had the details for tomorrow.

He took a long shower, wrapping the white, cotton towel around his waist as he watched the snow that had started falling. His room had a view of Main Street, the holiday wreaths lighting every pole down to the Smith home. His attention was diverted when his mobile phone rang, the ringtone distinctive. Instead of answering it, he laid down on the bed, his forearm under his head. He didn't want to speak to

Laura. He'd called last night, and again this morning without a call back until now.

Typical. No matter how busy the surgery schedule was, she found time to go to the bathroom and have lunch. The twenty-minute drive between their home and the hospital also offered time to return a call.

But no. No *Merry Christmas.* No, *I miss you's.* That phrase had become less frequent over the last two years. Then one trip, he'd left and she just never said the words.

Friends had given him books that had foretold the death of his marriage. It was always in the sections on grief, when the facts were stated right up front. The most common reasons for divorce was death of a child, first and foremost. Job loss was next and then moving. Affairs and betrayal didn't even make the top five.

After his daughter died, they still had Jarod. He'd been the lifeforce in their world. All the love Brayden had wanted to give to his daughter had been compounded into the energy he'd given his son. When Jarod died, it was as though the remaining optimism he and Laura had held on to for the future had died as well. Since then, their occupations had been even more consuming, the distraction and denial a toxic drink they consumed daily, providing the escape they both needed to remain productive citizens.

Brayden waited until he heard the beep indicating a message had been left before he picked up the phone and listened. His wife was going out with friends from the hospital; those who were on call for the holiday shift. The busiest time of the season was just getting going, just as Saachi had said. His wife would be working non-stop for the next forty-eight hours.

She had the luxury of avoiding what he, Brayden Cox, could not. While she was out on the town, he had a front-row seat in a production where the lead actor, a seventeen-year old kid was going to die right before him.

Eighteen next month, he thought, recalling Kyle's date of birth from the school site he'd accessed. Right about now, Mark would be speaking with him, inquiring about his activities prior to being at the pool. Brayden hoped the kid had the sense to come up with something believable and untraceable, nothing over done that would give Hancock or himself reason to verify his location.

Hopefully he was as good as Billy. That girl had been solid, her demeanor calm and cool when she answered Saachi's questions. It hadn't mattered what Saachi had said or how she said it, Billy was unflappable. He recalled what Hancock had said about her mother leaving. It had to have been traumatic to make her as hardened as she was. Given what might happen, she would be the better off for it.

Brayden raised himself up, putting on his boxers and t-shirt, thinking about his counterpart. Since arriving in the small mountain town, Saachi had methodically done her job, ignoring the pelting ice on the snow mobile ride as if it hadn't existed, then spending hours going up and down the long shaft and looking through the drawers, one by one. Yes, thought Brayden, it could be the miner who put Kyle up to it, but that required confronting Kyle with actual evidence of his crime. Exactly what Saachi wanted to do right after the results from the hair samples were returned.

That would take forty-eight hours at most. Friday, the day of Kyle's next basketball game.

He started going through his agenda for tomorrow, and as if on cue, his phone rang.

"Cox here."

"Spoke with O'Connell," said the FBI Director. "He communicated with Deardon, who's one town and three hours away. His father had a heart attack after eating his Christmas Eve meal and they're at the closest hospital."

"Overeating will do it every time," Brayden commented drily.

"Indeed. He's giving the task to his Deputy. Apparently the one you've been working with."

"Hancock." Forland asked if he'd present any problems. "Unlikely. As I said before, a small town will look out for its own, but he's been open-minded. Certainly not hiding anything."

"Good. Saachi will do her part."

Brayden affirmed she would. "Who's working on tracking down the missing cubes?"

His boss paused. "Reese." It wasn't someone on his team or the FBI at all. But NSA. "I know what you're thinking and I concur, but I had no choice. When it reached the President, he gave it to her."

Brayden debated explaining the FBI charter to the man in place to enforce it. "If our hands are tied so tightly…" he began, then stopped. He thought through the chess game of government bureaucracy. "They want the information and are going to do what they will, aren't they? No conclusion. No judge or jury. Just conviction."

"That's about it." Brayden could feel the man's intensity through the phone. His entire group, his people, were being played.

It meant something else to Brayden. A cover up. He'd seen it before. When a secret was rising close to the surface, a solid mound of concrete pushed it down into the depths.

Brayden resorted to the facts. "Saachi is confident we will have the data back by Friday," he said, his voice professional and brisk. "We'll make the necessary arrangements based on the findings."

"Acknowledged."

Brayden called Saachi with the news. "Do you have a preference on the time of day?"

"No. Earlier the better, the town may be quiet, but if Mark has something else going on, I'm flexible. What else have we got to do here?"

Brayden could think of one thing. "The hot springs."

"Oh, right," said Saachi brightly. "I have no bathing suit though. Never occurred to me."

"I'm sure they'd have one for you. Or," he drawled, "Hancock has a spare."

His counterpart gave something close to a snort. "Oh, you caught that, did you?"

"Small town subtlety as an oxymoron."

"I don't mind. We'll see. It's supposed to be seventeen degrees tomorrow. The hot water would be nice."

"I'll call Mark now and text you."

It took four rings for the Deputy to pick up. "Good timing Cox. Just left the Smith place."

"And? Anything enlightening?"

"Nope, just like I suspected. The kid went into Montrose to do some shopping, pulled into the parking lot of a pawn shop and didn't have his wallet. He came back into town, checked on the fish at the pool, his boss showed up and they arrived at Ty's not long before I showed up. Billy had told me he'd lost this wallet somewhere and she paid for the meal. It all checks out."

Brayden's chest released a bit of pent-up tension. "I have something else for you now." He told the Deputy about the need to get into the high school gym. "Both Directors at the federal and state level believe we have enough to warrant it."

"I'm not used to dealing with this kind of thing, so let me get this right. We don't need a search warrant or permission to gather evidence?"

"Correct. We get in, Saachi does her thing and we get out. No one besides yourself and Deardon knows."

"This is definitely above my pay grade."

"For what it's worth, mine too. The moment we identify who broke in, others are taking over."

"Is that normal? I mean, is that what you want?"

"The answer to both questions is no, and that's all I can say."

"Got it." They agreed to meet at the school at eight a.m. The fewer the people who saw them, the better.

One last call with Saachi to confirm the details and he laid down on the bed, his thoughts turning back to Laura. She was a beautiful forty-five year old, no hair coloring or unnatural fillers to her face. She wanted to grow old gracefully she said, like her mother and grandmother before her. He still loved her…at least he thought he did, but they were more like roommates now, cohabitating in the same home where they spent few hours together.

Not unlike other working couples. Yet there was more to life than this. Could they rekindle what they had before…before their children died?

Brayden turned on the television, watching a series of weathermen share meaningless data. The voices eventually lulled him to sleep.

CHAPTER 29

"Nothing I like better than cherry pie for Christmas breakfast." Kyle looked over the top of the faded, yellow fridge at his father.

"Morning, Dad."

"Ashley does it right."

"You mean her mother. I'm not sure Ash could boil an egg."

"Probably true."

Kyle took out the leftovers from last night's meal and warmed it up. "Mom still asleep?"

"Am I breathing?" he father asked in return. "What you up to today? Besides giving us your undying gratitude for the Christmas gift we got you."

Kyle turned on the microwave and leaned against the counter. "Is that sugar making your loopy? What are you talking about?"

"Look outside."

"You want to give me a hint? I'm hungry."

"The car port."

"You're kidding."

"About giving you a car? Yes. But you should take a look nonetheless."

"You don't want me to wait for Mom?"

"Your mother spent half the night getting your gift here while you were sleeping. She made so much noise I'm surprised an avalanche didn't come down. Go. I'll wait."

Kyle put on his boots and a light jacket and walked the twenty feet around the back of the house. He reached the carport, stopping dead.

It was an older model four-wheel all-terrain vehicle, red in color. It had a few scratches, but he barely noticed, his eyes going to the wheels. Round tires had been swapped out for triangular tracks, the kind that cost eight hundred a piece.

The magnitude of his parent's sacrifice for him created waves of financial worry. The next instant, he felt a rocket of adrenaline shoot right up under his chest.

He traced the inch-high tracks. *Barely used.* These special tires were worth more than the body, their unique capabilities allowing the rider to go through snow banks at steep angles, no matter the depth of the powder. *Where was this the other night?* he thought wistfully. The ATV would have made easy work of the steep hill down from the mine.

Kyle walked around the machine almost reverently. It had a bar of lights on the front, a thin strip of neons that he knew could cut through the snow from a blizzard. It would easily fit two people, and even one more within the metal rack with rails attached on the back end. Bungee cords were latched on the rails. He could also carry packs if necessary.

Kyle and his parents had never gone to church, and he'd not given God much thought in his life, but he took a moment to thank Him now. This was an answer to his prayers.

He went inside, quietly opening the door to his parent's room. He cleared his throat, but it failed to wake his mother, who was a small bundle under the comforter. Only her forehead and a mess of hair was evident.

"Thanks for the Christmas present, Mom." His voice broke. "You're amazing." His mother was the financial strongarm in the house. If she didn't approve the expenditure, it didn't happen. Her goals for savings were hard, fast and legendary. "You must have been saving for this for years." That got a little grumble from under the blankets and she stirred. "Seriously. I'm…in shock." Kyle felt her thin arms wrap around his neck, the grip pulling him down.

"We're so proud of you." She kissed his cheek.

"Go back to sleep Mom. I've got to be at the pool at ten."

She cracked an eye. "Are you going to take it for a spin first?"

"Can I?"

"Of course. Your dad has the key."

"Love you, Mom."

"Love you."

Kyle found his father in the small dining room, drinking his coffee.

"We did good."

Kyle laughed. "No. More than good. You did great."

"You looking for this?" He pointed to a green Lanier on the table, the key attached. "Figured you'd be less prone to losing this if it's strapped around your neck."

"Funny."

"You will need to change though." His father glanced outside. The snow had started to come down. "And it's early yet. Don't go waking the entire town. Maybe head south."

"I won't be gone long."

"One other thing. You'll have to buy another set of regular road tires in the spring when the snow melts. Those aren't road legal past March 15th."

"Birthday present?" Kyle suggested, smiling at the look of disbelief he'd anticipated. "Got it. Alright."

"Maybe your Aunt Ernie will send you a twenty for your birthday."

"I'll take it," he said happily and left the room.

He quickly put on his ski clothes, the loose-fitting white pants and shell, over his thermals and turtleneck. He didn't bother with a helmet, choosing his facemask and goggles instead. His thoughts were on Billy. He'd love to take her for a ride. Maybe he'd swing by her house before returning home.

"Be back in about thirty," he said to his dad. "And thanks again Dad. You guys…I still can't believe it."

"Neither can I," said his dad in a dry tone. "Get going."

Kyle knew the controls well; his friend Mario had one of these, as did Ben. In fact, any one with discretionary money in town had at least one four-wheel toy, be it a truck or an ATV. It was the only way to navigate the mountain paths in the high Rockies.

"My turn," he said to himself, his voice low and attitude smug.

He started it up, easing the ATV out of the car poor. It was already facing the back yard, and the off road vehicle seemed to float on top of the grass, barely pushing down the snow. He went around the corner, directly onto the one-lane freeway heading south. He hadn't looked to see if it had a license plate but took it for granted it did. They weren't road legal without a plate. Soon he was going thirty, parallel the pool, taking a left at first street that led into a small neighborhood of homes built mountainside.

Gonna see what this baby can do.

He was cautious at first, testing the sway and stopping distance, progressively finding deeper snow, going faster and putting on the breaks. He found a bank, went over it slowly at first to make sure it wasn't covering a rock, then realized it wouldn't have mattered. The tracks lifted the center of the machine high enough to clear three-foot boulders.

Feeling confident, he increased his speed, gunning it up the steep inclines, then cornering sharply between trees and boulders. Only once did he experience a heart stopping moment, and that was when he caught the edge of a bank, thinking it was snow or rock underneath. The tire snagged, jolting him with such force it almost threw him over the handlebars. His right side tracks kept moving forward, spinning around the outcropping, dislodging his left track enough to get it moving again. Looking behind, he saw a jagged tree stump, the angle just odd enough to catch the track.

I can take this thing anywhere.

For the next twenty minutes, he was going to enjoy his Christmas gift and pretend he was a regular high school student…even though he wasn't.

He found a steep hill and gunned it.

CHAPTER 30

"I'm going to start with you. Hold still."

Mark flicked his gaze from Saachi's eyes to her latex-gloved hands as they neared his head. "I'm a suspect?" he asked.

"No," she answered calmly, plucking one of the hairs on his head before dropping it into a vial. "You, me and Brayden will shed hairs as we move around the room. We might as well speed things along by identifying the three of us right up front."

She wrote his name on the outside of the container. "You can watch, but aren't legally allowed to collect samples."

"I could probably write the names on the bottles, can't I?" His suggestion carried with it a hint of humor.

"Sure. We'll collect, you name."

"Starting on this end?" he pointed.

"Brayden, you start there and I'll be over here," said Saachi. "We'll meet in the middle."

"Got it."

The three began their tasks, the two agents calling out names for Hancock, who placed the sealed vials into a plastic holder within a black, Teflon bag with handles.

"Saachi," Mark said. "Do Indian names have meanings?"

"Yes."

"What does yours mean?"

"Truth."

"Serious? Did this profession choose you or was it the other way around?"

"Gaby, Ben," she said, reaching into a locker. "I was in college on the path to law school, specializing in forensics, and the final year I realized I didn't want to try the person who had been convicted based on the forensics, I wanted to be the person to collect the forensics and do the analysis."

"That's interesting, and backwards, isn't it? Don't most people want the glory of being on the stand and convicting someone?"

"Not me," she replied, dropping a hair sample into a vial he held. "The hard work is up front. Any half-brained attorney can convict on good evidence."

Brayden laughed.

"I take it you agree?" Mark asked him.

"Let me ask you this," Saachi cut in, already turned to another locker. "Is it easier to arrest the person when you have a video recording or one where it's hearsay?"

"It's more fun to chase someone down, actually. It's all about the glory." Mark had included a hefty amount of dry humor in his voice and received the expected response. They laughed harder when he patted his stomach. "Although the glory faded slightly as the girth has expanded, but don't tell the local bad element. Don't want the word to get out."

"Martinez, Mario," said Brayden. Mark held the vial open, then screwed on the top.

"We'll do the floor and shower next," Saachi informed them. "Another hour and we'll be out of here."

"Then what?"

"Then we will take the samples into Montrose for testing."

"Won't they be closed?"

"Not for us," she replied. "Brayden, you don't have to come in to town. I can handle it."

Brayden nodded. "Johnson, Kenny. I've got more work to do, but then will head to the pool. Everything else in this town is closed."

"When?" she asked. "I might join you if I get back in time."

"It stays open until six today," offered Mark. "Hey, so back to what we were talking about last night. Are you going to collect samples from Billy?"

"Don't need to. Already have them."

"How's that?" he asked, genuinely intrigued.

"Law enforcement is covered under the need-to-know clause," she explained. "The government keeps the medical records of all its citizens. The DNA thread is a part of that."

"Oh, that's not such a big mystery," Mark said, somewhat disappointed. "Then why did you need my hair sample if you already have it on file? Oh," he said the next moment, a bit embarrassed. "Placement at the scene."

"Uh-huh," she said. "That's how we know that you weren't the person who broke into the mine on Friday night. It wasn't your DNA threading."

Mark's chuckled. "But we have already established I couldn't have run up and down." He turned mildly serious. "And you are still convinced that we are going to find a match among the hairs we are gathering today."

"Yes, and I have money riding on it."

"Well then," he said with a bit of confidence, "let's get this done. I'm as eager to see those results as you are."

At the edge of town, Kyle slowed down his machine, brushing off the snow that had packed to his arms and legs. The machine's tracks had lived up to their reputation. He felt a rush thinking about a wall of snow that had given way as he went right through it to the other side, then down into a ravine, his body lying almost flat against the seat as he held on. The ATV was solid and as sure footed as a trail horse on a steep incline.

Kyle checked the time and saw he needed to change and eat before heading to the pool. He took the back roads to Billy's, past the church and the school. He barely slowed when he saw Hancock's car, thinking nothing of it.

But movement caught his attention. He slowed, craning around. The lights inside the school were on, and shadows were on the walls. Someone, actually more than one person was in the locker room on Christmas morning.

He wasn't tall enough to see through the window, and it shouldn't matter to him in any case. Someone had probably lost something and had called Mark to pull in a favor.

Maybe.

Kyle turned off the road and went down the alley, parking behind the bar. He brushed himself off again and rung the bell. A few minutes later, Ty answered.

"Merry Christmas," greeted Ty.

"And you. I'm sorry for bothering you and don't plan on coming in. I just wanted to show Billy something. Is she up?"

"For hours. Let me get her. You sure you don't want to wait inside? It's warmer."

"Sure." Kyle stepped in, conscious of keeping his feet on the rubber mat. When Billy came around the corner, his felt the air move into his mouth. She smiled, and he did the same, feeling a warmth as real as the sun rising over the mountains. Billy didn't give him a chance to say a word. Her lips were still curled in her smile as his arms automatically went around her waist, one hand moving up to the base of her neck, barely touching her hairline.

"Merry Christmas," he murmured. She nudged her nose against his, the smell of her breath intoxicating. "Are you wearing red lipstick for me?"

"Actually, I did it for me," she answered. "If I'm going to wake up one day with a new face, then I better become an expert at changing my looks."

Kyle pulled back, serious and worried. "Your note. We never got to talk about it." He glanced over her shoulder, not seeing her father, but unsure how much could be said. "Put your shoes and coat on. I want to show you my Christmas gift."

"For me? You shouldn't have."

"I already did, but this isn't it. Hurry."

Billy caught his tone and look. Her smiled dropped as she bent to slip on her shoes and pushed her arms into a jacket. Once the door shut behind them, he pointed to the ATV.

"Wow," was all she said. Kyle told her about the tracks and its capabilities in two sentences. "That was the best part of the last twelve hours." Then he told her about the visitor he'd had the night before.

"Billy, you have to give me the cubes."

"After I transfer the data," she said quietly. "I've told you before, I have this."

"Billy, you connected with someone from the dark web. Then a guy shows up at my house with a warning. You said you are going to meet him and I say no way. He'll take the cubes and you'll end up dead."

Kyle received Billy's version of an eye-roll. "We are going to talk and transfer. That's all."

"Billy, the last time you were so blasé was with D. Now he's dead."

"Kyle, no one is going to die this time around. But you can't know what's going on." He pulled back, all romance gone. "This has to be me. Even telling you puts you at risk."

A snowflake landed on her nose and before she could flick it away, he leaned over to kiss it.

"Billy, if you don't give me the information, I will go in right now, search your room for the cubes, and if you don't hand them over, I'm going to pull in Ty and tell him the whole thing."

She shrunk back at his tone, then lifted her chin defiantly. "You asked for my help."

"Yes, to figure out what's going on, not to put you in harm's way, which you have already done that and then some."

Her eyes softened slightly. "And what if he's too strong? He could overpower you."

"Unlikely. He's in his late fifties, I've got speed and strength on my side."

She sighed, her frustration evidenced in her eyes that had narrowed. It was her thinking expression. "Hold on."

Billy returned with a soft, black case with a thick Velcro top. "We use this when traveling," she explained, opening the flap. "It protects anything against magnetic pulses and x-rays. Even though the cubes are solid state, it's good not to take chances. Then there's this."

She presented him a 45 in a holster. "Are you serious?" He asked.

"I was going to be prepared when I met this guy. You would be stupid if you didn't do the same."

"I couldn't use it, even if I had to. It would be traced right back to you."

"Nope. It's been in the family for years, purchased on the reservation, my mom's side of the family. Untraceable."

The gun felt heavy and awkward in his hands. He hoped he didn't have to use it.

CHAPTER 31

Mark had just dropped off Brayden and Saachi when he turned down Main Street. A red dart to his right caused him to lift his foot off the gas, watching the ATV zip down the road. He accelerated again, keeping pace. He saw the vehicle again on his right. The driver was wearing a ski mask and snow outfit, but obeying the speed limit.

Mario or Ben out for a joyride. No, it had to be Ben. He had a red one. Mario's was yellow. Mark continued down the road but saw no sign of the ATV.

I have nothing better to do.

He turned off Main, glancing to either side at each cross street. No sign of the off-road vehicle. When he reached the base of the mountain, he put the car in reverse, backing down, his tires slipping then catching on the thin layer of snow resting on the ice beneath. In the rearview mirror, he saw the red dart again but wasn't in a position to turn around fast enough to catch up.

Waste of time. What was he going to chat Ben up about anyway? The kid was riding an ATV. Hardly a crime.

Nice tracks though. Those were new wheels, eight hundred a pop. Ben was lucky to have parents who could afford them.

He headed back the way he came, crossing Main, towards his two-bedroom home. It was small, but his parents had given it to him completely paid for. Without debt, he was free to spend or save depending on his wants and needs. Walking up the front steps, he always paused to turn and look around, grateful for his parent's gift of freedom. From the eastern ridge, he looked down on the entire town. Of course, it lacked a garage, but was all he needed.

A housemate would be good. One like Saachi.

He stripped off his coat. She was unlikely to give up the city life of forensics for the small-town world, but then, it wouldn't hurt to probe her thoughts on the matter, perhaps at the pool this evening.

When Kyle made it to the pool by nine-thirty, Amanda was already stocking the register with cash.

"Hey Mandy," he greeted. "Get everything you wanted for Christmas?"

"All reindeers, no sleigh."

"Don't get it," he admitted, opening up the back office.

She laughed. "It means I got everything except the man I wanted under my tree."

"You wanted a man under your tree?"

"Well," she said, "carrying it. Decorating it. Doing anything really. I just want a man."

"Deputy Hancock is available."

"I'm not sure he'd approve of my vices."

Kyle already had the testing equipment in his hands but paused. "Only the ones he needs to know about. But then again, this is Colorado. They legalized all the good stuff decades ago." She raised an eyebrow. "Don't say anything else. I'm your boss. I don't want to know." He gave her a wink and went into the cold.

Fred was alive and lounging in his aquatic hot tub, snapping at the morsels of food Kyle threw his way. The first buses parked as he rolled up the pool covers, wincing at the pain shooting through his right shoulder. He cursed himself, wishing he would have remembered the comfrey compress overnight. It wasn't as painful as it had been the day before, but the coloring was far worse, a sure sign of healing.

Two more days until the playoff game. He'd just wear a long-sleeve shirt, common at the collegiate and professional level. If they got away with it, he could too.

By ten, Kyle was perched on the center pedestal. Only then did he allow himself to think about what Billy had communicated on the media card and then what she inferred this morning. The man who'd appeared at his home was linked to her dark web contact. He could be a naturalist, a government plant, a lunatic or all of the above.

He could also be someone who wanted what Kyle and Billy wanted. The truth.

Don't dwell on that possibility, said his inner voice. The pessimist in him was rising to the surface, because no one could be trusted. Either way, Kyle wasn't going to search him out; if the man wanted to talk more, he knew where Kyle lived and probably where he worked as well. He knew Billy's whereabouts. The man could probably blend in at the local bars, until Hancock asked him for ID, which he might have already done.

Kyle traded places with the other lifeguards at intervals, watching the clock. Brayden's suggestion he stay busy had helped him avoid lunch at the Fine's, but he knew his parents were right; he should break it off with Ashley sooner rather than later. Before yesterday, he'd never seen the territorial side of his former girlfriend. However, watching her lips retract and her fangs practically drip saliva had been enough to give Billy's prediction surety. Ashley was going to be mean when he told her he no longer wanted to date.

Bitterness will do that.

Around four-thirty, bodies filled all three hot tubs to capacity, leaving the larger pool nearly empty, the tepid 99 degrees too cold for the majority of the patrons. It was nearly dark now, the sun setting behind the high mountains cooling the outside air further.

Kyle glanced up at the temperature. A balmy 21 degrees.

When Kyle noticed two figures walking towards the front entrance, it suddenly seemed much cooler. Brayden and Saachi were side by side.

A jolt of fear coursed from his chest, down his right leg, and he adjusted, inadvertently grazing the metal post with his right shoulder. Stupid move. If they were on a mission to arrest him, they would have Hancock with them.

In his peripheral vision, Kyle noticed a patrol car parking alongside the road, adjacent to his parent's home.

No, they are not here for that. They had said it was their intention to come to the pool last night when he left Ty's. That was it. Nothing more.

Chanting the mantra to himself, he focused on his job. Only ninety-minutes left. For the latecomers, that was eighteen bucks for an hour and a half. Hardly worth it.

Kyle wrapped the blanket around himself again. When the two adults emerged from the changing rooms, Kyle kept his thoughts on his patrons and saving lives.

Stop thinking about what they were doing at the high school gym. They couldn't find any more or less evidence on him or his teammates. Unless…

Kyle froze, and it wasn't due to the temperature, which had gone down another degree. Could he have left a piece of his clothing at the mine? Even a single hair strand would be enough to trace it to him. *Keep calm.* If they had that information, he'd already be arrested. Brayden seemed to be giving him a pass for now, but Kyle doubted that woman would be so generous. In fact, it could all be a set up; Brayden taking his side, only to betray him later.

I've watched way too many Forensic Files reruns.

The three went from the main pool to the hot, sulphur grottoes, testing the water with their feet. Brayden opted for the lap lane while the other two went to the medium-temperature grotto, which weren't actual grottoes. They were smaller pools, really, just made to look like natural stone work.

Kyle surveyed the area, keeping a loose count on Brayden's laps. His pace was good, hitting lap nine in the Olympic size swimming pool in about thirty minutes. Not collegiate level but certainly better than high school. He was starting his tenth when a woman gave a yelp. The second lifeguard was at her side as Brayden stood up, watching. The lifeguard ran to the closet, retrieved a bucket and soon had his arm in the water. He gave Kyle the signal which meant disappointment for everyone in the area. He nodded in response, and the lifeguard lifted the bucket and went to the office. Shortly thereafter was the announcement.

Due to contamination and Colorado rules, the pool was going to be closed for a three-hour maintenance schedule, which meant it was going to shut down for the night. Management apologized for the inconvenience, and all purchases made in the last two hours would be given a full refund.

Groans and complaints were loud as Kyle descended from the tower. Laggards would stay in until the last minute, it being Christmas, and a good many exhibiting evidence of one too many spiked egg nogs.

"Last one in, last one out," Kyle said under his breath to Mark and Saachi. Brayden hadn't heard the announcement, so Kyle waited at the far side of the pool.

"Hey," said Kyle, loud enough to be heard. Brayden paused, putting his arm on the edge. "We've had a slight contamination issue with the pool. I'm sorry to say that everyone has to get out."

"Seriously?"

Kyle laughed. "Yeah. You don't really want to know what contamination means. Not life threatening. Just gross."

"Can I swim back?"

"Sure. It was in the other pool, not this one."

As the patrons made their way out of the area, Kyle and the other lifeguard began the task of draining the empty pools to the required levels for cleaning, and then refilling. It would take roughly an hour, meaning his shift would be over around the same time as normal.

Mark gestured to him, pointing to the clock and then his wrist. "Sure," Kyle said. "This will take me ten minutes over here."

He went about his work, dragging the long suction tubes out of their containers. The pushing and pulling had one good benefit, his shoulder muscles were loosening up, the pain less intense. It wasn't long before he broke into a sweat. Finished with the larger pool, he went to the others. The paths outside the building were now full of people, sullenly making their way to the local hotel and condos, many still grumbling along the way.

Intent on his work, Kyle didn't notice a figure standing at the gate nearest the entrance.

"Hey, handsome."

He looked up, not having to feign surprise. "Hi, Ashley. What are you doing here?"

"We couldn't help notice all the people walking by, so Ruth stepped out to ask what was going on. That's when we heard what happened."

Kyle gave a pull on the closest hose, getting enough slack to bring it down to the suction tube. "Yep," he said, getting on his knees. "The glamorous life of a lifeguard."

"That was pretty sick. Was it true?"

He laughed. "Of course, it was. It's not that gross when it's a summer day, and you have a hundred little kids wearing diapers in the pool. Something is bound to escape. But when it's all adults, and one of their diapers gets a leak…" She squealed in response, giving Kyle a genuine lift. "For real."

"That…is…so…awful," she got out, still laughing. "And I was going to ask you to dinner."

"I'd need an acid body wash."

"Only from the shoulders down. But honestly, that's why I'm here. I went over to your parents, who said your family doesn't have any plans, so they cleared you."

Thanks, parental units. If they thought he was going to select Christmas night to end it with Ashley, they hadn't smoked enough illegal substances as teenagers.

"It's going to be another hour at least," he explained, gesturing to the pools. She knew enough about this particular issue to realize it was fact.

"No problem. We aren't eating until 7:30, that's when Ruth's boyfriend is showing up. I know you like him."

"Yep, as much as your mother doesn't like him."

"I know, right? Okay, if that's a yes, then you have my permission to open your Christmas gift when you get home. You can wear it to dinner."

"Really?" He screwed in the hose, turned on the suction and watched the action take effect. "And you know it will fit?"

"Everything else I've gotten you has. Why not this?" That much was true, and Kyle didn't have a reasonable excuse to avoid the dinner. He thought of Billy, shoved down his desire and took her advice. Play along until the time was right.

"Sounds like a plan."

"Well don't jump out of your skin with excitement." She used her pouty, I-want-my-way tone, which now grated on him like metal against cheese.

He stood full height. "Ashley, until you have to reach in and take someone else's turd out of the water, try not to be so harsh in your judgement, fair?"

Usually, a smart comment like that got her to laugh, but in a strange turn of events, she stared him down right back.

"Turd reaching and dish washing seem to go hand-in-hand in the last twenty-four hours."

The lips have retracted again, Kyle thought. *And this is her way of letting me know she hasn't gotten over the incident with Billy.*

"You don't have to date a commoner like me, Ashley. I won't hold it against you if you choose Mario instead. His father's financial bottom line is closer to yours than mine."

Kyle lifted a pole from the hanging metal hooks, screwed on the end and started pushing the brush along the floor. He'd issued the ultimatum and prayed she would take it.

"Hey, I was kidding. You know that." He kept pushing the brush. "Come 'on, Kyle. I didn't mean it."

"Yes, you did," he said, still pushing. "But this is who I am, Ashley. I live and work in a different world than you and that will never change. Not for the next six months and not after."

She walked along the chain linked fence, placing her gloved hands on it. "Of course it will change. You'll graduate with some fancy degree. You'll make a ton of money and this will only have been a means to an end."

Yep. The end with you, and long before I graduate.

He was moving further away from the fence, continuing his task brushing. He stopped, turning to her. "You still want to give me that Christmas present?"

"Of course," she said, looking surprised at the question.

"And you're sure you want me to come over for Christmas dinner with the family?"

"Kyle, how can you even say that?"

He shrugged, not wanting to continue the conversation. "If you want me to come, I need to hustle to get this finished."

"Sure. I'll see you at 7:30."

"See you then."

"Remember to wear the gifts, okay?"

Kyle closed his eyes on the inhale, trying to stop her toxic attitude from seeping into his body. "Yes, Ash."

"Hey," she said, using her flirty voice. "I'm just sayin…"

Kyle didn't turn this time, just kept working. "Sure you were. See you soon." He prevented another round of dialogue by walking directly to the utility room and flipping on the light. Seeing what he wanted in front of him, he continued his fabricated search for another five minutes. Long enough to ensure Ashley was gone by the time he emerged. To his relief, she was nowhere in sight.

CHAPTER 32

Kyle wasn't upset about having dinner with the Fine's. It would keep him busy until he met with Roy, which was the name he'd scribbled on the card for his mom, along with the address of a home he was renting at the south end of Oak Street. Kyle knew just where it was; a converted miner's shed, one with a legitimate coal bucket that carried residents from the ground up the side of the rock to the house.

All he had to do was leave Ashley's home by eight-thirty.

"Hey, mom. I understand I'm having dinner with the Fine family." His mom grimaced and his dad took a sip of his beer.

"She felt bad for Ashley," his dad said, pointing to the stack of gifts on the coffee table before Kyle could ask.

"Who's all that for?"

"You," answered his mother. "Your father tried to get her to take at least one back but she was having none of it."

There were six gifts. "She made me promise to wear what she got me."

"Then let's hope it's not a gorilla outfit."

"Here. Help me." He passed out the boxes. The gift included pulling out a camel hair coat, oxford shirt, V-neck sweater vest, tie and belt.

"I look like an idiotic professor."

His dad grunted. "Who teaches at Harvard. Could be worse."

"Sure. She could have gone cheap at the state school. Crap. It looks like it all fits too."

He modeled for his parents, belatedly realizing the blinds were up. "Darn it mom! They've probably been watching me get dressed this entire time."

She snorted. "Honey. They've been watching all of us do everything since they moved in. At least you have clothes on, which hasn't always been the case."

"Hey, Mom, do you have the present for Roy ready for me?"

"I'll wrap it and have it for you when you get back from dinner."

Another alibi conceived and told. He hated lying, especially to his parents.

She lifted the gift on the table, wrapped and inside another waterproof bag. "This is your gift for Miss Ashley."

"Mom, you know I'm not going to break it off tonight, right, but I plan to do so soon."

"Unless she beats you to it," interjected his father, still on the couch. "Or, she may just beat you."

"Thanks Dad. See you guys around eight-thirty."

Stu answered the door after a few seconds, and Kyle thought his mother's words were spot on. They probably had been watching him try on the new clothes. He should have been feeling mortified, but the notion of his girlfriend's parents spending money on him didn't hurt his pride. Reality was simple and harsh: he'd become Machiavellian, and it had happened in just a few days time. He was going to take what they wanted to give, knowing full well it came with an expectation that would never be fulfilled.

"Good evening, Kyle."

"Hello, Sir."

"Heard the story of the pool. Glad I wasn't eating at the time."

Kyle smirked. "I told Ashley to be thankful she was missing the glorious experience of working."

"Between you and me, it might do her some good." Stu spoke the words under his breath. "Our last dinner guest is here," he announced as they entered the large kitchen. Ashley's mother Britt was cutting into a large batch of rolls with orange goo on the top. Stu joined her, and Greg, Ruth's boyfriend waved, his mouth stuffed, while Ruth came over and gave him a hug.

"Don't you look sharp," she complimented.

"Your sister has good taste."

"Are you kidding me?" Ruth said in a conspiratorial voice. "What she picked out was terrible and I had to take control." He raised an eyebrow and she continued, her voice lower. "She has awful fashion sense but don't let on. She'd kill me."

"Where is she?"

Ruth smiled wickedly. "Where do you think?"

"At the stop of the stairs, waiting to be summoned." Ruth giggled and nodded. "Greg looks good, for a cowboy, didn't you think?"

"Who are hot, as long as they have on a pair of cowboy boots."

"Hey now," interjected her father. "Did I just hear what I think I heard?"

"Nope," said Ruth, her sassiness unabated.

"Britt, those look wonderful," Kyle complimented, "and the cherry pie was great. You're an amazing cook."

"Thank you, Kyle," she answered, her genteel, southern accent still present, even after her many years in California. Kyle accepted Britt's offer for a roll.

"It's great as is, but better with butter," said Greg. "Here, try this." Without waiting for Kyle's response, Greg used his knife to cut and placed two months' worth of calories on Kyle's plate. "Dip and eat while it's hot. That way it melts."

Britt scowled slightly, but Stu supported Greg. "You need it. Go ahead."

Kyle was in the process of dipping when he heard his name called. "You are being summoned," said Ruth. He took a bite and smiled appreciatively at Britt, who was watching him.

"Does Ashley know how to make these?" he asked.

"Not at all, but as long as you are in the family, you can have mine," Ashley's mother answered, pleased with his question.

He set the plate down. "I'll be back."

Ashley descended the stairs, one hand on the rail. In contrast to her sister, who wore black slacks and a tasteful, red and green sweater, hair pulled back with a black band, and natural makeup, Ashley looked like she was headed to the opera. Long skirt made up of some type of shimmery fabric, her curled hair lifted up and away from her face, high and formal, the type of style a woman in her fifties would wear. Red lips and dark eyeshadow set off her features.

Billy's red lips were superior, the gloss only accentuating what was underneath.

"You are Santa's best looking and tallest helper," he said, feeling pushed to his creative limits finding words that were both truthful and complimentary.

"Turn," she said. Robotically, he spun. "I did good."

"Yes, you did. But you went overboard. I shouldn't keep half this stuff."

"You can and you will. You'll need it for job interviews." She put her hand out, and instead of taking it, he lifted his elbow. His avoidance was mistaken for gallantry, proving another theory of Billy's: Ashley was either blind or ignorant in the subtlety of a person's actions.

"Shall we?"

CHAPTER 33

"Brayden, we have a hit."

"This quickly?"

"Yep. Forland's call to the Montrose lab was backed up by the Director of the NSA calling the district. They had people working for the last eight hours straight." Brayden heard the excitement in her voice and it caused his mood to drop.

"Who's the match to?" he asked, knowing it would be Kyle Smith. If Kyle was lucky, he'd take his own life. At least then it would be on his terms and not in front of the Patrol's line of bullets.

"Well, there's some seriously bad news along with the good. The good news is the lab confirmed the match, the bad is that not long thereafter, the files got corrupted, or the data entry person got mixed up. One of the two."

"Wait. What? That doesn't happen. Never happens. It's either a conspiracy or sheer stupidity."

"Forensics scientists are not usually big believers of theories, only evidence."

"So you're leaning toward stupidity?"

"That, or rush work. Regardless of the why, it's temporary. It will take them another day, but they will run all the samples once more, after they are all methodically entered again."

"Seriously?"

"One hundred percent. They have no choice. They've gone home for the night, but tomorrow, the administrative staff is going back in, and the names will be re-entered, along with the hair samples being re-tested."

"Both the hairs from the mine and the gym, correct?"

"Yes, and it turns out, we have four different samples from the mine, and one is none other than Kyle Smith. It puts him there at the mine."

"But not necessarily during the break in," he pointed out.

"No, of course not. His hairs could have been carried in by any of the other three people we sampled, one of whom was that miner who died. Mark told us the guy was both a drunk and spent a lot of time with Kyle and others at the bar and the mine."

"Saachi, even if the results come back from the gym, we can't prove Kyle was there."

"No, but those two other strands were unidentifiable, and we may get another match. I'm going to head into Montrose and watch the process myself. They won't appreciate it, but I can run circles around their local lab technicians."

Brayden thanked her for the update and called his boss, apologizing for the interruption on Christmas evening.

"It tells me you have important information."

"I do."

Forland's reaction to hearing the news was less controlled than his own. When he cooled down, pragmatism took over emotion. "We are dealing with a field office. We should probably be grateful they even came in. Turning to Saachi's comment, you've interviewed this kid?"

"Several times, myself and Hancock. Airtight alibi, straight-A student, prospects for both academic and sports scholarship."

"Out of character, then."

"Beyond, according to the local deputy. As Saachi said, perhaps the other two strands will reveal something. Changing the subject, has the mine been secured against another break-in?"

"No personnel are manning the entrance, if that's what you mean."

"What about metal drawers within the room? I still can't believe they were so low-tech. It's like they were intended to be easily accessed."

"That borders on a conspiracy theory," chided his boss.

"We are the FBI. What else do we live for?" They laughed for a moment, the levity brief. "Sir, there is truth to my comment. The scenario doesn't jibe with protocol of anything in the government. Do you have any ideas?"

His boss paused a moment too long. "I do, but for now, that's all they are: ideas."

Brayden knew what that meant and said goodnight. Some topics were above his pay grade, and that was just fine with him.

He put down the land line and picked up his cell phone. He called Laura, knowing she was likely in surgery, saving one of dozens of holiday revelers who had succumbed to the siren call of pumpkin pie and overindulged.

Still, he left his wife a voice message. The task in Ouray was proceeding, his timeline for being home was likely another week, maybe more or less. Have a Merry Christmas. On impulse, he suggested they skip the annual New Year's Eve party with her hospital staff and go out as a couple. It was time they had an honest conversation about their future, and if it would be one spent together.

Kyle found his name card on the dining room table and took his place.

The fifty-yard line, equidistant between Stu and Britt, who sat at either end.

"You seem distracted," Ashley whispered in his ear.

"I was envisioning goalposts in front of your mom and dad because this table size reminds me of a football field." She giggled, the flattery creating the response he expected. "I'm serious," he said with a bit more fervency, and she touched his arm. She did have a beautiful smile when it was genuine. He just didn't want to be on the receiving end of it any more.

He kept up with the conversation, but his thoughts were preoccupied about the hillside house where he was going to meet Roy.

"Kyle?" Britt had been holding out a plate of sweet potatoes.

"Sorry," he said quickly. He took a helping of every dish Britt handed him, passing it along as Stu cut the turkey.

"How's the winter looking this year, Greg?" he asked Ruth's boyfriend.

"Solid. Good crop and the market pricing is stable. How are the college applications going? Any prospects?" Kyle related the same information he'd told Stu. "What's the closest college that's interesting?"

That was easy. "Carroll College in Montana."

"Montana?" interjected Ashley. "I thought it was the University of Colorado in Boulder."

"That University is on the list," he said, not quite a lie. It was on the list, but he'd just never applied to it.

"What are some of others?" Ruth asked. Kyle listed his top picks as he took a scoop of caramelized sweet potatoes, turkey dressing and beans, keeping the flow of food moving. "Johns Hopkins, Georgia Institute of Technology and the University of Washington."

Ruth laughed. "Could you pick three further apart?"

He shrugged. "Probably not, but they have the best biochemical engineering programs and offer scholarships. In fact, Carroll College covers nearly half of the tuition with scholarships. It drops it within a few thousand of the University of Washington."

"All of them are so far out of your price range," Ashley knowingly added.

"How do you know that?" inquired Ruth. She sat across from Kyle, with Greg beside her. Kyle thought Ruth's intolerance for Ashley's lack of aspiration was mostly veiled, but every so often, the thickness of the material went thin. Like now.

"Everyone knows those colleges are ultra-expensive."

"Then why not add Harvard to the list while you're at it?" teased Greg. "If you're going to be in the debt for the first ten years anyway."

Ruth passed Kyle the gravy. "More than that if you get your masters," she said appreciatively. "Especially if you are going to come right back here and pay off that debt one paycheck at a time."

"Hey now, ease up on our guest," Stu suggested. "Don't want to permanently scare him off this place. Ashley, pass me Kyle's plate. Brown or white meat?"

"Both, please. Ruth, who says I'm going to come back here after I graduate?"

"The obvious person, of course," Ruth answered, tilting her head to Ashley, who handed him his plate.

"Of course I said that," Ashley admitted. "After school and some travel, this is home, where Mom is."

"This is home, that's for sure." Kyle began thanking Britt for the meal, asking who made what; anything to turn the topic from plans after graduation.

"Kyle, Ashley mentioned a bit of travel," began Britt. "After Stu finished his program in mining at the University of Arizona, we went all over the place, didn't we? Australia, where they have big mining operations. Overseas…"

Kyle listened to Ashley's mom recount their travel and living experiences, nodding and asking questions. He was getting full, but asked for seconds, appreciating homemade food when he had the chance.

"Any downside?" Greg asked Britt.

"To traveling? No, that part I loved. What I hated was not having a choice, following Stu around like a puppy, ending up here," she shrugged with a false contentment.

"Ouch, Mom," said Ruth. "You might not like it here, but I found exactly what I need." Ruth didn't need to glance at Greg to make her point. Kyle saw her body shift and figured Ruth nudged Greg under the chair with her knee.

"Hopefully, Kyle," Britt continued, "you won't have too much travel and will have a choice. Montrose has a growing community of technology from what I've been reading, and so does Grand Junction."

"Two hours away?" asked Ashley.

"Better than across the country," Britt answered her daughter, the sentence carrying a tone of discipline. "Kyle, have you ever been to the east coast?"

"No. But I will visit a few schools over spring break if I get acceptance offers. But to your point, Ruth, I won't be able to afford to come back here if I want to clear the debt in the first ten years. I'll go where the job takes me. Full stop."

"Full stop…*not*," slurred Ashley. Ruth erupted in laughter.

"Ashley, unless you pay your way through college, and then choose a career that allows you to work anywhere you want, location is generally subject to the job," said Stu.

"Like Ruth," she said, rolling her eyes.

"Yes, like Ruth," he confirmed.

Greg lifted a fork. "If the idea of nursing doesn't appeal to you Ashley, you could come learn husbandry."

Ashley turned to him. "Is me being on a farm funny?"

Kyle nodded, joining Greg's laughter. "The notion of you inserting your arm into the nether regions of a bovine to aid a cow give birth is hilarious. You couldn't even watch me handling the contamination incident earlier today." Kyle turned to Britt, talking over Ruth and Greg's laughter. "And that's the reason why we shut down early and I'm here with you. Thanks again for the invitation. This is really amazing."

"I don't think you give me enough credit," Ashley said, poking him, annoyance and challenge in her tone.

"Then let's prove the theory. I'll go off to engineering school to do math for eight hours a day while you put on boots and learn to milk cows."

The dining room filled with laughter, but Ashley just stared at him with a look similar to the one she'd given him at Ty's, when he'd declined to stand up for her.

"Are you kidding me?" she challenged.

"Of course, just like you were kidding about learning how to raise cows."

Kyle felt Ruth watching him with interest, her eyes sliding over to Ashley, then down to her plate. Stu didn't approve of her dating Greg because he didn't want his daughter to have what he called a farm life. Early hours. Economic ups and downs, dependencies on uncontrollable forces of nature like rainfall and droughts. Only through her convincing him that she'd continue her nursing profession for a period of years if they got married and had children had Stu eased up on her finding a different guy.

"Seriously, Ash," Ruth started. "What colleges are you looking at anyway?"

"I thought I was looking at the same ones as Kyle, like UC in Boulder, but I guess I'm wrong."

"What, you won't follow me to the east coast?" Kyle asked her.

"No, you'll follow me to Boulder." Kyle couldn't help catching Stu's eye. She'd used the same, petulant tone of a teenager wanting her way that she used with her father. "Besides, how do you know you'll get into any of those colleges, and even if you do, didn't you tell me you only had twelve grand in the bank? Even with a scholarship, that will barely last one year."

"Ashley," her mother hissed. Clearly, Ashley's comments were below the level of manners deemed appropriate by the mother of the home.

"It's okay, Mrs. Fine. It's not like the financial affairs of my family is a state secret. But," he said, glancing at Ruth and Greg, "it is a reason why I work and take extra jobs. And speaking of which, I need to excuse myself no later than eight-thirty. I have an appointment."

"On Christmas Day?" exclaimed Ashley.

Kyle smiled, gratified he got a rise out of her. He turned to Britt then Stu. "I am sorry I can't stay longer, but I'm sure you understand."

"Of course, Kyle. We admire your work ethic."

Kyle's personal life wasn't brought up again until dessert, when they had moved into the parlor off the kitchen.

"Is the team allowed to attend the tailgate party if you win?" Greg stood beside him, eating pumpkin pie.

"Sure, as long as I eat tacos and don't drink."

Ruth sidled up beside her boyfriend. "For the uninformed, tailgate parties are usually held *before* a game, and it's purely for the spectators to get trashed, so," she continued, in her dry way, "if the game is a total loss, the impact will be lessened."

Kyle laughed, nodding. "Thanks for giving me the positive vibes, Ruth. Appreciate that."

"You aren't getting anything else," she murmured, glancing towards the kitchen. "Things are not well in Neverland."

"I don't live in Neverland, Ruth. You know that."

"Someone else thinks you do."

"And that someone else also thinks she's a fairy."

"Which you clearly don't."

"Am I that transparent?"

"Yep."

He put his plate down. "Nice to see you again, Greg." Kyle shook his hand and gave Ruth a hug. "Thanks for being okay with me," he said in her ear.

"Ha," she said, her voice still low. "I've been okay with knowing this was a temporary fascination for the last year. You're a good guy."

Kyle found Britt in the kitchen with Ashley and Stu. "Thanks again for everything, the food, the clothes. I really appreciate it." Ashley's mother gave him a hug and Stu said he'd walk Kyle to the door. "Merry Christmas Ashley."

"Call me later?"

"Ashley, he already told you he's working," responded Stu. "Maybe tomorrow."

Kyle nodded, gave Ashley a quick hug and walked to the front door with her father.

"Sorry about that," murmured Stu. "As much as we want certain things for the future, they may not always work out." Kyle only nodded. "I do have one question for you. Why didn't you tell her straight out you hadn't applied for UC Boulder?"

Stu just confirmed Kyle's' worst fears. The man knew where he'd been applying. For once, feelings of sickness in his stomach were wholly unrelated to the mine, DNA and mortality.

"Don't worry," Stu said, breaking the silence. "I am intuitive that way. You aren't doing anything that was all that different than I did at your age." He glanced over his shoulder, back to the kitchen. "By the way, it didn't work the way she says. Britt followed me." Kyle's eyes went wide with surprise. He never would have guessed. Stu dropped his head a little, as though the gravity of his choices were only now being recognized. "She liked the money but has hated other aspects, and certainly hates it here. Be wise."

"I'm trying to be, Sir."

"Hence, the colleges around the country," he said with understanding.

"The *top* colleges, sir."

Stu's lips crunched to one side. "Where there is no way I can get my daughter accepted, no matter how much money I give."

"Do you have that much money?" Kyle asked. It got Ashley's father to smile.

"Have a good night, Kyle."

"Thank you, Sir."

Stu watched the young man walk across the street. He'd been right all along. The kid was too good for his daughter, and there wasn't a darn thing he could do about it.

CHAPTER 34

Kyle saw the blinds were drawn in the office and his room, saving him the effort. He had twenty minutes to change into his snow gear and get over to the home on Oak Street.

"How was it?" His father was at the dining room table, reading the paper.

"Mostly uneventful. Where's Mom?"

"Checking a potential broken pipe over at your Aunt Ernie's place. A neighbor called and we're hoping the place isn't flooded."

Kyle went back to his room, thinking of his parents. In their relationship, his mother was like the sure-footed donkey on the rocky ridge, able to overcome just about any household issue, a gift she'd passed on to her only son. His father was the grazing sheep in the meadow, doing his thing, content to let the world revolve around him, encouraging and constant.

The balance was also emotional. His mom was tough, a little curt and fiercely loyal and on certain subjects, unbending. If someone lost her respect, it was gone for good. On the other hand, his father counseled patience, forgiveness and moving on with the same zealousness he had for everything in life.

Kyle felt he had the best of both parents, even though his father wasn't his blood relation.

"You sure you can't deliver that tomorrow?" asked his father.

"Tonight. It's Christmas after all."

Kyle returned with his gear on, taking the gift his mother had put out for him in another plastic wrap.

"Catch 'ya later."

"Later."

Nothing was ever as good or as bad as it seemed, his adoptive father would say. He'd begun repeating that line when Kyle entered puberty and getting a B on a test felt like the end of the world, while a girl looking at him made him stick to the ceiling in a state of euphoria. When the end of the semester revealed an A, and the same girl decided to ignore him, his father would shake his head.

"Be even and constant," he counseled. "You'll live longer without the crushing disappointment or unrealistic highs. It's not good for your blood pressure."

Kyle had scoffed at his words then, but now, he heard the wisdom. This didn't need to be a life or death situation. In fact, Kyle believed what he told Billy. If this man Roy wanted the data on the cubes, Roy could transfer the information. With pleasure. Once Roy had the data, Kyle could get rid of the cubes by throwing them in the half-frozen river or even return them anonymously to Brayden. Why not? Kyle suspected Roy was with the naturalists. By tomorrow morning, the man would be out of town, the cubes gone, and he and Billy would return to being normal teenagers.

Kyle eased the ATV out of the covered parking, went through his backyard and took a right, using the back road that paralleled Main Street. Less of a chance Stu would be looking out the window. At Fourth he crossed over, taking it slow on the incline. The road ended at Oak, where the contradiction of the little town with an international reputation was on display. To his right, he drove by rows of decades-old trailers, many held together with sheets of metal and fiberglass. Not a mile beyond were riverside homes, one and two story that were required to blend into the area. He slowed, nearing his destination. Here, at the base of the mountain, were larger homes, nestled into the crook of the meadow and hillside, intermixed with residences built by eccentric out-of-towners who used enormous rocks as foundations and built into, on top of, or beside them.

Only one car had passed Kyle on the way here. The street was now black, save for the lights on his ATV. He saw the hillside ramp, the 1900's version of an escalator. Because this home was literally built fifty feet up on the hill, it lacked a car port and even trees. It was rock from the home to the street.

He flipped the ATV around and went back down the street a hundred yards to the nearest house. It had several trucks in the driveway, but the building was dark. He kept the four wheeler on the road, killed the engine and walked back to the home at the base of the hill.

I can do this. I have the cubes, and the gun. In fact, he still couldn't believe Billy had insisted he take it, but he'd agreed, sensing it was the only way she'd have let him leave with the cubes.

He found the control panel and stepped in the converted coal car, pressing the green button. Probably a lot more cost-effective than steps that had to go under the snow, but much less efficient. One had a single way up and down from the home.

Annoying with groceries, he surmised, pleased he could think of such mundane things in the situation.

Soon he was being transported up the hill.

Kyle pushed back his thick glove, checking the time. 8:50. He was early. He'd have plenty of time to get his job done and get home before curfew. Whether or not he'd get to sleep was questionable.

CHAPTER 35

When Kyle reached the door, he didn't have to knock. The grey-haired man was waiting for him.

"In here."

Kyle followed him through the living room to a den. The blinds were drawn, the home sparsely furnished. He knew the owners rented it out on several vacation websites, but had never been inside.

"My name is Roy by the way."

"So I heard. Is that your real name?"

He smirked. "You've never seen me before now and it's unclear if you'll ever see me again, so why lie? You have them?"

"Of course."

"Let's get started then."

Roy sat behind an unassuming laptop. Next to it was a flat, square pad about the size of a coffee coaster. Another flip pad was propped upright, connected to the laptop. He separated the keyboard, putting it on his lap.

"I work better this way," he explained, his eyes on the screens.

"Are you a Naturalist?" Kyle asked him.

"Uh-huh." A red light on the square pad lit, followed by a blue. "Well?"

Kyle unzipped the right pocket of his ski coat. "The three states; Colorado, New York and California. I'll show you. May I?"

"Sure."

Kyle stacked the cubes, the resulting images coming to life once the cubes were connected. Roy peered forward, his eyes darting through the visible data.

"Shall we see if this works on the transfer pad?" Without waiting for an answer, he dissembled the three and restacked them. The images appeared again. "Okay," he said in an undertone. "Let's see if we can do this."

He worked quietly, watching the screen on the laptop change. It went to what Kyle figured was code. Billy would understand it perfectly. He did not.

The flip pad next to him activated, the data unintelligible.

"This is the raw information," Roy explained, pointing to the laptop. "It's going through an application that essentially categorizes it to a data file that makes sense."

"You're copying it?"

"That's right."

Kyle watched in silence. "How long do you think this will take?"

"No idea, because I have no clue as to what's stored on them. Billy said she had the files for the entire state, going back 37 years, updated every year."

"What are you going to do with what you have?"

"Expose the government of course. Show the DNA files for select individuals to prove what we have."

"Won't that just make the government hunt you down even more? Where will you go?"

The older man gave him a look of experience. "We don't necessarily reside inside the United States. But to answer your question, yes, but by then it will be too late. We're going to reverse engineer the DNA threading, create new faces in a lab and then find volunteers to undergo face transplant surgeries."

It was the very thing he and Billy had hypothesized. "Are you going to record it, the before and after as proof?"

"Of course. The virus the government says is out there isn't, but that doesn't preclude them from creating a new one that actually does what they claim. Ah, good, it's working," he said. "See here." The man pointed to the flip pad. "Let me see if I can do something. This might be very interesting." Kyle kept silent as Roy pulled up a series of screens, transferred data and cut and pasted results.

"This is why the government will eliminate you, Billy, and this entire town. Watch this."

On the left, the photograph of a man in his mid-twenties appeared. "I picked this person at random. This is him today." He tapped out a query. "And this is what he would like with his natural face." A visual appeared, and Kyle peered close. It was the same guy, but wasn't. The photo on the left had perfectly rounded eyes, brows and lashes in proportion, a strong jawline and smooth skin. On the right, the eyes were marginally sloped, the brows and eyelashes thinner, as was the lips. The skin was clear, but not as strong.

"If that's the natural version, I'm not sure anyone is going to want to ever go back," Kyle stated factually.

"That's one example. Now let's go to another. This time female." He pulled up a woman, mid-thirties. "This is her today, the actual person."

"Okay."

"And then this."

Kyle and Roy assessed the two versions in silence. While the first picture was almost perfect, the second face was a bit…off, Kyle thought. The oval structure was the same, and the cheeks were equally smooth, in the second face, her brows were thin, and her eyes were spread just a little too far apart to be considered ideal. The tip of her nose curled slightly in the 'natural' second version, and she had a mole on her right cheek, near her ear. She also had higher arches on both eyebrows, giving her an exotic, look.

"She is *so much better* on the right," Kyle said.

"Exactly. She's unique, and that's what makes her stand out. In a world of perfect faces, we have bits and pieces of our own DNA but it's been improved to a point where we have no outstanding features, people become ugly."

"Maybe not ugly, but mundane," Kyle added.

"It's the weight gain, or scars or whatever that are added upon what we were given that make us interesting."

Kyle's thoughts shifted. "Can you pull up a name?" Roy nodded. "Ruth Fine."

In minutes, a current picture of Ruth was on the screen. It was her alright. Shoulder length brown hair, brown eyes, her lips and lashes all what he considered nice looking without make-up, which she rarely wore. Then the other photo came up.

"Now that's interesting." She was nearly identical. Without makeup, she had mostly the same features and look.

"She wouldn't change at all," Roy hypothesized, "and if she did, she could dress it up or down depending on the makeup and hair. Imagine her as a blond with red lips. She'd be a knock out."

"Try Ashley Fine."

Roy repeated the steps, and Kyle held his breath. For her sake, he hoped she was going to look like the same person. "Oh, man."

"That's not good," Roy agreed.

The after didn't resemble Ashley's current version in the slightest. It was as though she and her sister Ruth had swapped places. Ruth would have the brains and the beauty, her sister reduced to insignificance intellectually and physically.

Plus, Ruth's personality was genuine. Kyle briefly wondered if Stu's attention would have been given to another daughter had the world been different. *If the faces had been different.*

"Discrimination comes in all forms," Kyle said quietly, a trace of bitterness in his heart. Ruth deserved more.

"What do you do in a situation where the person doesn't want to go back to what they should be?" he asked Roy. "I mean, are you going to give them a choice?"

"It wouldn't be up to me. It would be up to the new government in place, but I expect a new election would be in order. Or," Roy went on, "maybe only people with the money to afford the surgery could get it done first."

Kyle sat down in thought. "She'd freak out. Do you show people the before and after so they can see before they decide? That's only fair, don't you think?"

"Lots of things are possible. This is almost done. Anyone else?"

Kyle did a time check. "One more person. Billy Rowe."

"I was wondering if you were going to ask about her."

The seconds ticked, and when the results appeared, Kyle leaned on the desk. "That's impossible."

"Why? She's the exception," Roy said. "She got lucky."

"No," Kyle said, disagreeing. "She showed me the files. She had the transduction notation like the others. Check again." Roy did, the same images appearing. "She can't be. Look, I swear that she showed me."

"Before I do that…" Roy said. "Now you. Another lucky soul."

"Is it possible that for certain people, the government didn't interfere? They used the same characteristics so it was the perfectly modified face, but with the gene mutation?"

"To what end?" Roy mused, his fingers tapping out a query.

"I don't know," answered Kyle. "Make the perfect human, resistant to anything that comes along? Like me, I'm 100 percent natural, she's 100% natural, and somehow we have the immunity to the virus."

For the first time, the man turned to him. "That certainly seems possible. But," Roy continued, turning back to the screen, "someone would have had to purposefully gone into the code and manipulated it in such a fashion as to make it appear she was modified and was then left alone. The premise to seem like the rest of us."

"Who would have that kind of access and power?" Kyle wondered aloud. "Billy told me that her grandfather once owned the mine, and her father was disinherited for marrying an Indian woman. Maybe somewhere in the family line there were the connections required to make this happen, but she has no idea. I guarantee it."

"Something to solve later," Roy said. "You have anything else you want copied?"

Kyle retrieved three of the six cubes. "Masters."

"For?"

"I suppose the entire country. Maybe the secret to reverse engineering?"

Roy quickly placed the blocks on one another. The computer began whirling. "Holy…" his words trailed off. Hundreds…thousands of lines of code streamed on the page.

"Does it make any sense?"

Roy shook his head. "Not yet."

Kyle stood, pacing the room as the program copied the files. "You aren't going to look yourself up?"

"Don't have to. I'm like you. A natural."

"How do you know?"

"Trust me. I know."

Kyle looked down at the man. His skin was tan, but not olive, like an Italian. His nose was prominent, the arch sitting high, a perfect crest for a pair of glasses. Grey hair was always a bit unruly, but Roy's was wiry and coarse. "Is it me, or is this taking longer?"

"The system isn't reading these files as easily. It's continuing to get caught up in something. I don't know what."

"I have to get back or I'll be out after curfew."

"I need to keep these and finish."

"Sorry, man. I can't let you do that. You seem like good guy, but I don't know you and you don't know me. What if something happens to you?"

"Wouldn't matter," Roy answered, still watching the screen. "I've been uploading these to several servers on the dark web. The three states are encrypted and unbreakable but accessible to the right people."

"Great. But that still doesn't mean I'm letting you keep them or the masters." As much as Kyle wanted to be rid of the entire mess, he needed a back-up plan in case Roy did nothing with the cubes after all, and the country remained the status quo.

"I'm sorry to hear you say that." Roy turned in the chair, and when he did, he had a small gun in his hand.

"Are you kidding me?" cried Kyle.

"No, and I also know you're lying. Billy said she had six master blocks, and you gave me three. Give them to me and you can leave."

"How do I know you won't shoot me anyway?"

"I won't cause problems for myself. You go missing, your parents alert the cops, they swarm the place since you are already a person of interest and the whole state gets locked down. That I don't need. Be the smart kid everyone says you are. Hand over the masters."

Kyle thought of the gun at his hip. There was no reasonable way he could get it out and fire before he'd be dead. "Fine," he said, reaching into the same, outer pocket he'd used before. He walked towards the man and pulled out his hand, showing the remaining cubes.

"Thanks kid, I knew you'd do the right thing." Kyle made as though he was going to drop them into Roy's palm but instead lunged sideways, angling his left shoulder into Roy's collarbone. The man fell forward, head into the computer, the crunching sound followed by the gun firing. It hit a window, shattering the quiet. Kyle pushed him into the desk with all his force, snatching the cubes on the desk and metal coaster.

Kyle gasped as the chair pushed back into his midsection. Roy lifted the gun again, craning over his shoulder. Clenching the cubes, Kyle dropped low, pressing his legs to force the man back into the desk. He jammed the cubes in his pocket, then used both hands to pry the gun away while it was angled down. It fired again, and he thanked God it missed his toes.

Up went the gun, and another shot. Four more shots and it won't matter who had the weapon. Kyle knew it would be out of bullets.

Kyle took an elbow to his face and saw spots. He'd never been hit in the face before now, the momentary blackness frightening.

This guy wasn't going to just get the blocks, he was going to kill me.

Kyle kept his grip on the gun in Roy's hand and punched. Roy fell back, his grip loosening. Kyle twisted the gun out of his hand, breaking free. He didn't want to fire and wasn't planning on it until Roy lurched forward. Kyle pulled the trigger, self-preservation overcoming his hesitation. Roy flung back on the desk, hands flailing. Kyle ran, making it to the landing as he hit the descend button.

No cars, no lights. Not yet. Please let people think the shots were in celebration.

He ran to his ATV, speeding down the street. *What if the man came after me, or Billy*? No, no sense going after Billy, she didn't have the cubes, unless he kidnapped her as a means to get to me.

Dead men don't track anyone down.

No, I couldn't have killed him. Kyle had never even punched anyone other than Mario, and that had been over a girl in eighth grade.

He was so intent on getting home, he ignored all speed limits, sure that Oak Street was safe under the cover of the trees and the time of night.

Kyle guessed it was close to ten p.m. and that Mark was home instead of trolling the streets. Fate was on his side. A burst of fear-induced confidence flooded him, and he hit the gas with his right thumb. He'd get home, hide the cubes and no one would be the wiser.

CHAPTER 36

Mark was watching The Grinch when an out of sequence pop caught his attention. It was followed by another, then another, the sound ricocheting along the valley.

Not on this night, and not in this town, ever. Then a third, then fourth sound pinged, overlapping with the sound of the Grinch crying about his heart increasing in size.

Mark opened the front door of his home and looked down on the valley below. Lights on his lower left caught his attention, the flashing effect due to the trees overhanging the road. The sound was higher than a car, and louder. Had to be an off-road vehicle.

Ben probably racing around with his new tires.

Mark followed the ATV as it took a left off Oak, onto Seventh then across Main Street. Expecting it to turn right, he frowned when it went left. Speeding. Shots fired. He sighed. Could be Ben was visiting friends, out later than curfew by a few minutes. No law against shooting guns, and speeding in a small town never warranted a ticket. The kid could be having a sleepover.

The officer in him couldn't stop his line of thought. The only teen who lived in the vicinity to the left was Kyle Smith. Saachi's hypothesis came to mind. Could Ben and Kyle be in this together? Unlikely. Was it his civic duty to make sure everyone was home, safe and sound by ten p.m. during this period of uncertainty with FBI agents in town? Unfortunately, yes.

Mark grumbled as he put on his police belt and jacket, not bothering to change out of his jeans. It was times like these he would have liked to have a younger deputy, but dismissed the notion. That would mean less money for him, and there was barely enough work for him and the Sheriff to begin with, except during the summers.

He drove down Oak, up Seventh then turned left on Fourth where he'd last seen the ATV. He drove slowly down the street, inspecting the Ouray Elementary School on his right, easily seeing the wide tire tracks in the snow. It continued until the road ended at 9th and he took a left, heading back towards Main. The tracks turned right, onto Potosi Place, and he felt smug, relieved and annoyed.

The ATV tracks headed in the direction of Kyle's house. They would be busted for curfew if they were still out and not inside. He wondered if it was even worth it.

I'm this far. Might as well make sure they are at his house and then call it a night.

Since Potosi was a dead end, he turned around and took a right down the alley instead paralleling Main. He saw the tracks again on the snow, and asked himself why they were here and not at Kyle's house. Ben wasn't going to be hitting up Ty's for a drink at the bar. It was closed and Ben knew better.

Wait, there they are again. The tracks hadn't stopped at Ty's, just went down the alley and to Kyle's after all. Mark made it to the side parking spot in time to see the ATV cut from the road, across the backyard.

Ben must be awfully friendly with Kyle's parents to get away with that.

He parked the car and called out when he heard the engine turn off.

"Ben," he yelled. "Ben?" he repeated, walking to the carport. From the dark emerged a figure with a mask and goggles, and Mark instinctively put his hand on his holster. "Hold it right there, Mister. Hands up."

The hands slowly raised. "Mark, it's me. Kyle. It's okay."

Mark tilted his head. "Kyle?"

"Yes. Can I put my hands down now?"

"No, you can't," he said, walking forward slowly. "You're wearing a mask and I can't make a visual verification. I heard shots a few moments ago, and that black on your chest doesn't look like dirt."

"Mark, it's blood and to be honest, I have serious issues. Check my jacket and belt. I have a gun around my waist and another in my left pocket taken from a guy who just tried to kill me over a stupid Christmas ornament I was dropping off for my mom. I'll keep my palms out while you search me if you want."

"What?" Mark asked, surprise overtaking worry. "What happened?"

"He tried to shoot me, we fought and I shot him. Can I please put my hands down and will you listen for a second?"

He approached Kyle, trying to keep the formality of being a cop. "Keep your palms where I can see them. Did you say Christmas ornament?"

"Yes, you search me and I'll talk."

Kyle kept his arms wide, palms facing out. Mark patted down the outside of his jacket, feeling the cubes and pulling a few out.

"Paper weights," explained Kyle. "Saw them in a store and thought my mom would like 'em so I bought a bunch. That other thing is a metal coaster I thought was cool." Lying had become second nature. Mark put them back in Kyle's pocket, opening his jacket. "The gun in the holster is mine, so it has my prints. The one in the left pocket is the one from the guy."

"You get a name?"

"He called himself Roy. Don't have a last name."

"We can get the ID from the gun, but if he was smart, it's untraceable. His blood is another thing. Tell me exactly what happened."

Kyle did. "You can ask my mom and dad. They were here when he stopped by Christmas Eve, paid for one ornament and advanced cash for another. Asked me to drop it off so I did." He told Mark about the house. "You want me to go with you and check it out?"

"Hold on a minute," he said. He went to his patrol car and returned with a white cloth. Kyle held still as Mark carefully lifted the handgun from his pocket. "Your coat," he muttered.

"Shouldn't you get a kit to take the blood off it?"

"I should do a lot of things, but first I want to go to that house and see if the guy is still there and what he's going to tell me. If he's alive." He'd muttered the last words under his breath, like he couldn't believe he was saying it.

"You want me to stay here?"

"In theory, a cop would never leave a participant in a crime by himself, because you could do anything while I'm gone."

"I won't."

"But I put myself at risk if I leave you here."

"Then I can go with you."

Mark's lips parted when he exhaled in frustration. "Do you need to tell your parents you're with me so they don't worry?"

"Yeah, be right back." Kyle leaned in the back door, yelled that he'd come home and was going out with Deputy Hancock.

"You want me to sit in the back?"

"Kyle, anywhere you are, will be, or have been can be rounded up with the right forensics evidence, and I'm just not sure it's going to matter. Get in the front."

CHAPTER 37

On the drive back over to Oak Street, Mark asked him to repeat the sequence of the evening, clarifying certain points. Had Kyle seen the other man before? What was he wearing? Describe his face in detail.

"It sounds similar to a guy I saw at the bar just before I came down to see you." Kyle nodded, staring out the truck's front window. "Where did you park?" Kyle pointed and Mark pulled the police cruiser across the street. "Any idea where he parked or what vehicle he drove?"

"No clue. He was in the house when I got there, like I said."

Mark used his flashlight back and forth along the road. "Watch it," Mark said, putting his hand on Kyle's jacket. "Dark spots. Down here."

"I wasn't anywhere near here."

"It's possible he left, but you never know. You stay here. I can't risk you getting shot."

"Are you kidding me? Maybe he's sitting in the bushes, and you took my gun. No way I'm going to stay here."

Mark grumbled. "I'm not allowed to lock you in the car unless I cuff you. Crap," he said with resignation. "Let's go up, but you hang back behind me."

They rode the old time metal car in silence.

"You ever been through something like this before?" Kyle asked in a low voice.

"Only with druggies from the meth labs. Easy to catch. No surprise. Very little danger. Ok, like I said, you stay on behind me."

Mark had his gun drawn. "Police! Don't move!" Mark shouted, crashing in the door. If the shots didn't wake the neighbors, the crash and shout certainly might, although, the next house was a ways down, so perhaps not.

"You can come in," Mark called. Kyle entered and felt more unsettled than if he'd seen a dead body. Nothing was out of order. The table and chair were in place, the computers gone. "Did you say a window got shot out?"

"Yeah. Over there."

The blinds were still drawn, but a bullet hole was clearly evident. Roy couldn't do anything about the shattered window.

"He cleaned up the glass on the floor," Kyle said without thinking. "Why would he do that if he was injured and needed to get out of town?"

Mark didn't answer him. He glanced below at the street, looking towards the tram then he turned, pacing through the living room and den.

"Kitchen rags are wet. I bet if we sprayed this place with luminol, we'd get a lot of blood spatter."

Kyle shifted on his feet, unwilling to stand still, but not able to sit. *Less evidence of being here.*

"Kyle," he asked with some exasperation. "What were you doing with a gun in the first place?"

"I was going to meet a stranger at night. I have a hunting license, Mark. It seemed prudent."

"And tell me one more time. What he said, word for word."

"He said give me your money and the keys to your vehicle. He pulled out a gun and I knew I wouldn't be able to get mine before getting shot, so I lunged at him, crunched him against the computer like I said. The gun fired several times, I punched him, got his gun away from him and fired. Then I got the heck out."

"All we have is your story."

Kyle nodded. No amount of stretching the truth was going to change what happened next.

"Deardon is going to freak," Kyle began. "I'm going to be screwed, the town is going to lose it, thinking we have a thief or worse on the loose. My life is a mess, and all for a Christmas ornament."

The emotional roller coaster of the last five days suddenly overtook him, and he put his hand over his eyes. He'd never shed a tear over anything, not since he lost the playoff game when he was in middle school. It was then he decided nothing in life was worth such emotions. Over the last four years, he'd been constant, steady, and in control of his life. Just like his dad had advised. If only Mark hadn't seen him come home, covered with blood, the smoking gun literally on his body.

His hand was still shading his eyes as tears of anger threatened to seep out. "It's over."

He felt a palm on his shoulder. "No. It's not," Mark said, shaking him. "Kyle, we have no body. The only blood we have is on you and, presumably, what's lying around here but thankfully, not apparent to the naked eye. The snow outside will cover the blood, and even if someone saw it, the assumption would be a nose bleed, right?"

That got Kyle nodding. The altitude of 7,000 feet caused everyone to get them if they didn't keep hydrated. Nose bleeds were almost as common as the snow itself.

"What now?" Kyle asked with a bit of hope.

"Police procedure is to file a report. Forensics would have to come in from Montrose. That's going to shine a light on everyone in this town. More than it already is. That's means it gets attention from State." Mark's eyes were tight together, the scar on his chin pronounced. "The guy probably thought you were going to be an easy score. Good hometown kid. You'd have a wallet. It was stupid, but maybe he was desperate and made the wrong call and got the bad end. If he can drive, he's long gone by now, never to return. This," he stopped, touching the window, "will be chalked up to a late night of drinking. A renter comes in, trashes the joint and leaves. Totally reasonable in a small town where most people are on vacation. The owners will file a report, insurance will cover it. End of story. Do you recall anything else missing?"

Kyle looked around. "I don't think so, but I can't say I was paying much attention."

"Fair enough. One more thing." Mark took out the cloth he'd used with the gun. "You said you touched the table? Show me." Kyle pointed out the areas, and Mark wiped them clean. "Just in case. It's not strange to have a completely clean table if the housekeepers were here before the guy arrived. The table doesn't even look used. Turn around. I don't want you to see this." Kyle did so, hearing the sounds of cabinets opening and the clinking of glasses on the table. "Nobody knows what a scene looks like better than a cop."

Mark joined him at the door. "You first." The ride to town was quiet.

"I don't know what to say," Kyle admitted. "You're covering for me."

"Yeah, pretty much," Mark answered, the tension in his voice replaced with a bit of humor. "Of all people, you, the boy scout."

"I *have* been a boy scout and everyone knows it." Kyle reflected on what Mark hadn't said when he was going through his summary of the situation, the potential of unwanted attention and the downside of filing reports. "You don't want the Patrol coming into town, do you?"

"No, and they wouldn't bother making a special trip for a simple theft or damage to property. It's the unresolved issue with the FBI agents and unable to determine who broke into the mine. Until that's cleared up, we are all under some level of scrutiny, even me."

Kyle glanced at him. "*You?*"

"Saachi retrieved hair samples from the mine and are intent on matching them up. She's convinced that only an athlete was able to make it in and down the mine then back out, which points to you and the other guys. She took one from me just in case."

"I guess you're right. Everyone is fair game," Kyle said, barely getting the words out. He didn't have to fake the feeling being gut punched. "Is that why they were at the school this morning?"

"You saw us?"

"Only your car outside, but I saw the lights on. I'd just gotten the ATV for Christmas and was taking a joy ride, otherwise I wouldn't have noticed. What you said makes sense now. Athletes, me and the guys being the obvious choices."

They had made it to the car and got inside. Mark turned on the heaters and Kyle put his hand over the vents.

"Kyle, if I process this incident, you'll get written up with a police report and it's game over, even if you were acting in self-defense."

"The colleges will run," said Kyle, going with Mark's line of thought.

"Like I said, game over, literally and figuratively. You'll be stuck here forever, like me."

The regret in Mark's voice interrupted Kyle's self-absorbed concern. Mark pulled out and flipped on his headlights.

"I thought you liked it here. Your parents' house, your job, four-wheeling in the summer and fishing, the life of a bachelor."

Mark turned on Seventh, driving slow. "The life is fine, it just doesn't progress. The dating pool doesn't change, it just ages up. You really think I want to be taking out girls your age after they graduate?"

Kyle hadn't ever thought of if it that way. Mark's casual comments always made it seem like he was living the life he'd always wanted; the small town ideal, homeowner, cop, single and free. "You have other towns where you could go, other people."

"Not much of a bigger pool, but my life isn't the issue right now, yours is. Get home, soak that jacket in vinegar. When you are done with that, use WD-40. Both work equally well. Reality is this will never be known beyond the two of us and no one is going to come looking for what you were wearing."

Mark drove to Potosi, stopping when he reached the end. "Better to walk from here. Stu won't see you coming in from the back."

"Thanks, Mark. Really."

Mark stared out the front windshield for a moment, as if projecting what his own future could have been. "I want you to make a life away from here. Something like this, through no fault of your own, isn't going to stop it."

Kyle got out, feeling sick with relief and guilt. Would Mark let him off had he known the truth, and what would Mark do if he learned Kyle had omitted critical parts of the story and that he wasn't the boy scout Mark thought him to be?

Kyle already had his coat off when he entered the house, going straight through the tiny kitchen and eating nook, into the closet-sized laundry room. He shoved his jacket in the washing machine, got the vinegar and soaked the top with it. He wasn't sure what else to do--leave it and have his mother sniff out the vinegar? He put it on cold soak and rinse cycle, it was what he'd used for stains in the past. Inspecting his pants, he didn't see any blood marks but wasn't going to take a chance. He stripped them off and dunked them in the water, shutting the door behind him.

"Mom, Dad, I'm home." Both parents called back to him. They were in their bedroom, only three feet and one thinly-insulated wall separating them. "Taking a shower," he called as he headed down the hall before hearing them reply.

He stayed under the shower until the water turned lukewarm. He'd unnecessarily scrubbed his body multiple times; no amount of lather would eliminate the memory of what had taken place.

Mark had presumed Roy had left town with a bullet wound. Would Roy go to Billy?

Concern for her flooded him. He dressed and went back into the kitchen, unable to slow the adrenaline chasing through his limbs to his chest. The data was in the hands of others, and Kyle had no control over what happened next. It was great of Mark to give him cover for the next forty-eight hours, but forensics would eventually nail him. And Billy, if he could keep her out of this, she'd live her life and someday, maybe through the grace of God and some very smart, brave people, the next generation would have new faces.

It could happen.

In the meantime, I'm going to live my life without regrets. No more pretending. No more acting like I'm dating Ashley. If I only have a few days or weeks or months left to enjoy myself, I'm going to do it. *Starting now.*

At ten after ten, Kyle picked up the ancient yellow land line. The connection would leave a record, but who cared? He was always fixing the Rowe's appliances. Billy picked up on the third ring.

He spoke in soft tones. "Is your fridge working okay?"

"Yes, thanks for asking. How was your night?"

"Eventful."

"Really?

"Yes. Half of it went as I expected, the other half, completely off the rails."

"But you're home."

"Yes, thanks to Deputy Hancock."

"Huh. He was out trolling around?"

"He saw me as I was pulling in the covered parking and we went for a ride in his car. Not often I get to spend time with the Deputy. It's all good though. I have my sugar cubes ready for a late night snack."

"I thought you were going sugar free?"

"I was, until the store manager wanted to prevent me from buying them at all. Actually, tried to take them from me."

"You're kidding?"

"No, and we got in a fight. I punched him. Got some blood on me."

"And Mark knows all this?"

"Yes, except I was too embarrassed to admit it was all over some sugar cubes."

"Kyle, your better get some sleep and repair your body. The big game is Friday."

"Speaking of which, you've trained the players like ducks. They're reliant on your food."

"Say no more. When is practice?"

"Ten to noon."

"Be there."

"Billy, this time around, I'll help you carry all the extra trays back to the restaurant. You shouldn't have to do that every time without help."

"Don't you have to work?"

"At one. More than enough time to help you."

"See you then."

Kyle didn't go to bed. He checked the blinds in his room, opened his laptop and used the USB cord to connect the square plate. The light went from red to blue, but he wasn't sure what to do with it. The plate was level on the table in front of him, the sounds of a basketball game rerun overlapping with the keyboard.

"Mixed up," he muttered in frustration. He'd kept the three cubes representing the states separate, but now they were with the back-ups. By trial and error, he identified those with the individual DNA files, realizing they only worked with one another. It didn't matter which was on top or bottom. The data emanated from out the sides.

"Now which state are you?" With the cubes stacked, he scrolled through the names until he found his own and Billy's. He got a pencil and marked each side of the cube- CO. He found a half dozen names on the next cube, used the Internet for a search and was confident he knew the New York block, leaving the last for California.

"Three down," he said. "What else can you tell me?" He painstakingly placed different sides against one another, hoping to get more information.

"Nothing." He stood, getting a Coke from the fridge. It was past midnight, and he hadn't learned anything new.

He set those three aside, and then tried different permutations of the masters: on top of one another, side by side, different sides. Nothing. Roy couldn't make sense of them either, his software applications useless. What did he say? The program was getting caught on something?

Kyle rolled one of the masters in his fingertips like dice. He picked up the one of Colorado state. Playing around, he held the cubes an inch apart and felt a pull. At first, he thought it was no different than the magnetic connection of the states. He rolled a master in his hand, expecting the pull to be constant, but it had disappeared.

Interesting.

He rolled the master cube to another flat surface. *No pull.* He then tested the surface of the Colorado state cube in his left hand. Only one side of the cube was magnetically drawn to one side of the master.

With an increasing sense of excitement, he found the magnetic side of master, connecting the cubes.

He jumped. Above him were streams of addresses. Cautiously, he rotated the master cube forward one surface. This time, lists of people were connected by prongs. It looked like a genealogy chart. He turned it another surface forward. It was birth and death dates. The last appeared to be the family history, notes that were made about the person.

"No one like me to test this." It took him a while, but he located his city and then address. With a pencil, he marked that side of the cube. By turning the block, he found his family line on one side, going back to his maternal grandfather in England, and on another surface, his extended family members on another.

"A cousin?" he whispered. According to this data file, his Aunt Ernie had given birth but the baby had died at… "three months." Could it be possible? It was like the medical records had been joined with this master record.

His fingers were jumpy when he started putting in the names of those he knew, feeling like the virtual voyeur who had unlimited access into the lives of others. Mario's father had an illegitimate son living in Arizona and was on his second wife. Kyle wondered if Mario knew. The Fine's had extended family on the east coast, Stuart's own line going back to the Mayflower. No wonder Britt was uppity. She'd married well. It made Kyle think better of Stu. He probably had a coat of arms somewhere in his office and was modest enough to keep it out of the way.

He hesitated on looking up Billy. Did he want to know more? There was safety in secrecy. *There was also risk.*

Billy Rowe. He turned the blocks, anticipating absorbing the facts of her life. "That's it?" Ty appeared, his relatives, previous addresses and history. The story of Billy's grandfather founding Diamonte mines was in the notes section, along with a copy of the deed of sale. But her mother was a blank.

"How's that possible?" He thought about Roy's findings. Her file had been manipulated. Had her master records also been accessed? Had to have been, unless… she said her mother was Native American. Since they had retained their sovereign nation status through the last war, perhaps they weren't included as part of the master files on U.S. Citizens.

Or perhaps the story on Billy's family ran much deeper than anyone knew, including her.

On instinct, Kyle put in one more name. In the moment, he wasn't even sure why. Perhaps it was because Brayden had saved him once already.

As he read through the file on Brayden Cox, Kyle leaned forward, as if proximity directly correlated to truth. Brayden had reason to help Kyle out, more than enough. Family members identified two children, both deceased. The notes section detailed why. Cause of death for his son was listed on the medical records as a self-inflicted bullet wound, but in the notes, it was contradicted and the details certified it. And the daughter. *Whoa.*

He sat back, feeling waves of queasiness. *I'd asked for it.* He was now burdened with a knowledge he wished he didn't have; information he knew was being hidden from Brayden. The notes said it all.

CHAPTER 38

During the first ten minutes of practice, each step sent spikes of pain through Kyle's shoulder blades and right arm. What healing had occurred prior to the incident with Roy had been reversed, the impact he took on his upper body worse than he expected.

If this is how I feel, I wonder how Roy is.

Kyle was also spent with fatigue. At three, his mother had wandered into his room telling him if she was going to bed, then he better turn in as well.

"Kyle, open," yelled Mario. His peripheral vision had been off. Ben slapped the ball out of his hand on the pass, and soon he was running the opposite direction.

"What is up with you?" hissed Mario, running to the far side of the court.

The visual of Roy hunched over, that's what.

"I'm tired," he retorted.

Over breakfast, he'd sorted through all he'd learned the night before, gratified he'd broken a part of the cubes' code, confident that he knew what had to be done. He'd run it by Billy when he walked her home after practice.

Kyle refocused, leapt and hammered down Ben's shot.

"That's more like it," shouted his coach from the bench.

At the break, he asked his coach for a muscle relaxant.

"Your arm?' his coach asked.

"And shoulder." Kyle was careful to take the cream and go under his long sleeve, around, over and down his arm. He turned to the stands, closing his eyes as he held his arm. Only another hour and the practice would be over.

"Looks like we are going to have food again," said Mario at his side, jerking his head at the side gym door. Billy was there, two bags in her hand. She set them down, glanced at the coach and motioned she'd be back for more.

The coach yelled and they were back running for another hour. When he didn't have the ball, Kyle rolled his shoulder, encouraging the synovial fluid that lubricated his joints. *More comfrey would help*.

"Kyle, the bench," yelled his coach. "Sit. Put some ice on that shoulder. You will be out tomorrow for the game if you don't give it a rest."

"It'll be fine."

His coach grunted, folding his arms, watching the team. "No practice tonight. Understand?" Kyle nodded. "Do you do much pulling or heavy lifting at the pool?"

"Pulling the covers back on the pools at night and off in the morning."

"Get some help. We are going to be in a bad spot if you aren't playing at full capacity for the playoff game."

He held the ice on the outside of his shirt. "Kyle, what are you doing? That's not helping. Take the shirt off."

"I can feel it plenty."

His coach turned and glared. "Man up, Son. Take it off and ice it direct."

Kyle had no choice. He stripped off this t-shirt which was over his long sleeve, hoping to do it fast enough where he could put back on before his coach saw.

"Holy Mother of Mary, Kyle. You said the weights slipped. Ben, to your left!" Kyle put on his top and put the ice underneath. His coach lifted the back of his shirt up again. "Does your kidney hurt?"

"No."

"Any spitting up blood or in your stool?"

"None."

His coach pressed against Kyle's shoulder, along his arm and under his rib cage. "Didn't notice your hands before." He eyed him then. "Looks like you went ice climbing and fell, but were lucky enough to break the fall with your hands and shoulder." Kyle remained silent. One fewer lie to tell. "That about it?"

"Yes, Sir."

His coach exhaled. "Ice climbing is a flagrant violation of team rules."

"I'm sorry, Sir."

"Not once, in four years have you screwed up. We have the playoff game tomorrow and you go and do this?"

"Yes, Sir."

"One word, Kyle. Disappointed."

"A team captain knows better."

"*You* know better, Kyle."

He sat on the bench with the ice pack for the remaining thirty minutes. The team was good without him. It was great with him. But they wouldn't win tomorrow if he wasn't playing.

The coach blew the whistle, signaling the end of practice. Billy had set the food on the table nearest the locker room doors, but he hadn't noticed. His eyes were on the court, never veering away once.

Kyle made no motion to stand when his teammates went to the food. "Eat Kyle. You need it to heal."

"Coach, I'm sorry again. I haven't ever fallen before."

"You shouldn't have been ice climbing at all, not then or any other time. But why am I all that surprised?" he asked rhetorically. "You were a sophomore when you started stringing yourself on cables over ravines."

"And you got mad at me then too."

The scowl turned to a slight smirk. "Yeah. It's your determined spirit that won me over. Go eat some food."

Kyle had a mouth full of pulled pork in his mouth when he caught sight of Billy. She was sitting on a bleacher bench, head down toward her phone. Black cap today, no neon green, and this one had a small bill in the front, partially hiding her face.

"Hey guys."

Oh, man.

Mario greeted Ashley as she walked over to Kyle. She was too happy to have seen Billy yet. "Can I walk you to work?" she asked him. "We have some left over pie and you could grab a bite before your shift at the pool."

Kyle felt like he was the stalled car on the train tracks, the locomotive barreling towards him. "Sorry Ash, I can't. But thanks for coming up and saying hi."

"I'll walk you over and eat some pie," offered Mario.

"Oh, Mario," Ashley said, rolling her eyes.

"What? Kyle's busted up and has an errand to do with another girl."

"Right, Mario. You'll do anything for some food."

"Not kidding, Ashley. Just look over there."

Ashley turned, her face dropping.

"Thanks, Mario," he muttered. His friend's ever-present desire for Ashley was rising to the surface at the worst time. "I'm walking with Billy because I'm taking trays back. She's hauled these things herself every other time."

"And she can do it again," Ashley said.

"Look, I have to change and get over to the pool. You coming, Mario?"

"I'm still eating."

Kyle showered and changed in less than five minutes. When he came out, Ashley was gone and Mario hadn't moved.

"That was fast," Mario said.

"I'm surrounded by people who don't have jobs," Kyle called Billy over. "Like you."

"And if Ashley has her way, you won't have a job either."

"What are you talking about?"

"She says she knows Barrett, and you have been working too much anyway. She left to go talk with him."

Kyle laughed. "Try another tact Mario. Just ask her out. I give you my full blessing."

"Right."

"I am right. It's officially over. The only person who doesn't know it yet is Ashley. I'm telling you first. That way, when she shows up at your house unannounced, or at basketball practice, or anywhere else in town, and then has her dad follow you around just because, or Ashley cuts you down in front of the local police, you let me know how wonderful it is."

Billy arrived with a bag in her hand. "Mario. Shut your mouth. It looks like a fly went into it."

Kyle good-naturedly slapped his friend's back. "It *is* hanging open, Mario. Like I said, best of luck to you. You're going to need it."

Billy joined Kyle in scraping the leftovers into the garbage can and stacking the trays. "Here," he said, holding out one of the sacks.

"Kyle, can I speak to you for a minute?"

"Sure Coach."

Kyle walked with his coach until the man stopped. "You are likely to have scouts at the game tomorrow. They will see that arm and shoulder of yours and think the worst. They get paid to do that, so we have a problem."

"Why, sir? I can just wear my long sleeve shirt."

"It's against regulation, and you can get disqualified by the other team any time if they want to call it."

Kyle didn't know that. "I've never had to wear one before." Kyle knew they were on the same team, mentally and physically. They both wanted to win the game. "So, what do I do? Wear it and hope no one notices?"

"Trust me. The minute we get ahead and you're hitting your shots, they'll remember the rule. No, I have another idea. I can say you are badly injured and healing. They might infer a burn without me being explicit and I could get a medical pass. That would eliminate the risk of you being thrown out of the game."

"And what if it doesn't work?"

"Then you take off the shirt and the scouts see the extent of the damage and pass because of your crazy life-style, or you leave it on, exit the game and we lose."

"Pretty crappy options," Kyle admitted.

"I'll do my best," said his coach, patting his left arm, walking him back. "You ice that for the next twenty-four, alright? And no heavy lifting, no nothing until the game tomorrow like I said."

"Yes, sir."

He and Billy left the gym and walked down the street in silence until they turned right on Main.

"Did I hear what I think I heard between you and Mario?"

"Yes," he answered, "and that bit of smug happiness that I detect in your voice is warranted. Of course, I'll be catching the backdraft at some point. It will be added to the flame thrower that's going to be aimed at my head anyway."

"Barrett owns the pool. He will ignore whatever she says," Billy predicted.

They reached the front door of Ty's, and Kyle held it open for her. "You'd think so."

"My good news is that Dad thinks he found a new full-time cook. Dan has already resumed his shift as back-up."

"Hey Ty," Kyle greeted.

"Kyle," he said, tipping his head as he put ice in a glass.

Billy and Kyle unloaded the sacks in the kitchen. "The food was great Dan."

"Thanks Kyle. Billy got a head start on things today for me."

Kyle followed Billy through the hallway, into her home. "Sounds like you need an ice pack for your climbing accident," she said to him.

"Yeah."

"That does look bad."

"It wasn't so much until it got reinjured last night. I want to skip to the part about Brayden, but I'm going to start with Roy. Ready to hear it all?"

They sat on the worn, leather couch, her knee touching his thigh.

For the third time in their short relationship, Billy sat in total silence, watching him as he related the chain of events from Roy to Mark.

"Well, what do you think?" he asked when done.

"I agree with what Mark did. It's perfectly logical. The guy leaves town, maybe dead in a ditch somewhere. He got his data, and we hope he does something good with the information. I don't think he'll bother me at all, because as you said, I don't have the cubes."

"Billy, what if you can be traced by association with the cubes?"

She shrugged. "I can't do anything about it now, can I?"

"No." Kyle took one of her hands within in his, gently rubbing the top. Although he felt emotionally bonded to Billy at a core level, physically touching her was still new and unexplored. It felt…innocent, special and awfully adult. "I have so much to tell you about the cubes. Two parts; the first is what Roy discovered when he transferred the data off the state files. The second is what I found."

She raised an eyebrow. "You?"

He smiled, the expression one he wore after sinking a three-pointer from the centerline. "I may in fact, deserve that valedictorian award."

He related Roy's exercise with the government-created faces versus the natural ones. First with Ruth, then Ashley, then herself. Billy was happy for Ruth, smug about Ashley and skeptical about her own incarnation.

"Impossible," she disputed.

"Roy was certain someone got into the data files and purposefully changed it to make it appear you had been one of masses, but actually you aren't. You are like me. Natural."

"And here I was getting ready for a dramatic change."

He kissed the top of her hand. "Don't you think it's crazy that of all the people, you and me won't be subject to change? What?"

While he was speaking, Billy had started to smile. "I'm not going to apologize for it," she said, tilting her chin up. "That girl needs more than a verbal take-down."

"She hasn't done anything wrong…" Kyle began. "She's just highly misguided."

Billy shook her head. "And that's why everyone likes you. Diplomatic to the very end."

"You might not believe you are a natural, but other facts were proven out when I started looking at the master cubes." He related the sequence of events with the cubes, what he found, detailing her father's family, and her lack thereof.

"That's interesting," was all she said.

"But you don't sound surprised."

"Yes and no. The government hasn't cared about Native Americans since it stopped getting tax revenue from them. The curious part is why someone would bother. I mean, I'm not special in the grand scheme of things."

He smirked. "But I'm right?"

"You're full of yourself."

"We both knew that. Billy," he started again, turning somber. "I feel like a rope has been thrown around the town, and it's drawing tight. I'm half-tempted to get you and me on that ATV and ride out of town."

"To where?"

"I knew you'd ask that, so here's my next idea. I take Brayden aside. I tell him what's on the cubes. Even give them back. He gets the FBI to leave."

"Why wouldn't he turn right around and take you in? Oh," she said, "you think because he lost a son, he'll be sympathetic. Kyle, he may have helped you out with the wallet, but he can only do so much."

"But his daughter…"

She nodded cautiously. "What's the end game then? If they identify you from the hair samples, you are going to appeal to him to wipe away whatever forensics they have in return for the cubes?"

"Yes, like you said, appeal to his sense of loss."

"But not his sense of career longevity. Kyle, don't do it."

"You have another plan? Get on line again and find another Roy-type of person and we go through this, round two? It's not going to get easier. Besides…"

He sat back. The thought he had was so bleak, he closed his eyes. Kyle felt Billy's fingertips above his ear, gliding through his hair.

"Besides, what?" she asked softly. Her voice made him look at her, the motion causing her fingers to touch his lips.

"You are so gentle, Billy. The game tomorrow will come and go, and whatever happens to you will be all my fault. I can't let that happen."

"Nothing is going to happen. Trust me." She ran the tip of her thumb along his lips.

"You're right," he confirmed, "because this time, I have it figured out."

"You really think you only have one more night here, don't you?"

"Yeah. I'm sorry, Billy."

She pulled him close. "Don't be."

CHAPTER 39

Brayden stared at the mobile phone in his hands, feeling as though his connection to all things emotional had been severed with the call. Laura had phoned late in the day and he'd answered without looking at the ID, thinking it was Saachi with news on the DNA match up. He played the conversation back word for word, as antiseptically as if it was a case he needed to file.

"Half of us were pulled in," Laura was telling him, the explanation sounding like the excuse it was.

"No worries, I was at the local hot tub."

"Are you going to be gone much longer?" she asked. He thought Laura's tone held a trace of anxiousness, and he wondered if she were actually missing him.

"Unknown. This is presenting some interesting challenges, forensics and otherwise."

"Are they using the facility out of Montrose?"

"Yes. How'd you know that?"

"Good guess. When we get backlogged the staff sends items over there. It's a slow facility, so they can pick up the slack on our gene work and other diseases when we have issues. You said it's presenting challenges?"

"Let's just say some data has disappeared at unfortunate critical time."

"That's not good."

"No, it's not. But I should be out of here by New Year's," he added, expecting to transition into a discussion of their plans for the evening.

"About that…" she began hesitantly. "We need a change, Brayden. It's been a while coming, and the truth is, I can't stay here any longer. The memories of the past are preventing us—well me, from moving forward."

"You'd like to move?" It was abrupt, but the bureau had offices all over the country. He was top ranked in the region, making the transition possible. "I'm glad you told me now. I have until the end of the year to put in a request for transfer."

She cleared her throat, a mannerism he knew she employed just before she had to deliver hard news to a patient. "I've applied for and been accepted to a job in Idaho. Coeur d'Alene, actually."

"Really? I never knew you'd consider a move that far north. More snow than here in the mountains, I think. Wait, you said you already received an offer?"

"Yes, week before last."

Brayden catalogued his wife's words. She'd been planning this move without his knowledge or input. She'd accepted the job on her own, no discussion with him.

"You're going alone?" he surmised.

"Only for the time being," she clarified. "You can come up and visit when I get settled."

"Laura, you are effectively ending our marriage. Why would I come up and visit?"

"No, not at all. I am changing one aspect of our lives, which I hoped you could understand."

"If you wanted me to understand, you would have talked with me about it before you made the decision, behind my back."

"There was a very good reason."

"Enlighten me."

"I didn't want to distract you from your work."

Brayden wasn't shocked at the end of their marriage, but he was surprised at the manner in which she'd chosen to tell him. Her soft, empathetic side had been slowly stripped away, leaving only her cold intellect and medical skills. Laura was a beautiful, hollow shell of the woman he'd married.

"Why Idaho again?"

"They have a growing medical facility that supports western Montana, southern British Columbia and the entirety of northern Idaho. It has some of the best surgeons in the area, perfect for us."

"Perfect for you," he corrected. He wouldn't be surprised to learn she had met a male physician at some conference who just happened to be located in that town. The notion of her being with another man wasn't a mortal wound, but it did hurt.

"Could you have at least honored our marriage while you were still part of it, after all we've been through together."

"You have no idea how I've honored our marriage," she answered, an uncommon thread of anger in her voice for someone so perennially detached. "And respected it more than you could ever imagine."

"Laura, respect means communication. Friendship means going out to dinner. Marriage means sleeping together, at least occasionally. We haven't done any of those things for months now. Changing environments won't alter that fact."

Two heartbeats of silence were interrupted by the sound of her throat clearing. "Brayden," she said, her tone lower. "There are reasons for everything. Some are not so obvious. I'm not ending our marriage, I'm changing the location. I'm not filing for divorce, pulling money from the bank account or trashing the house. I'm trying to move on, and I want you to do it with me."

"By visiting. You're not asking me to transfer."

"Not immediately, no."

The silence was deafening.

"So, are you really saying this is a trial separation to see how we fair? If so, just be honest about it."

"It's a separation for good reason, but no divorce. No being with other people. I'm with you and I hope you are with me."

"But not in the same city. Laura, I give up. Just don't change the locks."

Since the call ended, he'd done a lot of thinking. Staying together but living apart, taking time to reevaluate and reassess? To a degree, he got that part. People needed space, and it wasn't unheard of to live in different cities for a time. But for how long? And what was the trigger for reuniting?

Brayden ordered room service, leaving half of it on the plate. At four p.m. he called Saachi, hoping for an update.

"It was all entered, the original samples stored away. The analysis is running, and we have matches for the mine, and another person, Joe Draper. Ring a bell?"

"Not at all."

"He wasn't on any of the lists for those who worked on the mine?"

Brayden had the papers in neat piles on his desk. "No, I'm looking at them right now. I guess I'll be adding him."

"Brayden, you know what I'm going to ask next, don't you?"

"I have a pretty good idea. I'll call Forland for a directive on how far we take this. Like you said before, hairs don't place a person at a scene because they can easily be transferred and picked up. But if he really wants us to go one-hundred percent aggressive, we'll need to pull the entire basketball team for an interrogation."

"And testing," Saachi added. She was referring to a lie detector as the start, then continuing to the most aggressive means available.

"That would be normal for adults, when the number one directive is containment."

"That's going to be pretty hard with teens who have parents, don't you think? And the biggy here is that someone died, so the definition of containment might need to adjust."

"Not necessarily. The deceased was an old man taking painkillers. He had cirrhosis of the liver from alcoholism. I agree with going after cold blooded killers, regardless of age, but nothing in this situation supports that."

Saachi paused before speaking. "You aren't concerned about containment as much as getting too aggressive with the teenagers, is that it?"

"Look, I'm all for getting at the truth, but with teenagers, I simply question if it's worth a whole group of kids potentially dying."

"Agreed."

When Kyle greeted Mandy at the front desk, she pointed behind her. "Barrett wants to see you." Kyle moved his shoulders, testing out the muscles. His coach was right. He'd better ease off the pulling, which wasn't going to make Barrett happy, but then again, the man wanted the fourth playoff title as much as anyone else.

"Hey Boss. How was your Christmas?"

Barrett swiveled in his chair, fingers interlaced and resting on his hefty belly. "Better than yours, I hear."

Kyle took his coat off and hung it up, then sat down. "I have five minutes before my shift starts. Entertain me."

"First off, Deputy Hancock told me you got yourself a cool new toy, fell off it like a dimwit, and hurt your shoulder. Is that right?" Kyle nodded. Someone else was now lying for him. "Then I have Ashley Fine marching into my office right at noon, telling me that you need to be promoted to management because you have put in too many long hours shoveling s.h.i.t. out of this pool." Kyle's eyes widened, and he cracked a smile. "True story."

Kyle laughed, the built-up tension bursting from him like helium in a balloon. "Promoted. Awesome. I want to be the employee who sits in your chair. Excellent."

"Not exactly what I thought. What's the real truth here?"

"Other than Ashley following me around and pretending that we are going to run off after high school, get married and attend the same college?" Barrett cocked his head, then shook his head in sympathy. Kyle told him about the ATV, and Barrett asked him about the vehicle's specifications for a few minutes.

"Where in the world did Ashley's demand for a promotion come in?"

"I've been dropping hints that have become a lot less subtle that I want to break up, and she's not getting any of them. Not a single one." He spread his hands. "She must have taken my increasing absence as too much work from you, but I swear boss, I've told her until I'm blue in the face that I need the job, the money and plan to go to college far, far away."

Barrett grunted, looking up at the clock. "You're late. I don't want to fire you unnecessarily."

"And I don't want a desk job. You make me sit inside and I'm quitting." The comment got a chuckle. "But I will need some help pulling on the covers. I did jack myself up pretty bad." He lifted his shirt as evidence.

"Geez, Kyle. You going to be able to play tomorrow?"

"I hope so. The coach is going to try and get me a pass to cover my arms so any scouts showing up won't think I'm an adrenaline junkie."

"Then you better hope they aren't sitting by anyone who knows you. Get going. I'll be here until closing to help you cover the pools."

CHAPTER 40

Deputy Director Forland twirled his pencil as he listened to his senior field officer. Periodically, he wrote a note. *Kids. How far to take the interrogation?* Technically, it was his judgement call on next steps, but given the scrutiny on the project, Janet would ask for a justification, and ultimately, she had the ability to go over or around him.

"I have to get back to you. Need to talk to the NSA first."

"Yes, sir."

He hung up, preparing for the next call. Janet might accuse Brayden of going easy with the teenagers because of his own son's death, which might be valid concern. Still, his argument against a complete round up of the team was sound. If Janet pushed it, Forland had a response.

He placed the call. "Janet Reese." Forland related the events. Hairs in play, several matches, the entire basketball team.

"We are walking close to the edge with this entire town," Forland warned. "We have hairs placing individuals at the scene but no other supporting evidence."

"Which we don't require under these special circumstances," she pointed out. "It's all formality."

"True," he acknowledged, annoyed at being interrupted. "That's what I told the Colorado head of police, O'Connell. Nonetheless, we are at a cross roads. Tomorrow afternoon we will likely have the data set back."

"Fine, then Friday afternoon, gather the team and administer polygraph tests."

"There's an issue with that strategy. It's the team's regional playoff game which starts at 6 p.m. tomorrow. The entire town, plus the ones from the neighboring counties will show up. If you take the winningest team out of commission all afternoon, their parents are going to scream and riot. You want that?"

"No," she said coldly. "The President doesn't want overkill, only containment." The only way to limit the spread of rumor would be to wipe out the citizens. "What about after the game?"

"The parents and even police are going to want to know why."

"Have the local deputy work with the forensics to write up the paperwork so it looks official."

"The timing is going to be tight," Forland pointed out. "The results will come in later afternoon, four-ish, the game at six and over around seven-thirty or eight."

"What about equipment?"

"No idea what's available. I'll get my team on it."

"In the meantime, I'll call my local staff and make sure we have resources in the area."

Forland took a drink of lukewarm coffee before he called Brayden. His approach had worked so far. Reese hadn't opted to call in the Patrol, but that didn't mean she couldn't put another form of officer in place as a backup. She was under no obligation to tell him, other than the pretext of maintaining good will.

Not something the NSA was known for.

Brayden answered and acknowledged the timeline. "It rests on the paperwork for conducting the interviews, with the associated evidence of hairs made clear, correct?"

"That's right. I'll get O'Connell to lean on Deardon and his team so they are on board. Do you need reinforcements for bringing the kids to the station?"

"Sorry, sir," Brayden said, cutting short his laughter. "Have you ever been to a town of five hundred? The station has two rooms, one for each of the officers, and then the front desk, which is no more than a thin barrier to the outside world along with a coffee machine."

"Oh, no room for a mass group interrogation."

"Exactly. Let me work out the details with Hancock after it goes through the chain of command. We are going to be hustling."

"I know you'll do just fine."

"Thank you, Sir. One final question. How much can I share with the local police?"

"This entire situation is about containment. To the degree you think he, or they, need to be aware of what's really occurring, use your judgement. Just keep in mind that whatever you tell can come back to hurt the individual if this takes a wrong turn. Use your discretion."

Brayden understood. Whatever he shared put the recipient at risk. "Yes, Sir. I'll keep you in the loop."

Twenty minutes later, Brayden was on the phone with Deputy Hancock.

"You need to take me through this again, Brayden, slowly, because I can't quite believe what I'm being asked to do."

Brayden reviewed the plan again with Saachi. "The Sheriff wanted to be here, but he still has family in the hospital."

"What about location?" They discussed the space limitations of the police station.

"We need the privacy of a room with a door, and a place where they can wait," explained Brayden.

"Why not just do it at the school?" Saachi suggested. "That way we aren't hauling them to the station. Anyone at the game will just think the players are milling around."

Brayden liked the idea, appreciating Mark's offer to connect with the facilities manager of the school to work out the details.

"I've got the easy part," Mark concluded. "You're the one who gets to hook them up to the testing equipment and get the interviews."

Mark was right. It was going to be the most unique questioning session Brayden had ever led.

On the upside, it will keep my mind off my home life. *What's left of it.*

Things aren't always so obvious? Laura's final words meant to torture him.

He checked his financial accounts. They hadn't budged. He and Laura combined money, one checking and savings. It hadn't even occurred to him to bring up the split of finances. She made more than he did, and her retirement account was triple his government plan. Given her prudent financial nature, she'd probably use one of the on-line divorce services. No kids, no pets.

No life.

Her words continued to nag him. What wasn't obvious? By the time he closed his eyes, he still hadn't answered the question.

CHAPTER 41

Kyle entered the back door to his house, calling for his parents.

"In here," his father answered.

"Hey Kyle, ready for the big game today?" It was Mark, sitting on the couch beside his father, having a beer. It was a small town, after hours in the private home of a local. Had the events of the last week not occurred, Kyle wouldn't have given the situation a second thought. As it was, he knew Mark had something to tell him.

"Am I ever ready for a playoff game? "

"Fair enough. Well, nice catching up Ed. See you at the game tomorrow. Kyle, I noticed that snazzy machine under the carport. Want to show it to me?"

"Sure.

Under the carport, Mark leaned over the ATV.

"Good news and bad," he said in an undertone. "I heard no chatter on the police scanner. Our missing person is just that, presumably gone. I took the liberty of calling the owner of the home to tell them shots were heard and I investigated. Needless to say, they were grateful."

"And so they didn't have to fly back to check things out."

Mark pursed his lips. "That's what a small town officer is for. The health and safety of his community. I already called the cleaners and the window guy. It will be fixed and cleaned up by Saturday."

"That's awesome. Thanks again."

"Now the bad. Friday night after the game, the entire team is going to be held for polygraph testing. Brayden and Saachi will be doing it. Based on how things go, it will proceed to the next level."

Kyle felt a spread of tension from his inner chest outward, constricting his muscles, pulling his shoulders inward. He purposefully pushed back his arms, stretching out the anxiety.

"What does that mean?"

"Unclear. Kyle, I don't know what they're going to ask. Have you ever taken a polygraph test before?"

"No."

"I figured. I'm going to give you information any self-respecting criminal knows, or, for that matter, recreational drug users who have professional careers like a pharmacist. Stay up all night using Vivarin or some other form of caffeine. It makes all your vitals go off the charts and is a lot harder to interpret. Calm people who pass the test are either innocent, or pathological liars who can outwit the test. Everyone else, the guilty or nervous, go the staying-up-all-night route with caffeine pills."

"I'm going to be a disaster for the game."

"Or so amped up you will play like a champ. When you see Brayden and Saachi and myself waiting at the doors, don't freak out. We are going to hang around and then subtly usher the team into another area for the tests."

"Won't the parents or other people see what's going on and get curious?"

"Sure, but we will have the necessary paperwork and it's all going to be legit. The caveat to all of this is if the paperwork isn't completed by the lab beforehand, nothing will go down."

Kyle exhaled, nodding. "All night. Lots of caffeine. Play like a madman and pass the polygraph."

The cop patted his back. "Good man."

Kyle returned to the house and asked his mom for her stash of caffeine pills.

"Don't have any. All out."

It was the day after Christmas, for her just another work day, like any others. "Can I check just in case?"

"You may, but I can tell you I burned through all of them on Christmas Eve when I had to go get your new toy. Sorry."

He called Billy, asking if she had any No Doz, Vivarin or form of caffeine.

"Don't you want sleep before the big game?" she asked, teasing.

"Billy, a simple yes or no. I had a visitor stop by tonight and I just really need to concentrate."

"Hold on," she said abruptly. A minute later, she told him to come over. "You going to walk or ride the ATV?"

"Why? Want to go for a ride?"

"Actually, yes. We have time before the curfew."

"Get your snowboarding outfit and hat. It's cold."

Kyle told his parents he was heading out for a ride, put on his clean snow gear and left. When he stopped the ATV in the alley behind Billy's home, he almost felt like an adult. He'd never had a car in which to pick anyone up, and this was as close as it came.

Billy came out, her goggles and gloves already on. When he felt her hands lock around his waist, he squeezed her thigh. It might be the only time in his life he'd be able to have a girl ride behind him. He was going to make sure it was memorable.

In Denver, the FBI Director had just arrived home and taken off his coat when his cell phone rang. He went directly into the den and closed the double glass doors.

"I've run this by the team, and your strategy is fine except for one thing," said Reese. "We may be making an arrest tomorrow night."

Forland stared out on to the quiet, suburban street. His home was in a development closer to town, new enough to have the modern amenities but the lot retained a few old growth trees. Unfortunately, a branch from one of them was lying across his front lawn and he would need a chainsaw to cut it up.

"Assuming someone fails the polygraph or admits guilt?"

"Yes, that's one of the reasons."

"What else would there be?" Reese didn't immediately respond, and he was losing patience. "Look Janet, are we on the same team or not? This information being given to me in drips and drabs may work on my counterparts, not me. What are you intending?"

"Fair point. We intend on taking the person, or persons, into custody, who is penetrating our servers through the forensics lab in Montrose."

"Come again?"

"It's not credible that data simply wasn't correctly entered into the system or lost overnight."

"Sure it is," he interrupted, fed-up with her unprofessionalism. "You had an employee in your own organization leaking out confidential documents on the election, which was far worse than a first-year agent who wiped out six months' worth of criminal files with a single command. At least my employee could claim stupidity."

"This was not stupidity," she admitted. "I'm suspecting it was intentional, as in one of mine."

Forland gave her points for honesty. "A direct report?"

"Tangentially. We have a group that hired scientists in the medical field. We are narrowing it down now to those who were brought in on a gene sequencing project."

"But you aren't positive."

"No, but we will get it if we trace back the other lead that's come up. We'll get two internal terrorists at once."

"What does that mean?"

"When a person goes against the laws of our country, they are a terrorist. Pure and simple."

Forland thought about what else she didn't say. "You must be sending people to the forensic labs then?"

"Yes, but they won't arrive until around three."

"By that time, they will be assembling the documentation to take in the basketball team."

"That's right. My people will assist yours."

Forland hung up, staring outside, knowing he should feel satisfied they were inching closer to finding the culprit.

If one of the kids turned out to be a match. But then, as Brayden said, even if they got an admittance from a teenager that they were connected to the mine break-in, the true source of the problem was still at large.

Gary heard his wife upstairs in the gym, the whirring sounds of the treadmill confirming her position. He'd not told Brayden about his suspicions regarding the files in the mountain, and Brayden had stopped short of asking, but wondered if he and his agent had guessed the same thing.

It was almost like the whole thing was a set up. A code to get in, yes, but so simple once inside.

Leading a bee to honey. Put out the scent and let the hunter bees find their golden food.

And now Janet had people heading on site, putting them in place just to be prepared. Patrol would kill on sight, her people would handcuff and take away. Who did it was semantics: the person, or persons, would never be seen again.

CHAPTER 42

At seven-thirty a.m., Kyle put on his back-up pair of boarding pants, the black bottoms and red top matching his ATV. He decided to walk to Billy's, craving the cold air. Taking a night's worth of caffeine pills had left him jittery and hot, his temperature feeling close to having the flu, but without the ache.

In the pocket of his weatherproof jacket, he had the cubes. All of them.

He took the backroads to Billy's, knocking as loud as he dared.

"Kyle?" Ty asked through slit eyes.

"Yeah. Sorry, I know it's early. Is Billy awake?"

"Don't know. Come on in."

"Sorry again," he murmured. Ty put up his hand, reminiscent of his daughter, walking away. Doors opened and shut, there was the sound of running water and then Billy appeared. Her hair was half under a hat, half out. Her red flannel pajamas had moose prints on them, antlers and hooves. It was cute and girlish, traits people didn't associate with Billy, including him.

"You're going through with it?" she asked, glancing at him up and down. "Your hands are shaking. Please tell me that's from the caffeine pills and not nerves."

"At this point, I can't tell the difference." He stepped forward, his arms out, wanting Billy against him, appreciating her affection and strength at the same time. He kissed her forehead, lingering. "I don't know when I'll see you again. Maybe later tonight."

"Why not after you speak with Brayden?"

"I'm paranoid of being followed and don't want to be anywhere near here."

She laid her cheek against his chest. "Then come in the front door. It's about as obvious as you can get, and standard for you to order food before a game."

"That's true." They held each other in silence until he pulled back just enough to kiss her again.

"I have something for you." He carefully lifted a tissue-wrapped ornament from the left side pocket of his coat. The snowboarder ornament was different from the one Roy had purchased. He'd asked his mother to make this with a teal snow cap, identical to the one Billy wore.

"It's a mini-you," he said quietly. She held it up, twirling it. "Do you like it?" he asked.

"I love it." When she kissed him, Kyle felt the tears, kissing her harder as they rolled down his cheeks. He felt like he'd touched her heart, the first person to do so in years. He didn't want to leave her, potentially crushing it again in the same way.

"You do realize why I have to speak with Brayden, don't you?"

Her nose brushed up and down against his cheek. "You want to keep me safe. That's why you won't give me back the cubes."

"That's right."

"Please stop by the bar today and let me know how it goes, okay?"

"I'll do my best, but only if it's clear."

When Kyle arrived at the Stagecoach Hotel, he used the lobby phone to call up to Brayden's room.

"Why don't you come up?" Brayden suggested, telling him the room number. As Kyle turned to the elevator, he felt like his heart was literally hitting the inside of his jacket.

Those bloody caffeine pills. He had several in his pocket, knowing that he'd be coming down and need another. At six that morning, he'd started to suffer a crushing headache and finally understood what his parents had been talking about when they mentioned withdrawal. It was brutal until he popped another pill.

He extended his fingers open then shut as he rode the elevator. Rolling his shoulder, it felt less sore, a credit to the non-stop comfrey compress his mother gave him.

Kyle found the right room and knocked. Brayden opened the door, his tie missing, and the gun Kyle expected to see at his belt. "Come on in."

The room had a sitting area by the window, the desk faced the street and a side chair and small coffee table were in front of a love seat. Kyle took the leather chair while Brayden sat by the desk.

"An unexpected visit," Brayden said.

"Really?"

Brayden pressed his lips together, sighing. "No. Not so much."

Kyle put his hands into his pockets and pulled out two sacks, which landed with a thunk on the glass table.

"Two sets," he started. "One has three states, the other six are the masters. Do you want to know what's on them, or do you just want to take them?"

"I already know what's on them."

Kyle shook his head. "I don't think so."

"Why's that?"

Kyle looked out the window, unsure how to bring up sensitive subjects. Should he wait or forge ahead?

"I want you to take these and leave. I know you said that can't happen, but you need to make it happen."

"Kyle, I told you no before, and now it's worse. We have the hairs gathered from the team. The forensics will be done this afternoon. If I were your friend…"

"What?" Kyle asked when Brayden faltered. "You'd tell me to run?"

The FBI agent shook his head. "I'm not sure what I'd tell you. Running would guarantee a search and seizure."

"You're telling me that with or without these cubes, I'm done."

"I'm sorry. I can't do anything else right now."

Kyle looked out the window and up to the mountain beyond. The one that had started this mess. "I guess I'll be taking these right into the hands of the naturalists then. Of course, if I wait long enough, they'll come here again."

"Again?"

Kyle squinted at the man. He obviously didn't know about Roy, and if Kyle told him the whole story, he'd be putting Mark at risk.

I have no choice.

"The night after Christmas, a guy showed up at my home under the guise of buying an ornament. He wanted the cubes, pulled a gun and I shot him. He got away. I don't even care if you know this now, because you're no help at all. I kept my cubes but I should have let him take them. Because I will tell you something right now," continued Kyle, with conviction. "I'm not the only one who's been lied to. So have you Brayden. You have family members who are alive, who you think are dead. You might want to think about that as I'm getting arrested. You will never know the truth, and it will be your own fault." Kyle snatched the sacks up and put them in his pocket. "Be seeing you." A hand was on his right shoulder and shoving him against the wall before he could take a step.

Brayden had him by his neck, his thick fingers easily indenting his flesh. Kyle felt the man's knee push into Kyle's midsection, pinning him tighter against the wall.

"Do you really want this to end now?" Brayden demanded. "Get shoved into the deepest pit in the U.S. for your entire life, or face an anonymous black squad of the Patrol?"

Kyle turned his head, unable to talk. Brayden seemed to understand and moved his thumb slightly.

"Yes, if that's what it takes," said Kyle. "What would leaving here and running away do? You know at least some of what's on those cubes. You're dead along with me. The government wants control, not anarchy. People like Stu and his daughter, they will want to keep their place in life, their protected position and faces. They and lots of other people won't want reality, but I know her sister Ruth will because I saw the before and after."

"What are you talking about?"

"It's on there Brayden. The naturalist I met put some of the data into his software. It pulled up the natural version and then the modified, government version. I saw it with my own eyes, but guess what? Not all of us mutated. Not me. Not some others."

Brayden held him, looking deep within his eyes for the truth.

"I also got data off the masters. It's more than anyone thinks the government would ever keep. Genealogy, family history, facts and lies, mixed together. No one wants to see that Brayden, even you."

"I don't care," Brayden replied, the muscles clenching, his grip becoming tighter.

"Why, because you think you lost a son and a daughter?

Kyle choked when the fingers compressed. "Don't you dare talk to me about what I lost."

"But you are wrong, about two things."

"Shut up."

Kyle kneed Brayden in the groin and shoved with all his force, knocking the man back.

"You think your son committed suicide, but he didn't. The forensics notes said it wasn't a clear cut suicide. The overdose could have been accidental, and he wouldn't even have known it."

"That's ridiculous. Jarod took his own life with a gun," Brayden said, preparing to move forward.

"Wrong!" retorted Kyle. "The forensics examination was black and white. The gunshot happened after he'd been dead. Someone shot him after. Why would they—whoever it was—do that?"

Brayden was breathing heavily. "It can't be."

Kyle took a step forward, his voice a notch lower. "Why not? The cubes in the vault were updated every year. You, your wife and your son are all there, as well as your daughter."

"Don't you talk about my daughter. I will shoot that smile off your face right now."

"Then listen up. We've all been lied to, you more than anyone. Your daughter is alive. I saw her files."

"She died at three. We had her cremated."

"No. Your little girl wasn't cremated. That was someone else's child."

"Shut up!"

"The girl is alive, somewhere in this country. There's no death certificate for her, just the original DNA records which are on the cubes. Why would you help destroy the very thing that could bring her back to you?"

Kyle was uncertain how Brayden was going to handle more revelations, and so he kept one hand out, as if to steady them both.

"I think your wife wanted to give her daughter a chance, but knew that the only way she could manage it was to make it seem as though she had died. Who, more than a doctor, would know how to hide her own daughter?"

"How could she have pulled it off?" demanded Brayden, now wavering.

"I don't know, but if she's half as smart as you, it could be done. Her information said she's a surgeon, as well as a biotechnology research scientist. Is that right?"

Brayden seemed to be in a slight daze, as though the door to a world he didn't know existed was real and he was being asked to step through. Kyle tried to open it further.

"Listen to me," Kyle pleaded. "Are we going to learn that it wasn't a virus planted by foreign countries but from within our own government? And here's something else to think about," he continued. "Those files folders in the mountains were ridiculous. No locks, no nothing. What if the person who told me to go look for them was a plant by the government? I've had seven days to think about this. D was a good guy but a drunk. What if someone told him the codes, and what was in there, knowing he'd be certain to tell someone else. The only thing the government didn't know was who, and they didn't care. So, the codes remained the same, but the files were left open."

"And unlocked."

Kyle saw he was listening, thinking it through. "Yes. I go in, but the choppers are already there, immediately. Soon you're here to investigate, and then what happens? Somehow old D eats his pills up, when he could have done that at any time."

"Was that Billy who visited him?"

"Yes, and she said he was drunk, talking about starting this mess, that he shouldn't have listened and needed to finish it. He was alive and well when she left, and he refused to go with her."

"She thought he would leave with her?"

"That was her plan," said Kyle.

"She's got guts of iron."

"Brayden, what if this whole thing were a set up by the government to draw in the naturalists for a wipe-out fight? We are a small town, miniscule in the grand scheme of things. No one in the entire world is going to know or care if it gets erased, right?"

"And the government gets the naturalists once and for all," Brayden concluded.

"It's the only thing that makes sense," said Kyle earnestly. "I get that you can't let me go because then you will become one of us. I no more want that for you than I did for me or Billy. But what are you supposed to do, deny it, and continue living your life because you can get retirement in a few years?"

Brayden stepped back, feeling old. He worked out the math. Sasha would be almost nineteen now. A mixture of himself and his wife.

"Sit down," Kyle requested. "I'm going to show you on the cubes, because Billy said you wouldn't believe it until you saw it yourself."

"I really like that girl," Brayden said with quiet admiration. "But I can see not as much as you love her."

Kyle's face was somber. "I'll show you what I learned about your daughter if you can keep it together."

"I'll keep the gun on the table, just in case," he said with a smirk.

Kyle smiled, the relief genuine. "Shut the blinds."

CHAPTER 43

"Want a water or something?"

Brayden was in the bathroom, anger and sadness creating a toxic mix of emotions. His eyes stung, his chest felt constricted and a rage unlike anything he'd ever known had created an unstable situation within himself.

"No. Give me a minute." He told himself to breathe through it, push down his emotions and come to a resolution. He was either going to believe this kid, and choose one course of action, or ignore everything he'd seen, do his job and take Kyle in, cubes and all.

At the end of the day, the only thing Kyle had done was listen to the meanderings of an old man. Kyle was curious, just like any teenage boy, but instead of sneaking into his parent's liquor cabinet, he'd gone into a mine, one that was supposed to be empty. Pandora's box, which wasn't to have existed at all, had been discovered and opened. And what was inside was worse than a civilization-crippling virus. Brayden agreed with Kyle, it included the antidote, which was likely feared at the highest levels of government. His own boss had doubts about the NSA and the ease of entering the mine.

It had told him something else. The President was in on it. The NSA didn't operate without his consent.

Kyle had showed him the files on himself, Jarod, Sasha and his wife. It wasn't inconceivable that Laura played a role in his daughter's supposed death, but how could she have left their child to be raised by someone else?

Because if this was all true, Laura knew that if Sasha were to survive and give birth to a baby of her own, the medical records would have to be falsified. Laura had clearance as a research scientist. She had consulted for the government early in her career, during the time she'd given birth to both children.

Yes, it was feasible.

Laura had relinquished her little girl to someone else, doing what she had to do; what she knew he couldn't do.

And she was right. If I'd known, I wouldn't have let it stand.

He cringed thinking of their last conversation. In light of this new information, Laura was right to become offended when he'd accused her of having no respect. All that she'd done was for the family and him. She'd kept their daughter alive, *somewhere.*

Idaho. What part did that play in their family?

"Do you think she knows where your daughter is?" Kyle asked from the other room.

Brayden washed his face. "No idea."

"Know what I think? I think that you were set up for this by your boss, or someone in your organization. If they know this about you and your family, and then at some point they use the information against you, what do you do? Who do you choose? Maybe they've been tracking you this entire time."

Brayden walked out of the bathroom, rubbing the towel around his face. The kid might be right again.

"Or," Kyle continued, "they think your wife is involved, they tracked it, set a trap, and used you to lure her in."

"That's awfully far-fetched."

"Is it really? Think about this another way," Kyle continued, standing and pacing, sounding a lot more like an FBI agent than a high school senior. "Billy was born in Denver, at Denver Medical. It was in her birth notes on the cube. That's where Laura works, right? Okay. Perhaps, just perhaps, Laura saw what was happening. Things were going wrong with other babies, or she wanted to give her daughter a chance. What if she found a way to reverse the code?"

"You are really stretching," Brayden cautioned, but even as he said the words, it wasn't that impossible. Laura was brilliant. To his knowledge, her clearance had never been revoked. The fact that he worked for the Bureau made the two of them tied at the hip to some degree.

"She couldn't tell you about your daughter, because it went against everything you stood for. The government. Toeing the line. You might have turned her in."

"Where is the tie back to Billy?"

Kyle shook his head. "I don't know, but this can't be coincidence. Your wife was the person who delivered Billy. The records of what happened to Billy's mother are missing. Your daughter is supposed to be dead, but no record confirms it. Maybe we can get more information off the cubes."

Kyle turned to Brayden, his look ashen. "Do you think those cubes have triggers on them? Oh, man…I have to get back now."

"Tell me what you're thinking," Brayden requested.

"I left the metal square from that guy Roy plugged into my laptop. I got distracted rolling the cubes in my fingers and then learned all the other information, but the light had turned from red to blue."

"It was transmitting," said Brayden, pressing his lips together.

"But I didn't have the cubes on it."

"Might not matter. If the laptop was active, there's no telling what they put on your laptop or took off."

Kyle was half-way across the room, when Brayden put a hand on his shoulder. "Whatever's been done is done. Rushing back won't change it now." He could see the kid was distraught, but they had to make plans for tonight.

"I'm sorry, but I have to go anyway. Brayden, I'm sorry your wife might be a naturalist. That's going to make things hard for you."

He gave a grim smile. "It's already a mess. Kyle, you don't know what's going to happen tonight. We may show up and take the team, or just you. I don't know." He caught the look in the kid's eyes. "You were already planning on running, yes? You think you can escape the Patrol?"

"Absolutely."

"Why are you so confident?"

"If a group of people can dig a city-sized hole in the Wasatch mountains for their genealogy records, the naturalists can build and use an underground network to transport and hide those who need to avoid the Patrol."

"You've already gotten in touch with them?"

"Billy's working on it."

"You're going to risk this guy Roy showing up again? He might kill you for real this time, Kyle."

The kid narrowed his eyes. "I already have a list of people trying to kill me Brayden, and that includes you." His comment almost got Brayden to smile. "Brayden, you haven't mentioned one other possibility in all this. If the trap has been set, and others are coming in to take out all the connections to the mine, why wouldn't they take you?"

For that question, Brayden had no answer.

CHAPTER 44

Kyle jogged down Main Street, unconcerned if anyone saw him. The hard snow was packed, his boots making slight indents as he ran. At eight-thirty in the morning, the town was just coming alive. Shop owners were brushing off their doorsteps while visitors bundled up in down-filled jackets made their way to the coffee shops.

Kyle saw a police car at the end of town, slowly driving up the street. He figured Hancock was inside, but he saw the Sheriff instead. Kyle waved back, and in five more minutes was home. Stu was outside, shoveling the snow off the path from the sidewalk. On impulse Kyle cut across the road, waving to an on-coming motorist.

"Stu," Kyle called. His informal greeting created a raised eyebrow on the man's face. It's time, thought Kyle. No matter what happened, in a couple weeks, he was going to be eighteen, an adult, and he wasn't going to be calling this man Sir forever.

"Kyle," he greeted formally, standing his shovel straight in front of him.

Kyle attempted to control his breathing. "Can we find a time to talk about…to talk privately, when you have a chance?" He glanced over Stu's shoulder purposefully, hoping the man would get the hint.

"Is it urgent?"

"Yes, well, no. But it's important."

"Is it about college?"

"No, Sir," he answered automatically. Old habits die hard. "It's about Ashley."

"No wedding proposal I hope."

"I need your advice. I'm going to return the clothes that she gave me, but I want to be respectful of her, your wife and honestly, yourself."

"They're yours, son. Purchased for you."

"I know, but it was too generous."

"We have money to spare, Son. Don't worry about it." He began shoveling again, probably expecting Kyle to leave.

"I do worry about it, and…to be honest, it's not right to keep something when it's not received with the same intent as the giver." Kyle watched the older man stop his motions, his head down. He envisioned Stu trying to compose himself before he went in and got his shotgun. "I really cared for Ashley but things have changed. What she wants and I want are not the same. I thought she might change or evolve this year, but she hasn't. In fact…" Kyle hesitated to say the words, then plowed forward. He didn't have the time in his life to avoid issues. "The fact is that Ashley and I are two different people with different goals and ideals."

As her father looked up, Kyle braced himself for fury. What he got was understanding. "I saw some of that the other night."

Encouraged by his even tone, Kyle continued. "The more I talk reality, she reverts back to going to school nearby, staying home with her parents and starting a family. I am years away from contemplating any of that."

"I got that too."

Kyle glanced to his right. The traffic was picking up; perhaps locals from the surrounding areas coming to spend a day in town, to participate in the tailgate party.

"Look, I really like you and Britt and Ruth. The entire family actually…"

"But you're not in love with Ashley."

He thought of Billy and Brayden's comment.

"Sir, I'm not even sure I understand what real love is. Anyway, I wanted you to know first because I can't do this anymore. It's not fair for her and not right for me."

Thankfully, Stu nodded his head. "How are you going to tell her?"

"I haven't figured that out yet. I want to do it before the game." He dreaded winning and being on the receiving end of a game winning hug, the entire audience cheering. "If you have any suggestions, I'm all ears."

"I can tell you no one has ever broken up with her before," he said dryly. "She's going to be pretty upset."

"Hmm. I'm off work today because the coach wants me to take it easy before the game. Maybe lunch? Or before?"

"You want to get this over with, don't you?"

"It's going to be awful no matter when I tell her. At least early in the day she might have Ruth here to talk to her. That might help. How about right after she gets up?"

"Sure. Let's say ten," Stu said, pushing the tip of the shovel into the snow. He paused and looked up. "Then she might get her appetite back before lunchtime."

"Stu, Sir. I appreciate you…being cool about this. I don't want to hurt her. It wasn't and isn't my intention."

"I know, Kyle. You're a good young man. To be honest, you've done a better job with her than any other boy in this town possibly could have. I only hoped it might have lasted a little longer."

"I am sorry about that. I just can't be who she wants."

"No, you can't. See you at ten."

Kyle looked both ways then jogged across the street. One hard conversation down, another to go.

Kyle rushed in through the back door, almost missing the sticky note.

Dishwasher is down. Will trade you food for services. Bring your metal coaster. Ty.

"Looks like I'll be going up to Ty's," he said out loud, then seeing his father to the left, he jumped. "You've already been for your walk?"

"Yep, left and returned before you. How's the shoulder today? You look a little off."

"Well Dad, you'd be proud of me. I did the deed." He walked to the dining table, resting his hand on the back of the chair. "I spoke with Stu. Straight up told him I was no longer going to be with Ashley."

"Well, you're alive," his father drawled.

"Dad," Kyle moaned, rolling his eyes up to the ceiling. "I'm going back at ten to speak with her. He didn't say it, but I think he's going to prep her a bit for me. Or not. Whatever."

"Seriously, was he okay to you?"

"He was great. I'll tell you all about it later."

"What's going on now? I thought you were supposed to be nice to your arm today for the big game tonight."

"I am, but my fingers work just fine and I have to check my computer."

"Can't. Your mom took it."

"What? When?"

"She said she needed it for her meeting today. She's with her glass distributor in Montrose and had to place orders on the spot. You know it's the only way she can do that, same as always."

His dad didn't understand his frustration and for good reason. They'd always shared the laptop, but in reality, his mom only needed it once a or twice a month. Why did she need it today?

Kyle left and went to his room, relieved to see the metal square on the table where he left it. The lights were dark, but as Brayden said, it was too late.

He turned right around and walked through the kitchen "I'm going to head up to Ty's."

"You coming back before you have the ending-it showdown with Miss Fine?"

"Not helping, Dad," Kyle muttered, hearing his father's low laughter.

He cut through the back and used Potosi to reach Billy's back door, knocking on the restaurant loading door. Dan answered.

"You here for pre-playoff game food?" the chef asked.

"I wish. No, Ty said a washer is down or something."

Dan waved him in. "Must be in his home. We're up and operational in the kitchen." Kyle said he'd go through the back and check with Billy, leaving Dan in the hallway.

Billy answered the door, dressed in jeans and a black turtleneck, her hair contrasting with a deep shade of orange lipstick. He was about to remark on her sexy look, but caught her eyes and simply nodded.

"Hurry," she said, closing the door behind him. The Christmas music had been replaced with hip-hop, the beat matching her step as she went quickly into the living room. Her computer was up and running, the black screen with green letters ominous.

"Is that what I think it is?"

"Yes. Sit. First, how are you feeling?" So intense was her scrutiny that he felt momentarily insecure. "You've been up all night, I'm assuming, taking your pills. Jittery? Weak?"

"Jittery yes, but I had enough strength to shove Brayden to the wall, so I have something left in me."

"Crap, Kyle. What happened? Hurry, I have things for you."

Kyle replayed the entirety of the events, concentrating on all that he'd learned the night before, which was new to Billy.

"We'd never talked about where you were born," Kyle said, a bit defensively. "I didn't want to intrude on your past, but—"

"Stop. Don't go there. You know more of my life than I probably do at this point, and if anyone is going to screw me, I'd like it to be you." Kyle blinked at her words. "No, not that way, duh. I'm talking informationally. I agree with Brayden, the connection between his wife and my mother are a stretch, but then seven days and six hours ago, everything I now know to be reality was also a stretch, so who's to say."

"You don't want to talk more about it?" Kyle asked, worried.

"No, and it's not because it doesn't deserve a conversation. It's because we have other things to worry about—the most important is right here, in front of me. Look."

She directed him next to her, and they sat close, the laptop across their connected legs.

"I accessed the dark web and had a message waiting for me."

"Was that safe?" he interjected. "Shouldn't you have been at the library or something?"

She shook her head impatiently. "No, that's the whole point remember? It's encrypted. I could be sitting anywhere."

Kyle didn't want to offend her, but he had to be honest. "But Billy, Roy said you were smart enough to contact him but not smart enough to keep your location a secret."

"He's an idiot," she said dismissively. "I purposely put my location with the IP address line so he could figure it out, and then I followed it up with telling him the city closest to where I live. He had to come here to transfer the data anyway. My one and only mistake was I *did* use the public library, and he, or one of his friends, hacked into the library's camera system which stores its data on the cloud. I failed to wear a wig or large enough hat, and he caught me by connecting the time of our correspondence with the video."

"How do you know all this?"

"Because he's not stupid, and he's clearly not dead. He tracked me down, got the sales records for my computer from the stinking warranty number, which he also had to have hacked, and bang. I had a message waiting for me and he included this video." They watched the minute-long clip of her sitting down at the library's computer.

"You're done for," Kyle said blankly.

"If I was done for, I'd already be gone. They want to trade keeping my identity secret for the cubes you still have. And before you ask, I'd do it right now if we could get the data off them, but those cubes are solid state. I can't transfer the data and Roy couldn't make sense of them."

"Doesn't matter now. We have to give them over. When?"

"Forget when and listen a little more. I offered a compromise."

"Are you kidding me?" Kyle interjected, incredulous. "There is no compromise. We keep you safe and out of this."

"Sorry to be the brilliant one here, but we have the negotiating upper hand, and since we are negotiating with my identity, I feel more than qualified to do so. May I continue?"

Kyle worked to keep the pressure in his chest from erupting, and nodded.

"Okay. So, when I said I'd compromise, he asked if you still had the square pad. I said yes. I guessed he could hook me up with the software application he was trying to use for the data transfer, and we could do this remotely. He agreed." She held out her palm and he placed it within. "But before I do this, it's my turn to share with you what Roy told me."

Kyle listened, his eyes growing wide at what she had to say. Billy's identity had been anonymous until they saw the video. It wasn't hard to track her down using visual identification software, matching her to the high school, street and then her family line.

"The naturalists did a family search on me and found Roy."

"What? You're…related?"

"He's an uncle, Kyle. My mother's brother." Kyle thought about the empty files on her mother's side. They had been completely non-existent, her mother, mother's parents, siblings…nothing.

"Now that you told me my files were completely empty, this is why. Someone went into the records and wiped them out. Was it Brayden's wife or someone else? Don't know. For now, it's not important. They got a hold of Roy, who was and is, a leader within the naturalist movement."

Kyle thought about his skin tone now. It was a shade darker than Billy's, but very similar. The noses were totally different, and the hair color as well, but Billy had her father in her as well, which accounted for hair, eyes and other facial features.

"He didn't know where I was until I got on line."

"I almost killed your uncle," he said, only half-kidding.

A random thought came to him, but he was sensitive to Billy's feelings.

"Yes?" she asked.

"Did he…your mom. Did that come up?"

"No. Right now, we are dealing with the here and now, not dredging up the past." Subject closed.

"You're telling me you trust him implicitly because he says he's your uncle, which may be true because of a slight family resemblance, and now you are ready to transfer the files. Not that I disagree, but he's really going to leave you alone once you do this?"

"No. He's coming here again."

"Wait, what?!"

"I'm going to transfer the files in a few minutes, Kyle. On a side note, the shot went through his side. Lots of blood but it missed every major organ and the bones. It was more of a flesh wound really."

He sounded like a tough old bird to Kyle. "Tell me why he's coming back? To finish the job on me?"

"You're not worth that much dead," she quipped, giving him a nudge. "According to what they've learned on the dark web in the last twenty-four hours, Ouray is going to be hit with a post-apocalyptic mess this evening with the interrogation, and if it goes as planned, you and I will need to get the heck out of here."

Billy thought of his mom, dad and Ty. They'd be put through the wringer if their children went missing. They knew nothing, but would be deemed guilty by association.

He checked the time. "You are going to take me through this again, and then we are going to figure out what to do tonight, but before that, it's my turn for one last reveal."

Billy leaned back slightly. "What? You think you can out-inform me?" she teased. "After what I just gave you? Bring it on." Her challenge brought a smile to his lips. Once he told her about the conversation with Stu, and his planned discussion with Ashley, he turned smug.

"I think I just proved you wrong."

"And I'm really glad of it. Let's take a brief pause to celebrate you beating me. For once."

They were still smiling when their lips pressed together.

CHAPTER 45

Walking into Stu's house felt like entering a funeral home where he was the director, guiding Kyle to the appropriate waiting area: the front room. The only difference was that he wasn't really there to mourn; the visit was going to be a cause for personal celebration.

"Did you say anything to her?" Kyle asked Stu.

"Not a word. Put those right here," he suggested, referring to the packages Kyle held.

"Hey Kyle," Ruth said as she walked into the room. He stood, and received a genuine hug from Ashley's sister. "You look like you've seen a ghost."

"Yeah, a very live one who can give me the Heimlich if I need it," he quipped, unable to stop thinking of the image he'd seen on Roy's screen. Ruth had a wonderful personality. Every guy in a fifty-mile radius would be chasing her if the government hadn't stolen her face.

"You here to see Ashley? By the way, did she ever thank you for the bird feeder?"

"Come to think of it, no. Not really. That probably tells me how much she appreciated it."

Ruth glanced over her shoulder. "That's Ash for you. Will it crush you if I take it? I love those things and handmade ones are really hard to get."

"Be my guest. I'd rather have a person appreciate a gift and use it then ignore it or throw it away."

"Kyle?" Ashley called from the other room.

"That's my cue."

"Hey, Ruth, uhm, the reason I'm here…you're going to find out soon enough. It's not working out with Ashley and me."

"It was pretty obvious to everyone but my mom and Ashley."

Kyle's relief was genuine. "You'll still fix me up if I come in your clinic, right?"

"Yes, maybe with a girl as well. You need someone older and wiser."

I already have one that's wiser, he thought happily.

It was good his mind was in a positive place, because Ashley's face turned down the moment she saw the packages in the foyer.

"What are these doing here?' she asked.

"Ash, we need to talk." She glanced over at him, a wariness in her eyes. "In private." Ruth left the room with a little wave and Kyle closed the door behind her. He turned to find Ashley sitting on the couch, legs crossed, arms folded. He sat on the side chair adjacent to her.

"You aren't even going to sit by me."

"Ashley," he began, leaning forward, his elbows on his knees. "I'm returning the gifts because it was too much. The clothes are nice and I really appreciate it, but it's not right."

"Why?" she asked coldly. "I already told you I don't expect much, and you agreed. You got me a bird feeder."

Kyle suppressed a flash of anger. "My mother spent hours making that for you, Ashley."

"And I spent hours shopping for you," she retorted. "I understand," she continued, slowing her words. "You don't feel equal."

There was no easy way around it. "No, I don't feel like we are a good match for each other." Her eyes widened, then narrowed. Whether it was to hold in tears of sadness or anger, he couldn't tell. "It's not right to keep the gifts under those circumstances."

For a few moments, she continued to stare at him, then she turned away, looking out at the gifts. "What a waste of time," she said in disgust. "What has happened to you in the last week? First you get injured, then you start ignoring me, then you start complaining all the time about having to work. I know you have to work and I don't, but that never bothered you before."

"Things change Ashley, and one of the biggest things is where we were and where we're going. You want to leave and come back, I don't. I never want to return to this town except to visit my parents once or twice a year."

"Don't you think I know that?"

He took a deep breath. "Ashley, you're not fooling anyone, not me, not Ruth and certainly not your parents. You want to come back here and have kids. End of story. I would be lying if I pretended I share those goals. I don't."

She turned away again, this time, her eyes were glassy and lips pressed thin. "But you have years of college. Things may change."

Kyle interlaced his fingers. "Not for me Ashley. It's better to do this now rather than letting things go further over the next few months and then breaking up anyway. At least this way…" he regretted starting the sentence. There was no diplomatic ending that wasn't going to offend her.

"This way, what?"

"We just finish the year as friends," he finished lamely.

"*Friends?*" she hissed, her voice raising.

"Yeah. Friends."

"I don't have friends who are guys. I have a single boyfriend. Or used to."

"Well, that's too bad. We were friends before we started dating. But if that's what you want, I'll respect that."

"Sure, Kyle. Just like you respected me too much to touch me this entire year. I should've known."

Kyle looked down at his fingers, rolling his thumbs. This conversation was digressing quickly and he needed to get out before she escalated it into a fight. They'd never had one before, but he could see her temper and tongue rising to the occasion.

He stood. "Take care, Ashley."

She stayed seated. "That's it? Now you're just going to leave? You can't even give me a good bye kiss?

"I'll let myself out." He expected an explosion of words behind him, and was sure he'd have gotten it if her father hadn't appeared as he opened the door. "Hello, Sir."

"Leaving already?" he asked.

"Yes, Sir."

"Good luck tonight, Kyle."

"You coming to the game?"

"It's the playoffs. We'll be there. Ruth and Greg will be joining us." He extended his hand, and Kyle shook it, grateful his relationship with the man wasn't going to change.

The relief Kyle felt as he crossed the street was immense, the burden of a concrete sack weighing him down. He was sure it was his imagination, but his shoulder seemed to ache less.

Of course, his butt would be dragging on the snow and he'd feel like he was going to pass out from exhaustion after the game due to lack of sleep, but it had to be done.

Kyle noticed the parking spaces around the perimeter of the pool were full, and vehicles were starting to occupy the spaces along the road, to and from the town.

Instead of going home, he walked to Ty's. He was a local who wanted chicken wings. It was his God-given right, and he had ten bucks in his wallet. Ty greeted him with his typical head nod. "Extra wings if you can today," Kyle asked. The bar was half-full, most of the patrons sitting near the back where the acoustic on the television were better and the room darker. Kyle sat up front, checking out the activity on the street, wondering where Brayden was, and what Saachi had found. No, it would be four or five more hours before the testing was confirmed.

Last night, Billy told him Roy was going to be in the auditorium. He'd be ready to take her if the Patrol showed up and arrests were made.

"Hey," Billy greeted. She put down two plates of food. "I'll be right back."

She went to the counter and ordered up two cokes, grabbing three packets of ranch and ketchup.

In their corner in the front, he gave her the play-by-play of the conversation with Ashley, and Stu's words before and after.

"That girl is so dense. I don't know how you stayed with her for so long."

"I told you before. I didn't know what I was missing."

"A wonderful cliché."

"Clichés can be true. That's why people use them." Billy smiled. "I know you can't believe it happened, but it did."

"It's not that. I can't believe we'll have about five hours of coupledom."

His mood dropped, the emotional helium let out of his happy balloon. "About five hours until Brayden will know."

"And he's going to tell you how? He can't, unless he incriminates himself."

"He's smart. He'll figure out a way." Kyle stopped eating, wiping his hands and taking a drink. "Billy. Would you go back to your house with me?"

She assessed his sudden mood change, eyes roving his face. With Ashley formally over and done with, he didn't want to hide how he felt. Since it wasn't safe to display his affection in public, he needed to do it in private.

"Really?" she quietly teased.

"Look, I'm not going to get you pregnant if that's what your worried about." She giggled in response, his own laughter deep and full. He covered the top of her hand with his. In that moment, all the craziness of his life quieted down and he had a moment of fulfillment.

Billy's eyes darted and she muttered under her breath. She slid her hand to her coke and kept the half-smile on her face. "Look normal."

"Hey Kyle." It was Mario, with Ben following behind him. "Grabbing a bite?"

"Yep, couldn't wait until the next practice."

Mario stared at Billy, who ignored him. "What else are you doing?"

Kyle laughed. "Breathing. You know, the normal." Ben's attention was on the flat screen game, but he chuckled at Kyle's response. "Anything else?"

"Actually, remember our conversation yesterday? I made good on it. You're welcome to make your play now, if you know what I mean."

That caught Mario off guard. "You're kidding."

"If you want to find out, why don't you keep walking. I'm going to finish my meal."

"Mario, this is the second time you've had to put your jaw up in my presence," said Billy. "As much as the look can be relatively sexy on the right person, I'd prefer you not drool on my food."

At this, Ben let.out a full-blown laugh. "She's funny. I'll give her that."

"Hilarious," slurred Mario, moving his jaw back and forth. His eyes went back and forth between Kyle and Billy, like he still didn't believe the two were at the same table.

"Well?" prompted Kyle. "The clock is ticking."

"Right. Maybe later."

"See you guys at 5," Kyle reminded them.

The two headed down the street. Kyle doubted Mario had the nerve to back up his talk about Ashley, but at the dance, he would have no such worries. He expected Ashley would show up, if only to try and make Kyle jealous and regret what he'd just left behind.

He looked at Billy. What he had before him is so much better.

"I don't think I got an answer to my previous question," he said quietly.

"You didn't need one."

"Brayden, from the looks of it, we have a match on two of the basketball players," said Saachi. "But we did it blind, so I'm waiting." Brayden understood. They were conducting an impartial match set, where personal opinion wouldn't play a role in the outcome.

"You're taking extra care," he complimented.

"I only do this when I've met the people and know the background on the case. I don't want to be accused of bias."

"How much longer?"

"Thirty minutes tops." That would give them an hour to create the forms required for the parents to read and sign, get back to the game and be in position to talk to the players after the game.

"What did you find with that Joe the miner guy?"

"That he was very drunk in preparation for the big game tonight and could hardly keep his eyes open."

"Gotcha. Have you heard any more from Forland? No one's showed up here yet, and from what you told me, I was expecting someone."

"Me too. But I'm not told every detail. Where do you want to meet me? Up here or do I come down there?"

"Stay. Let's connect at the hotel at 4:15 unless you hear otherwise."

Brayden hung up, then texted his wife. He'd been rehearsing his lines, every word he planned to say to her. He used the bathroom and waited. At the prescribed time, she called him.

"I've been thinking about our last conversation, and I want to apologize. I am sorry if I offended you with my comment about respect. I have had no idea what you have been through."

"No, you haven't."

"Laura. I'm telling you now, I've thought through our conversation, and I mean, *a lot.* Every word. Every detail. And I..." he paused, uncertain of saying too much in a digital world. "I'll come visit you in Idaho when I can. At my earliest convenience." His wife was silent. "You're sure we won't see each other before then?"

She cleared her throat. Could it be that was her way of sending him a message? There was so much to say, so much to talk about. He had to make it easier for her. "Oh, right, in our last conversation you said you'd be up in Idaho by New Years. If that changes, let me know, and send me the address so I can look it up. Sound good?"

"Yes, that sounds good."

"Laura, one more thing. It will be really nice to be together again, and maybe this next year as a family."

Her pause this time was much longer. "Yes," she whispered, her voice breaking.

"I know it's been hard, and I'm sorry I didn't understand." He heard her quiet sobs, his own heart wrenching for the years of suffering she'd endured alone, with him but unable to communicate what she'd done. "We'll make it through this, okay?"

"Yeah."

"Laura, I love you. I never stopped."

"Me either."

Brayden brushed his eyes, the love for his wife resurging like a whale that had been deep in the ocean, now coming up for air. With it came a rising sense of anger. He'd started to accept that things were not as they seemed, first with the mine. It was a set up. And now they were going to help nail a kid who was being used by one, or maybe two parties.

He called up Saachi after he turned on the scrambler.

"What's up?" she asked.

"I have a theory and I need confidence between two peers. Can you do that?" He waited while she thought about it. The sentence and phrases were code within the Bureau that someone wasn't to be trusted within the organization, or the government at large, and if you couldn't keep your mouth shut, it wasn't personal. It was job safety, security and ignorance. But to accept under those terms and conditions meant you'd go to your grave without sharing the secret.

"Yes. You have it."

Brayden started with the truth about Kyle. The wallet. The slide down the mountain. What were on the cubes, and the fact that Kyle had likely been told about the mine by the now deceased miner. He finally related his theory about the ease of entering the mine and the lack of security all being a trap to entice the naturalists to the town. "Kyle takes the fall and anyone left in the town is collateral damage," she surmised.

"Including us," he finished.

"Which is why your telling me."

"I like you Saachi. And it doesn't make sense that your files just up and get wiped out. Now the NSA has people on their way to you, and then what? Will they come here tonight, to oversee our interviews with the team?"

"I have an interim solution."

"You want to share it with me?"

"Unsafe." That word, when used between two agents in the Bureau, meant one thing, she was going to act in a way contrary to Bureau rules, and if he knew, he'd be implicated.

"See you at the same time. Around 4:15."

"See you then."

Brayden hung up, telling himself it was a waste of time to hypothesize about what she was going to do. He was the field agent, she was the forensics specialist. He needed to concern himself with wrapping this investigation up and finding a way to tell his boss he needed a transfer out of state.

But what about Kyle? He wondered if Saachi's plan involved him.

CHAPTER 46

The short, stop and start screeching of shoe treads against the glossy basketball court was the only sound heard during the warm-ups. The opposing team from Ridgeway was on the other side of the court, their white and green uniforms blurs in Kyle's peripheral vision.

He made a jump shot from the three-point line, sinking it.

"Save it for the game," muttered Mario as he dribbled by, then taking his own shot near the three-point line. He missed.

It was still forty minutes before the start, but the gym was already half-filled. The Ridgeway team on the east side of the gymnasium, the supporters wearing white or green with colored flags in hand. The townspeople from Ouray were mainly in black and orange. Kyle had always wondered why the officials had chosen Halloween colors for the school; the decades-old joke about the team coming to life on a full-moon was worn and tired.

Sort of like me.

His body was high on adrenaline, his eyes dry from the lack of sleep. Ever present were Mark's words on beating the polygraph test. As he dribbled, Kyle glanced at the doorways. He caught sight of Mark walking past with a box against his chest.

Equipment for interrogation. He missed a dribble, Ben easily stealing it away. He ran to catch up, trying to keep his eyes focused and not at the doorway. When the imposing figure of Sheriff Deardon appeared, Kyle felt comfort and concern. The man parked himself near the main entrance, greeting the increasing throng of spectators.

Kyle wondered if Mark had told Deardon the latest. He suspected not. It would place the Sheriff in a precarious situation.

Kyle felt the sweat drip down the side of his ribs. The long-sleeved, black undershirt was breathable, but it was still hot. He was unused to the texture, but was infinitely grateful to be wearing it. Coach had received the medical exception for the shirt, but the referee had warned him that if the other team really wanted to make an issue, the shirt would have to come off. Small town rules.

He made another shot, the start clock ticking as they ran up and down the court. He swayed, felt a wave a light headedness and went to the bench, directly to the Gatorade. His mother had made him three sausage and eggs patties for lunch, and he'd topped it off with bowl of cereal. Odd, but his body craved the sweetness of the cornflakes and dried blueberries.

"You okay?" his coach asked in an undertone.

"A little lightheaded, to be honest."

His coach took out an energy boost protein pack from the cooler and poured the yellow crystals into Kyle's cup. "You take it easy once we are ahead you understand?" Kyle nodded, gulping down the drink.

Ten minutes later, the team assembled in the locker room, listening to the chanting of the crowd and the start of the introductory music. Instead of a traditional band, it was hip hop, banging and high intensity. With only fifty-six upper classman total, he'd never had the experience of live music, but that was just fine with him.

"The entire corner of the state is here," Mario said, nudging his right shoulder. It didn't hurt, but it was still a little sore. "And your stable of girls."

"Girls aren't horses," he retorted. He'd seen neither Ashley or Billy as he made his way from the gym floor to the locker room. "You can have your pick of the fillies at the dance after."

Unless we are in a room hooked up to sensors on our heads and arms.

The coach gave his final words of motivation as the music hit a crescendo. While the other team was announced, Kyle joined his teammates in placing his hands on top of the coach's and brought their arms up to the center of the room. When the Ouray Trojans were announced, Kyle led the team out of the room, the other guys following him in a line. The cheers were deafening. The team collected in the center then formed a line on the sidelines. As the players on the opposing team were introduced, Kyle surreptitiously glanced around, looking at the doorways and over to the sides. When the announcer cut to his team and his name was called, he turned around, looking up into the stands. Billy was on his far right, third row up, sitting with Ty. He saw his parents, right in front of them. He felt other eyes on him, probably Ashley or Stu. In another moment, he saw Ruth, sitting beside Greg.

Moments later, the coin was tossed, they won, and he was at center court. The game had begun.

Brayden had been waiting in the car since 3:45 p.m., unconcerned he'd not heard from Saachi. At four, when she should been over half-way to Ouray, he called her phone. No answer. He sent her a text, but got no response. Then he phoned the land line of the forensics lab. It was out of service.

He stood behind the others waiting to enter the school. Worst case scenario was the Patrol came to town, confiscating everything and were now on their way. Second to this was the NSA was already here and had taken over the investigation. Did he stay and wait or did he go down and check on the situation himself?

Inside, Brayden glanced through the open doors and saw Kyle catching the rebound, passing the ball to a teammate and running down the court. Brayden turned left, looking for the signs to the science room. It was where Hancock had told him he would be setting up the equipment.

"Any casualties?" Mark was on the phone, his eyes dark. Brayden waited. "You sure you don't need reinforcements? Yes. Got it." Finished with the call, Mark explained. "The forensics lab is up in flames. Two casualties and two others taken to the hospital with serious burns on Saachi. Her forearm, neck and three-quarters of her jawline."

Brayden was stunned. There was no world in which he could imagine Saachi would take her own life or those of others to save one kid in a small town.

"I've never used a gun on a person in my life," Mark began, "but I'm telling you—"

Brayden stopped him with a hand on his arm. It was clear how the man felt about Saachi. He didn't need to voice his potential actions out loud. Brayden quickly thought through his options. They were few.

"I'm going to tell you the full story," Brayden began quickly. "But we don't have much time. I'm not sure who else is going to be showing up here or what's going to go down."

Mark's eyebrows drew closer together, sensing that he'd either been lied to or purposefully misinformed. "Don't take it personally," Brayden prefaced. "Deardon doesn't know as much as you do by virtue of him being gone but also because it's on a need to know basis. Forland has authorized me to communicate what's required as necessary, but I'm telling you right now, full disclosure puts you in jeopardy. Do you understand?"

"I do."

"I hope so, because I had just shared this information with Saachi last night and now she's in the burn ward. Are you sure about this?"

Mark put a palm on his holster, his face angry. "Someone has already come in this town trying to hurt its people. I'm ready."

"Problem is, we don't know who *they* are."

The first quarter ended with the Ouray Trojans up by eight, and half-time started with them down by 2, 42-40.

It was a running game; Kyle's legs were fine, but his head was light and his arms were sore. He wasn't missing shots—yet, but he felt his energy going down. During half-time, the bumping music played as the crowd chanted. The coach was talking offensive plays and changing the formation.

Back on the court, third quarter started off with a rough foul against Mario, who made his first shot and missed his second, bringing the score within one. A player from Ridgeway got the rebound, shoved Mario who pushed back, sending the player into the post. He got called for a penalty and five-minute suspension. The Ouray crowd booed the other player while the Ridgeway supporters booed Mario, the noise in the small gym amping up the emotions of the players of both teams.

The play got rougher, more fouls were called. At the end of the third quarter, Kyle's team was up eight points. They were heading into the home stretch when a time out was called. Kyle waited with his teammates as the referee spoke with the other teams' coach, then called Kyle's coach over. His coach looked down at the ground, a grimace on his face and Kyle knew what it meant. The next moment he was motioned over.

"You are getting a one-minute penalty for the shirt," he said. There was no discussion about what Kyle would do. He stripped off his tank, then his undershirt. The crowd quieted and Kyle had the satisfaction of hearing a few gasps in the room. He didn't need to look at his shoulder and down his arm to know it was mostly blueish black. His own teammates shuffled uncomfortably, and he caught a glance between Ben and Mario as he put his tank back on.

He'd been playing with a serious shoulder injury and had never said a word.

When Kyle went back on the court, the entire auditorium stood clapping a tribute to an athlete who was playing wounded.

By the time Kyle returned to the court, they were down another two, but the energy in the room aided Kyle. He took the pass from Ben, hitting a three-pointer. Mario intentionally drew a foul, and they scored on the turnover. Ben caught an outside shot, and they were up. The clock ran down, and Ridgeway scored a three-pointer. With nineteen seconds on the clock, Ben caught the rebound, passing it to Kyle. He should have opted for the safe two-pointer, but went for the glory shot of three and missed. Ridgeway got the ball, made the score and the buzzer rang. The final score of 84-82. The Trojans had been defeated.

Kyle slowed to a stop, stunned. For the first time in four years, they'd lost the playoffs and wouldn't be going to state. His final year, the one that really mattered, and he'd blown it.

He bent over, hands on his hips. His head was buzzing, the insane sound of the cheering for the winning team competing with his need for quiet. He felt sweaty palms patting his shoulders, a gesture of consolation given to the unlucky person who threw the final opportunity at winning.

The worst thing a player can experience is looking up and pretending not to notice the sea of faces in the stands, trying to avoid making eye contact with anyone. The goal now was to get the heck off the gym floor before someone yelled a profanity about the crappiness of his play.

His teammates gathered round in a circle, closing ranks as their coach joined them. They had a moment of silence, then put their hands in the center. On the coach's count, they cheered Ridgeway, then broke.

Kyle made for the bench and sat down, a towel on his face. With the adrenaline ebbing from his body, he felt nauseous, unsure if it was due to the loss or the caffeine that had been pulsing through his system.

"Let's get out of here," said Mario.

Those in the stand starting clapping in support as Kyle led the guys towards the gym exit, where he stopped in his tracks. Four broad-shouldered men in all-black tactical gear were standing on either side of the doors. Behind them stood Sheriff Deardon. Kyle heard his name called and turned.

It was Ty, giving him the thumbs up. Beside him was Billy, no cap this time, but her perfectly straight platinum hair, with a spot of color on her lips. Her usually hard eyes were soft and knowing, staring straight at him. He wouldn't have to explain the crushing defeat. Unspoken would be the strength it took for him to stay up all night, endure the pain of playing and face a town who placed all their expectations on him and the win.

Kyle didn't care who was at the door and what waited for him in the science room. He walked over to Billy and she stooped, wrapping her arms around his shoulders and gave him a kiss, the effect magnetic. The next instant she dropped her arms and touched his rib, gently pushing him away. "I've got a visit with Fred," she said in a low voice. The cheers continued, now mingled with the footsteps of hundreds of people descending the wooden bleachers.

Kyle followed behind Ben when he felt a tight grip on his right shoulder. He bent in pain and grimaced, hearing the voice at the same time he felt a harder press.

"You started up with *her*?" Stu Fine hissed the words. Stu spun Kyle to face him and grimaced when Kyle pulled his harm back, defiant. "Don't you leave while I'm talking to you."

"You're not talking."

"You had to humiliate Ashley in public?" Stu asked in disbelief.

Kyle gave him an equal look of contempt. "No more than she's put me down when we've been out and not cared. What's the difference? You have money and I don't? Tell her to stop lording it over people."

"How can you say that?"

"Easy. Ashley cares about Ashley and everyone knows it, including you."

The shock on Stu's face turned to pure hatred. "You won't be going anywhere. You're done."

"I've moved on, Stu. Why don't you?"

"Dad, come on," said Ruth, touching his upper arm. He shrugged her off, still glaring at Kyle.

"Who are you?" demanded Stu. "I thought you had integrity."

"Being honest is having integrity," Kyle said, staring at Stu until he broke eye contact.

"Ease up Stu," Mark Hancock said. He'd come from behind and placed his hand on Stu's shoulder.

"Get your hand off of me, or you'll be back at Lauren's ranch working security full time."

Mark kept his calm. "You know better than to threaten an officer, Stu. Let it go." Kyle expressed his appreciation with his eyes, but Mark glared back at him, the response unsettling. Kyle turned, heading the locker room.

“You’re done,” promised Stu. Kyle focused on making his way down the hall. It was going to be his safety zone, at least for a few minutes.

CHAPTER 47

The mood was sullen as the guys showered and changed. Kyle wondered how long it would be until one of the guys took a shot, and who it would be. He didn't have to wait long.

"The coolest guy in town shafted the girl and now shafted us," Mario said, wiping his hair. "You're going to find out what it's like to be a regular guy now."

"Shut up, Mario. I'd like to apologize, but then I'd have to remind you how many times you have blown the game in the past. Oh wait, you did, until I saved the day by planting the winning basket."

"Snap," chimed in one of the guys behind him, who yelled when Mario whipped him with a towel.

"Seriously Mario, did you see Billy tonight?" Ben asked. "She was hottest thing this side of Telluride. Who knew that all it took was a look from Kyle for her to change sides."

Kyle wanted to towel whip Ben for his comment. Instead he shot him a look of gratitude for deflecting Mario.

"Kyle lost us the game, Ben."

"At least he was playing," Ben retorted. "If you'd been injured like that, you would never even played or whined like a baby the entire time if you had."

Kyle appreciated Ben's defense but facts were facts. "Mario, you're right to be pissed I missed the shot. I own it."

"Tell someone who cares," Mario shot back.

Kyle removed his baseball cap from the top of his locker, his tolerance for Mario gone.

"Mario, you being a sore loser will fit right in with Stu and Ashley. In fact, the three of you can bond over a common hatred. Like I said before, good luck with that."

Mario started a profanity laced retort until the coach told him to shut up.

"Everyone get dressed, pronto. You all have a date with the local police down in the science room. Mario, since you're dressed, you first."

"I'm not going to meet with the police," Mario retorted.

Coach stared him down hard. "Then you'll be arrested. Sheriff's orders. You going to spend the night in jail?"

"Might do him good," muttered Kyle.

"You'll be there too, Kyle. Get on it."

"What's this all about, coach?" Ben asked.

"Police business. It's something to do with the break in at the mine."

"A great way to end the evening," said Kyle, his tone dour. His coach came to his side.

"You're pretty wrecked, aren't you?" Kyle nodded. "Did you ever get that arm checked out for broken bones?"

"Didn't want to," Kyle admitted, which was true. "I knew you wouldn't let me play."

"Kyle, we did a lot better with you than without you. You did good tonight, the last shot not-withstanding." His comment got Kyle to lift the corner of his mouth in a half smile. "Even the NBA greats miss the last shot of the game on occasion. You'll live to play another day." Kyle's smile faded, and the coach caught it.

"Don't worry about Fine. Fathers of small-town girls go overboard."

Kyle snorted. "Just one more motivation to get out of here."

"Get going then," said his coach, patting him on his left shoulder.

The narrow hallway was still crowded with the departing spectators who were mulling in the lobby. He caught the eye of Sheriff Deardon, who pointed over his head, towards the science room. Kyle took his place at the end of the line, resting one heel against the wall.

CHAPTER 48

Brayden stared at the street as he listened to Forland. He was getting updates on Saachi's condition from the hospital where she was under protective guard. Her burns were primarily on her left forearm, neck and jawline, all requiring grafting.

"She had the paperwork, Sir. Unless we can get the parents to agree on the spot for the interviews, we can't force the kids."

"Janet's men are already on site," said his boss. "She's given them authority to do whatever they want." He'd spoken loud enough so that Mark overheard through Brayden's cell phone. "My suggestion is you get the Sheriff or deputy involved to keep down the pandemonium, but let me be clear. The kids agree or they will be arrested."

"Hold on," Brayden said, cupping the phone. Mark put out his hand, forestalling an explanation. He nodded in understanding and left to prep the parents.

"Brayden, Saachi accessed the servers to upload the data but the entire file server was wiped. Regarding the attack, and that's what the local fire department believes, they're already think they've found the source." Brayden listened Forland's explanation of what had happened, becoming increasingly anxious about the young men in the corridor.

"Sir, are you sure we want to go through with this?"

"Brayden, you have four NSA agents waiting in the hall. One task is to ensure the polygraph are completed. The second is they have an informant who's feeding information real time on who to arrest."

"No more details?"

"I'm not sure I could give them to you if I had them, but I'm being kept in the dark."

His frustration was clear, but he was following orders.

"Yes, Sir." Brayden made the leap that his suspicion was dead on; the entire mine break in a set-up, a farce. It was all about containment of the real facts, with four people who already knew too much, one being in the hospital.

"Sir," Brayden began, "however this pans out, I have one request I'd like you to think about, assuming the dust settles favorably. I'd like a transfer to Northern Idaho when and if it's possible. I can still travel, but my wife is moving there in the New Year and I'd like that to be my permanent place of residence."

"Yes, we know." Of course, they would. All the major happenings of Bureau agents were tracked. "I'll see what I can do."

The phone hadn't reached his pocket when it buzzed again, along with the distinctive pattern of his wife's number.

"Laura, this isn't a good time," he began.

"I know," she said, cutting him off, her voice tight. "We just heard of the situation at the forensics lab in Montrose, and I was worried."

"I'm okay. Fine. I'm here in Ouray."

"I'm so glad. Brayden," she said, her voice prescriptively slow, like a doctor talking to a patient, "I thought about your comments on your headaches that have been flaring up, and I forgot to tell you that before you left, I put some pills in your wallet—"

"Pills, I—"

"Brayden," she said firmly, cutting short his comment. "I can hear it in your voice. You are probably already getting a migraine given what happened at the lab. As your physician-wife, you need to take one now, and I mean, now. It will kill your migraine for about three days. That's all you'll need."

Brayden thought through all she was trying to tell him. He never got headaches, let alone a debilitating migraine.

"And I know how triggers like the one today can set off an immediate migraine, don't you?" she said, her comment broaching no retort.

"Yeah. You know me too well," he responded, buying time.

"Also, I know it could get me in trouble, but between us, if you have anyone else who suffers from migraines, you might want to give them one as well."

Anyone else? If she was the person he and Kyle hypothesized she was, she knew about Kyle. Wiping out his short term memory? Perhaps; counteracting against a needle or other invasive mechanism to get into his mind.

"You're serious?" he asked, unable to help himself.

"Brayden, please be careful. We have crazies out there and if they, whoever they are, went after the forensics center, you don't know who will be next. Promise me you will take one right now, immediately, to prevent the onset of a migraine. Doctors orders."

In any other circumstance, he would have laughed. Not now. It was an order. One that might save his life, and Kyle's.

"I promise," he said, already pulling out his wallet. She had put them behind his insurance card. Three white pills.

"Right now. And anyone else who might be in pain."

He thought of Mark. "I love you Laura. Thanks for the doctor's advice."

"I love you too. Thanks for being my patient."

Brayden took a look at the pill then ate it dry. He waited until Mark had finished with the current set of parents then called him over.

"Here. Eat this," he said, handing him one, finishing his off in one swallow. "All I can tell you is it might save your life if you get questioned about things you don't want to tell others. Don't ask me anymore."

Mark ate it without hesitation. "After what I've witnessed, I wouldn't think about it."

Kyle had been leaning against the wall, tense and uncomfortable every time a person came up and offered their condolences. Had his mind not been on the room ten feet down, the words would have made more of an impact. As it was, he agreed the game was a good one, the play tough but generally fair, and yes, his shoulder hurt. Ty had only given him a quick wink before leaving with Billy under his protective arm.

His own parents were now speaking with Mark Hancock who'd muttered one word as he'd walked by: "Unbelievable."

Kyle overheard Mark's explanation to his parents. The evidence had led the investigators to believe that a person, or persons, with athletic capabilities, had entered the mine and stolen government property that needed to be returned. It was a prank gone wrong, and now the agency was taking the teens through a simple questioning exercise, not admissible in a court of law, but the fastest route to identifying those who were the prime suspects. Their son happened to be one of the best athletes in town.

"How do we know they are being asked the right questions by a qualified individual?" asked Ben's dad, a real estate attorney who worked mostly in Telluride. Mark described the examiners' qualifications and explained how there would only be one person in the room with the kid at a time, no emotion or bias from the interviewer at all.

Kyle thought the other parents were more interested in getting to Ty's for a beer, but Mario's father asked if he needed to stay. "Unnecessary," Mark replied. "They will be released as soon as the examination is over."

One by one, his teammates exited the science room, each session taking about ten minutes. After about an hour, the hallways were empty, and it was just Kyle and a backup player. When the door opened and the kid in front went in, Mark approached Kyle.

"You did what I said?" Mark asked under his breath, putting a piece of chew in his mouth. Kyle nodded. "I'll tell you this much, I regret helping you out."

"Apologizing for losing is going to get old real fast."

Mark spit in an empty coffee cup. "I don't give two farts over the game. You lied Kyle, boldface lied to me." Kyle's face felt the tingles of guilt, the downward motion of shame pressing like a wall of water through his chest, into his belly and legs. "The mine. That guy Roy. What's the real story, Kyle? Did you shoot him proactively, use me for the cover up and then what? Are you intending to sell the cubes to the highest bidder?"

"Mark I—"

"Shut up," he broke in. "I saw your injury during the break in the game. The coach told me it was an ice climbing accident, but that was after I told him you fell off the ATV."

"Oh, man."

Mark nodded unsympathetically. "Uh-huh. You now are in deep with your coach, but he's the least of your worries. And now I've got a problem with Stu who wants to kill you because you dumped Ashley for Billy. Billy? I should have known," he added, now seeming mad at himself. "Saachi had you nailed the first night but no, I was completely blind to it. And back to Ashley, you just had to make a statement in front of the entire town?" Mark shoved another large chunk of chew into the side of his mouth, shaking his head. "So methodical. So prescriptive in every part of your life. What in the world happened to you?"

"D told me a story and I checked it out," Kyle said simply. There was nothing but the truth left.

"You've lied about everything else. Why should I believe that?"

"Can't make you believe anything," Kyle admitted.

"Uh-huh. Brayden is going to find that out right about now. And those guys over there, I think they're here for you." He spit again. "Of all people…" he muttered, "and now I look like the fool for standing up for you to everyone."

Kyle couldn't say anything that wouldn't come across as whining for a second chance. His dad looked over, the expression of disappointment worse than any tongue lashing from Mark.

"Can I speak to my parents?"

"Nope. No one else got that chance."

It was only going to be a matter of time before they learned he'd been lying about all of it as well.

Mark left and he waited alone, watching the clock. Billy had said she was going to visit Fred, but what for? She also told him Roy was coming back into town. Was he here now, in disguise?

The door opened and out walked the last teammate. Kyle took a breath and walked inside.

Brayden shook his hand as though this were their first meeting and asked him to have a seat.

"Shoes off, please." Kyle did as he was asked, watching Brayden check inside the shoes. "Looking for tacks," he explained. "One of the most common and most effective way of tricking the polygraph." He handed back both shoes. "But also, the most obvious."

Kyle sat in silence as Brayden directed him to lean forward then back, fixing two straps around his chest. Around his right arm, he attached a blood pressure device, and then Brayden slipped his second and fourth finger on his right hand into pulse monitors.

"Three components," Brayden explained formally. "Pre-test, in-test and post-test. One to establish a baseline, then second is only ten questions and the last phase is the follow-up. I'll conduct the analysis afterward."

"Did everyone get the same questions?"

"Yes."

Kyle hadn't taken a caffeine pill since before the game, and although he was still awake, his body had been gradually shutting down, the physical degradation overtaking his mental concerns. If using a tack was effective, maybe pain somewhere else might be as useful. He bit the inside of his cheeks, the rush of pain accompanied by blood. Brayden started by asking his name, where he lived, his high school and relevant facts. He then asked Kyle personal questions; did he have a girlfriend, her name, and where she lived.

"What happens to someone like Mario, who doesn't have a girlfriend but wants my old one?" He thought Brayden would smirk, but his eyes remained fixed as he answered.

"Unless he answered it as I phrased the question, the test would give a false positive. Wanting something is not the same as having something."

Wasn't that the truth?

"Can you give me any analysis so far?"

"Your readings are consistent, how's that?" Brayden turned the screen around for display. All Kyle's answers read the same, an even plot line, with the same amount of spikes in heart rate and blood pressure. "No variance, as I said. Now I'll proceed to the next ten questions. These are yes or no questions, Kyle. No explanation necessary."

"Do you know about the break in of the mine?"

Kyle nervously bit his inner cheek. "Yes."

"Do you know people who have been in the mine?"

"Yes."

"Do you know a miner named D?"

"Yes."

"Did he tell people how to get in the mine?"

"Yes."

"Could you get into the mine on your own?"

"I don't know."

"Did you attempt, at any time, to get into the mine?"

"No."

"Did you have any direct involvement in D's death?"

"No."

"Have you ever been inside the mine shaft?"

"No."

"Do you know what was inside the mine?"

"No."

"Are you involved with the naturalists in any way?"

"No."

Brayden's eyes had been focused on the screen during the questioning, not on Kyle himself. All that mattered were the visuals appearing. He stopped, and then began removing the electronics from Kyle's fingers and chest.

"How'd my first-time experience with a polygraph turn out?" Kyle asked.

"Just as I expected it would. You have no idea what's going on in this town, just like your teammates."

If Kyle had been hooked up at that moment, he was sure the graphs would have gone off the chart.

"What now?"

"At this point, it appears as though we leave and the town returns to normal."

Kyle stood, waiting for the last sentence, not sure what it was going to be. "I'll be seeing you?" he asked as a question.

"Hopefully not, but then you never know. Are you keeping your things somewhere safe? Where they won't be found?"

"You don't want them?"

"I can't take them. Not now. That's different from not wanting them."

"So…you might need them at some point."

Brayden put his hand in his pocket first, then put out his hand to Kyle. "Take care of yourself, kid. You're a good one." He paused, curling his fingers. Kyle's eyes registered the small object in his palm. "Take it now," he said in a barely-there voice. "It might save your life." Kyle seamlessly slipped his palm over his mouth, swallowing it whole.

"What doesn't kill me makes me stronger, right?"

"Or forgetful," Brayden said with an intense look.

Kyle left the room unprepared for what faced him. He forced his swallow when he saw the six men waiting in the hall; the Sheriff, Hancock, and the four men in tactical gear.

"Excuse us, Kyle," Sheriff Deardon said formally. They waited until Kyle had left the front doors, but he paused on the steps, turning to see all six men go inside the science room.

Talking over the results, he suspected. Kyle adjusted the cap on his head, zipping up his shell jacket. Crap, he suddenly realized he'd left his bag in the locker room. He returned inside, heading directly to the locker room. When he came out, he turned left, nearly running into Mark.

"Sorry, I…" He stopped, not believing his eyes. Brayden was cuffed, hands behind his back, walking between two of the men, the other two behind him. Mark and Sheriff Deardon were in front.

"You keep this to yourself, Kyle," the Sheriff told him. Kyle saw that a few stragglers were still out front and Deardon frowned. "Never mind."

Kyle hung back as the men and Brayden went before him. Activity on the street stopped as on-lookers watched while Brayden ducked his head as he climbed into the squad car.

Kyle started walking back to his house, shivering. But why had they taken Brayden? It had to be connected to his wife. And maybe Brayden knew what was coming. That's why he wouldn't take the cubes and why he'd slipped Kyle the pill. Brayden was trying to protect him…again. But from who, this time?

That was bad, but wasn't the worst part. The town was angry they lost the game. He had the most influential person in the area after him for revenge. His coach, parents and Mark thought he was a liar.

I had lied, repeatedly. But what else was he going to do? Tell them all he had something that would change their faces and lives forever??

CHAPTER 49

Kyle took the route home by Ty's restaurant knocking on the back door. Billy answered, glancing each way.

"Brayden was arrested," he said before she could speak.

"And the forensics woman is in the hospital," she said, gesturing him inside. "The forensics lab was blown up. She's burned, but alive. My uncle says the NSA didn't get the information on the DNA, so you are safe."

"Not convinced about that." Kyle summarized the polygraph experience, and was about to tell Billy about the white pill when Roy came from around the corner. "What, you're going to try and kill me again?"

Roy smiled. His arm was in a sling, but he didn't exhibit any other injuries. "I wanted the cubes to try and reverse engineer the code. At the time, I misjudged your conviction."

"Kyle," interrupted Billy, "I think what you told me about Brayden's wife is where they made the link."

"Agree. Laura Cox was the one who delivered you in the hospital."

She nodded. "And sorry for not telling you Roy was here before you started talking. He had to hear it from you, directly."

Kyle dismissed the need for an apology with a kiss to her forehead.

"Laura and my sister, Billy's mom, were good friends," Roy said. "They both avoided having the HPV shot when they were young, for totally unrelated but valid reasons. We don't have the time to go in to it now, but I know beyond a doubt that Brayden is being set up. Beyond that, Billy told me what he did for you. He should have taken you in day one."

"I know."

"Kyle," continued Billy's uncle. "We believe what you found is correct. Brayden's daughter is alive and well, hidden in Northern Idaho, not where his mother thinks, but on a reservation."

Kyle looked between the two. Indian blood. Sovereign nation. "Where they can't touch her," he surmised.

Roy smiled. "Not even the government of the United States."

"But what do we do in the meantime?"

"I'm suggesting you join us," Roy began. "High school senior by day, naturalist by night. Together, we turn this country around and free people like Brayden Cox from the government, so we can reunite his family, who have been torn apart like so many others."

Kyle searched Billy's face for guidance. She had obviously heard this before and was on board.

"You don't need me at all. I'll give you the cubes and you can do what's necessary."

Billy and her uncle exchanged a glance.

"No, Kyle. You're the key."

He leaned against the counter. "What am I missing here?"

"They, the NSA, is going to come back to this town or move the files to another location until they trap us. They want us dead and off their backs. We need to keep them guessing, to move around so we have time to do what we need to do."

Kyle's eyes felt dry. "You are not suggesting I'm going to be the distraction."

Billy smirked. "You already are a distraction."

"I'm serious, Billy."

"So am I," she said earnestly. "You are pretty much going to be the most hated person in town. No one is going to care what you are doing, who you are with or why. You are going to be a literal pariah. You can come and go as you want, while we get working with the people for the reverse engineering on the cubes, all under the radar—"

"Because you've been eliminated as a suspect and Brayden has taken your place," Roy broke in.

"Billy," Kyle began, exasperated. "Sure no one will like me, and I have five more months until school is finished, but you will still be here. I don't want you to go through the pain and punishment along with me."

The smile left her face. "That's because I won't. I'll be leaving with Roy."

"Huh?"

"Kyle, they need me, they, being the naturalists, as another example of a person without the transduction. They need to run tests on me to be sure, and with the information on the cubes, they can do that. I'm at least as brilliant on the computers as my uncle here—"

"Or more so," Roy added.

"But I can blend in anywhere," she said earnestly, as though she had already planned a trip and wanted to get going. "He can't. I can put on a wig and contact the doctors, or whoever else I need to, but he can't. He's already on their list and targeted."

Kyle felt loneliness creeping in to his psyche. "How are you going to explain this to your dad? Leaving school with only a semester left?"

She inhaled and glanced at her uncle, then Kyle. "I'm not going to."

"Come again?"

"I'm going to leave. Disappear."

"You're not."

"I am. It's the only way. My dad can't know what I'm doing or where I've gone. I may leave a note with something to the effect that the hate I'm feeling from the town because of you is too much, and I had to leave."

Kyle's eyes roved over her face, her dark eyelashes and edgy hair, thinking of the way she knew him intimately without ever having been truly physical. It had only been a week, but he felt as though he'd finally begun living.

"Your dad is going to hate me."

"As much, or more than the everyone else," Roy concurred.

Billy slid her arm around Kyle's waist. "It's the only way we can accomplish this Kyle. You know I'm right. Otherwise, everywhere we go, every time we are together, we are going to be scrutinized or ostracized. We won't ever get to the bigger picture, which is for everyone."

"Who don't deserve it," he said quietly.

"It's only five months," Billy reminded.

He kissed her forehead. "Why are you sounding almost happy?"

"Because we are going to change the world Kyle. We are going to make it right again."

Kyle brushed his lips across her skin, down her temple and found her mouth. He pulled her close, giving himself to her through his kisses. "Remember what you said to me early on? That you said I was living a charade and had everyone fooled. But not you."

"No," she murmured. "Not me."

"I love you Billy."

"I know that, but it's okay, because I love you, too."

When they separated, Kyle squinted at Roy. "You're going to keep her safe? And you, you're going to keep in touch with me?"

"It's all in the fishpond with Fred," Roy told him.

"Right. Fred. You want the cubes, I take it?"

Roy shook his head. "Too dangerous if we get caught. As Billy said, you're going to be a pariah. So, you're the safest person we can think of. We'll be in touch."

Kyle gave Billy one last hug and a long kiss. The recollection of her love and support would have to keep him going.

ABOUT THE AUTHOR

Before she began writing novels, Sarah Gerdes established herself as an internationally recognized expert in the areas of business management and consulting. Her 22 novels are published in over 100 countries and translated by publishers in four languages. She lives with her family in Northern Idaho among a menagerie of farm animals.

BOOKS IN PRINT

Contemporary Fiction

In a Moment

Danielle Grant Series

  Made for Me (book 1)

  Destined for You (book 2)

  Meant to Me (book 3)

A Convenient Date

Suspense/Thriller

Above Ground

Global Deadline

Chambers Series

  Chambers (book 1)

  Chambers: The Spirit Warrior (book 2)

Incarnation Series

  Incarnation (book 1)

  Incarnation: The Cube Master (book 2)

  Incarnation: Immunity (book 3, release Fall 2022)

Non-Fiction

Author Straight Talk: The possibilities, pitfalls, how-to's and tribal knowledge from someone who knows

Sue Kim: The Greatest Korean American Story Never Told, the Authorized biography

The Overlooked Expert: Turning your skills into a Profitable Business, 10th Anniversary Edition

Navigating the Partnership Maze: Creating Alliances that Work

REFERENCES & RESOURCES

Web site: www.sarahgerdes.com

Instagram: Sarahgerdes_author

Made in the USA
Monee, IL
06 September 2022

12503011R00256